Love and Other
Alien Experiences

Love and Other Alien experiences

KERRY WINFREY

Feiwel and Friends
NEW YORK

A FEIWEL AND FRIENDS BOOK

An imprint of Macmillan Publishing Group, LLC

175 Fifth Avenue, New York, NY 10010

Our books may be purchased in bulk for promotional, educational, or business use. Please contact your local bookseller or the Macmillan Corporate and Premium Sales Department at (800) 221-7945 ext. 5442 or by e-mail at MacmillanSpecialMarkets@macmillan.com.

Library of Congress Cataloging-in-Publication Data

Names: Winfrey, Kerry, author.

Title: Love and other alien experiences / Kerry Winfrey.

Description: First edition. | New York: Feiwel & Friends, 2017. | Summary: Agoraphobic high school junior Mallory's life centers on an online forum about aliens and going to school by computer until a prank lands her on the Homecoming court. | Description based on print version record and CIP data provided by publisher; resource not viewed.

Identifiers: LCCN 2016037608 (print) | LCCN 2017017611 (ebook) | ISBN 9781250119537 (Ebook) | ISBN 9781250119520 (trade paperback)

Subjects: | CYAC: Agoraphobia—Fiction. | Mental illness—Fiction. | High schools—Fiction. | Schools—Fiction. | Dating (Social customs)—Fiction. | Family life—Fiction. | Unidentified flying objects—Fiction.

Classification: LCC PZ7.1.W584 (ebook) | LCC PZ7.1.W584 Lov 2017 (print) | DDC [Fic]—dc23

LC record available at https://lccn.loc.gov/2016037608

Book design by Rebecca Syracuse

Feiwel and Friends logo designed by Filomena Tuosto

Originally published as an ebook in 2015 by Paper Lantern Literary, The Studio.

First paperback edition, 2017

1 3 5 7 9 10 8 6 4 2

fiercereads.com

For Mama & Papa Winfrey

WHAT IT WAS LIKE

The front door handle is hot against my palm like there's a fire on the other side. There might as well be.

A small cough behind me.

Jump, turn around.

Mom's watching.

I wave. *I'm going.*

Step onto the porch. Let the door swing shut behind me. Breathe, breathe, breathe. I look up and around. Blue sky. Green trees. Still.

One step. No big deal.

It's hot. Sweltering, even. Diamond-sharp beads of sweat prick my forehead.

I move my foot, heavy as lead. *Two steps.* Then the other. *Three.*

My foot's at the edge of the porch stairs now. The flat edge of a cliff.

Once I get off the porch, then it's only a few more steps to the sidewalk. Then a couple of blocks to school. Simple. Piece of cake. Just do it.

I ease my way down down down, eyes closed tight. The soles of my sneakers kiss the ground. My breath gets shorter. And shorter.

Have my ribs always been so tight around my lungs?

BREATHE. Slowly. Gently, my feet crawl forward.

See? You're past the stairs! You're on the sidewalk! Look—see how far you've come.

I turn around, a halfway spin, and look up at the house. Its pale peach paint seems miles away, millions of miles, like it's an impossibly faraway star in the sky.

Then—I forget how to breathe.

I gasp. The house moves, shifts, a kaleidoscope vision turning and twisting farther from me. My knees buckle. Rough concrete claws the skin on my legs. I try to push myself up, but the pebbles push back, deep into my palms.

Missing lungs! Heart attack! I'm dying!

Something tugs under my arms. Hands pulling me up. *Mom.* Her red lips moving, her eyes searching my face, her eyebrows contorted in worry. *Like acrobats*, I think, and almost giggle.

She half pulls, half pushes me up the porch steps back inside and shuts the door behind us. Air inflates my chest again, a balloon of relief.

Eyes close against tears as my mind closes around a new promise: *I'm never going outside again.*

AlienHuntress: Okay, everyone. So let's say you're trapped on Mars, for all eternity, with no chance of coming back to Earth. You can only bring three things with you. What are they?

ManontheMoon: My metal detector, my phone, and a lifetime supply of junk food!

LunaEclipse: A journal, a camera, and my paints set, because I def need to record all of my adventures.

BeamMeUp: Nothing. Mars most likely can't support human life, so I'd be dead in less than a nanosecond. Material things wouldn't matter at all.

AlienHuntress: BeamMeUp, you are *really* bad at this game.

CHAPTER ONE

IT'S FRIDAY MORNING AND, as usual, I'm sitting cross-legged on my unmade bed, balancing a bowl of Lucky Charms on my knees and trying not to spill milk on my laptop. Again. And, just like I do every day, I'm half paying attention to the morning news show playing on the TV that sits on the corner of my dresser. The hosts are cooing over a cat that learned how to ride the bus. As interesting as that story is, it's no match for what's happening on my computer.

Things are heating up on We Are Not Alone, or, as its tagline describes it, *Roswell's Destination for All Things Extraterrestrial.* It's an Internet hangout for super nerds, space freaks, sci-fi lovers, and paranoid weirdos near Roswell—and, as a major alien obsessive from Reardon, an hour away, I definitely qualify.

I scroll through the forum categories—Abduction Experiences, TV Shows, Declassified Information, Equipment—and click on General Theories to check the stats for my latest post as I shovel another spoonful of chalky marshmallows into my mouth. I have 700 "likes" and just 150 "dislikes" for my totally perfect rebuttal of the claims that aliens were behind the recent disappearance of an Air America flight over the Atlantic. I mean, yes, I believe in aliens, but I also believe that planes crash all the time. (My brother, Linc, says the only thing nerdier than being obsessed with aliens is being the downer who destroys everyone else's theories.)

> **LittleGreenMen:** AlienHuntress OMG YOU ARE MY QUEEN

> **BlueSuperNova:** AlienHuntress wins at everything!!!

> **BeamMeUp:** AlienHuntress, that's nice in theory, but it's not totally rigorous. Planes crash all the time, but they don't usually disappear into thin air. No one's found any debris and . . .

Ugh. BeamMeUp appointed himself my own personal devil's advocate two weeks ago and hasn't looked back. His most recent comment is true to his pompous, know-it-all form.

Cringing, I read on. He actually uses bullet points to list all the ways I'm wrong. Bullet points! What is this, a PowerPoint presentation?

I shake my head and mutter, "Not today, buddy," and begin typing my reply. The click of the keys keeps pace with my mom's heels as they tap across the floor downstairs.

> **AlienHuntress:** BeamMeUp, you think we should just assume every missing aircraft is the result of aliens? Should we amend all of Amelia Earhart's biographies to state that she was probably abducted by extraterrestrials?

I'm getting into the groove when the morning show host's soothing voice announces that it's time for a check on weather and traffic, which means it must be 8:15, which means . . .

Shit. Class is at 8:25. And I'm going to be late.

I slip my laptop off my lap and pound down the carpeted stairs, straight through the dining room into the kitchen. My cereal bowl rings against the sink when I toss it in. My mom, who's adjusting a high heel while shoving some gross protein bar in her mouth, scowls.

"Are you running late again?" she says with her mouth full.

"Sorry, sorry, sorry!" I shout, shooting upstairs as she sighs a long, overly dramatic *"Mal . . ."* in frustration.

My laptop whirs on my tiny twin bed. Even though my fingers are itching to get back to We Are Not Alone and the virtual smackdown I'm laying on BeamMeUp, I put some effort into picking out a normal outfit to appease Lincoln. My brother's so eager to be a film director that he thinks he can art direct every aspect of our lives. He still hasn't forgiven me for a sweatshirt/sweatpants combo that he claimed made me look like "an '80s workout instructor."

Today, I'm going with the "Classic Mal": a pair of jeans and nondescript but fitted T-shirt. Then, on to hair. My BFF, Jenni Agrawal, a beauty vlogger who posts weekly tutorials on topknots and contouring for her adoring fans on her YouTube channel, *Just Jenni*, would probably try to give my locks a cute name, like "beachy waves." But I'm honest enough to know that "As Good As It's Going to Get" is more accurate. My shaggy brown bangs will not be tamed.

"Crap!" I mutter when I can't find my books in the pile of clothes on the floor. They must be on the kitchen table, where I did homework last night. I go back downstairs and slide across our perpetually polished hardwood floor into the kitchen, where my books are stacked next to my mom's giant red purse.

Sighing, I pick up the purse and open the front door just as my mom is pulling the minivan back into the driveway. The dry heat is already almost unbearable, and I immediately start to sweat.

"I swear, that's the last time I forget!" she calls out from the driver's-side window.

"I'm going to start charging a fee!" I shout. My toes curl nervously over the edge of the doorframe.

"Just bring it here, honey," she calls, holding her hand out.

I push one bare foot out the door, wincing when it touches the porch. A bead of sweat drips down my forehead and my stomach starts to churn with the force of a thousand chalky marshmallows. A pair of big, invisible arms squeezes my chest and my breath gets shallow.

"Mallory!" Even from a distance, I can see that her cheeks have gone slack—her disappointed look. I despise that look, how it's become so familiar. Before I can stop myself, I take a full two steps onto the porch so that look will disappear. But her minivan, which I *know* is only fifteen feet from me, looks like it's at the end of a tunnel that's getting longer and longer.

I'm shaking harder. It's loud now, like someone turned the volume up on the world. The purse feels heavier by the nanosecond while the taste of cereal climbs up my throat. With one deep, shaky breath, I walk down the porch stairs and fling the purse toward her open car window. Her slender hand plucks it out of the air, and the sound of her mascara tube falling to the ground explodes in my ears. My toes catch on the sharp edge of the entryway as I haul myself through, but the pain is drowned out by the animal need to just get inside.

The door slams behind me so hard that it bounces off the frame and swings back open, like it's mocking me. My chest heaves.

Back in the cool, brightly lit safety of my house, everything snaps into focus—the neat line of our shoes by the door, Lincoln's tennis racket on the living room sofa, the clock on the mantel that reads 8:27.

Double shit.

I launch myself up the stairs and straight to my laptop, logging in just in time to say, "Here!" when Mr. Parker calls my name.

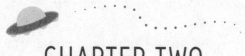

CHAPTER TWO

Many juvenile birds possess plumage that allows them to blend into their surroundings. Because they can't yet fly to escape predators, these vulnerable young birds camouflage themselves until they're older and stronger.

—*The Birder's Guide,* 1989

MR. PARKER'S FACE LOOMS on my screen, Coke-bottle glasses and all, like it always does when I log in. Satisfied by my telepresence, he moves down his class roster, ignoring the flood of snickers and whispers that greets me when I log on.

From my vantage point at the very back of the class, I can see almost everybody. To my left, there's evil Pia Lubeck, whose dark hair is so shiny it practically creates a glare. To my right, a bunch of football dudes appear as one giant mass of Reardon's blue and gold. Jenni, my official BFF, is subtly waving at me from her seat in the front row.

Maybe a more progressive school would have allocated some of the football budget for one of those "remote telepresences," but good old Reardon High just set up a laptop in the back of all my classrooms. Not very high-tech, but it works, albeit in an incredibly awkward way. If that's the price I have to pay for attending school via webcam because of, as Reardon High School's guidance counselor, Mrs. Boone, put it, my "personal issues," I'll pay it.

Personal issues. That vague phrase that always means "a person who's dealing with something super messed up." Like when our freshman year history teacher left school for a "personal issue" that really meant he got arrested for shoplifting, or when a celebrity takes time off from his career for a "personal issue" that's actually just a drug problem.

As Lincoln and Jenni tell me, some kids at school think I got pregnant and I'm at home with an ever-expanding midsection. Some kids think I started doing meth. Patrick Cruz suggested he has "proof" that I got arrested for a combination of those things and am currently attending Reardon High via a computer at juvie. Some kids think I have an allergy to sunlight and have to stay in my basement 24/7. And at least one person, noted weirdo Monica Bergen, is convinced that I'm actually dead. How she thinks I'm appearing on webcam, I'll never understand. If I were a ghost, the very last place I'd haunt would be Reardon High.

I haven't broken any laws or developed any drug problems, as much as the student population of Reardon High might think I have. The truth is much less sordid, but a whole lot more embarrassing: My dad left, and now I can't step one foot outside my house without feeling like the outside world is going to physically crush me.

I guess if we're talking about my anxiety, the even truthier truth is it started *way* before that, like pretty much when I popped out of the womb. While other kids were climbing trees and falling off their bikes, I was worried about hitting my head and developing a brain injury, or a scrape that would inevitably lead to gangrene, or coming into contact with bird poop (which, FYI, can carry over *sixty diseases*). I've always been *nervous*, but it was all under control—at least livable—until the morning I woke up and my dad was gone.

He's always been prone to going away for long weekends by himself and conveniently "forgetting" to tell us when he'd be back. When he left, I tried to keep my worry at a 4.5 level . . . that is, until he didn't come back the next week, or the next. When a month passed, my mom told me, in language I'm sure she learned from her therapist, that it wasn't my fault. Lincoln said good riddance, took our years-old family portrait off the mantel, and didn't give it a second thought.

But me? I couldn't—can't—let it go. I knew my dad wasn't happy here with us—I'm not an idiot—but I didn't expect him to just *leave*. And if that one unexpected thing could happen, what else might happen?

And then there was the Cheesecake Factory Incident.

No, I didn't OD on pasta carbonara or fall into a cheesecake coma. That would have been so much better.

Jenni, Lincoln, and I were at the Cheesecake Factory celebrating our last final of the school year. Lincoln was happily digging into his dessert when I saw it: the tan jacket, the growing bald spot—*him*, at a table across the dining room. I stood up, my silverware clattering to the floor, and ran across the room. I grabbed his shoulders, shouted, "Dad!" and he turned around to reveal . . . a man who wasn't my dad, looking at me like I was about to assault him.

"Is everything okay?" asked a Cheesecake Factory waiter, barely covering up his alarm. Jenni and Lincoln caught up to me and each grabbed a shoulder, tugging me back.

That's when everything got blurry, when Jenni and Lincoln tried to hold me up as I sunk to the ground. Everything in that cavernous dining room with its fake columns echoed so loudly that it felt like the clanking silverware and murmurs were screaming inside my head.

I couldn't breathe. I couldn't stand. I couldn't deal.

The next thing I remember is being in my room, safe in bed. The day after, when I tried to get the mail, I crumpled on the sidewalk. The day after that, I threw up all over the porch stairs. There was always tomorrow.

But tomorrow turned into weeks and months, and the reasons to stay inside kept piling up.

Mom, Lincoln, Jenni, some teachers—everyone who knows—think I'm overreacting. It's written on their faces every time one of them tries to "encourage" me out of doors and I break into a full-body sweat. But *you* try to leave your house when leaving your house feels like having eight heart attacks while your insides turn inside out. After four weeks and a diagnosis of an anxiety disorder complemented by agoraphobic tendencies, my mom and Mrs. Boone wanted me to go to school, even if I wasn't leaving the house. That's when my online education started.

As soon as Mr. Parker turns his sweater-vested back to the class to retrieve something in the classroom closet, one of the football players throws a wad of paper across the room.

Clearly, my room is a far superior learning environment to Reardon, panic attacks notwithstanding.

Plus, from the comfort of my room I get to be Jenni's "gossip mole," which means that I eavesdrop for her—because other than when I pipe up to correct someone ("Hermione Granger syndrome" according to my mom, whose book club read Harry

Potter for *Fantasy and Fromage* month), I'm basically in stealth mode. Monica Bergen (the one who thinks I'm dead) is talking about the French lessons she's taking for the Europe trip. Boring. Then she moves on to who she thinks will be on this year's homecoming court. Double boring.

I turn my attention to the football huddle, where Brad Kirkpatrick—also known as Reardon High's golden-boy football star and my next-door neighbor—is whispering to Cliff, a kid who had no choice but to become a football player after his parents named him Cliff.

"Having Jake back in town has been awesome," Brad says. "He helps me practice."

"Your brother?" Cliff asks. "Wasn't he in jail or something?"

Brad shrugs, or at least gets as close as his massive shoulders will let him get to a shrug. I'm even a little disappointed when Mr. Parker, now at the smartboard, *tuts* them. At least that conversation promised to be more interesting than football or homecoming, Reardon's hottest topics.

"Mr. Parker, are we going over the homework?" Jenni says from her seat at the front of class.

Pia Lubeck rolls her huge green eyes and mimes gagging behind Jenni's back. Cliff lets out a laugh that sounds like a pig's would if pigs could laugh. The back of my best friend's neck flushes red and she mumbles a small "never mind" before turning her eyes to her desk.

I mute my webcam and release a tsunami of insults that would definitely get me suspended if I were physically in the classroom. Pia's just jealous that Jenni is an incredible, breathtaking, perfect Indian supermodel walking the earth. Jenni, the only one of my friends who came to check on me, the only one who called every evening to ask me, calmly and without judgment, when I was coming back to school. Everyone else—including Sarah-Beth Greeley, who used to round out our trio—either faded away slowly or disappeared immediately.

Getting more time in person with Jenni is one of the only things I miss about Reardon. Actually, it's the only thing I miss about Reardon. I'd rather spend my time talking about UFO crash landings on We Are Not Alone than hanging out in the school hallways. I was planning on taking some college courses during my junior year anyway.

As Mr. Parker shuffles through some papers at his desk, Jenni darts her eyes to her lap. I can just see the flurry of her fingers as she types out a message. Five seconds later, I get her text.

Caroline asked me to be in her lab group!!! THANK YOU!!!

I smile to myself, impressed by Jenni's relentless social striving and my cyber-stalking skills. Reading tons of inane conversations between Caroline and her friends on Facebook and Twitter and tumblr and Instagram helped me deduce that she missed a deadline for a summer course at Reardon Community College. It's amazing how much one girl can complain in missives of 140 characters about how she'd never be able to get into Vanderbilt without that class. It just took one conversation with his favorite daughter for Mr. Agrawal, head of admissions at RCC, to bend the rules a bit. And apparently it paid off.

Jenni treats the popular kids like they're celebrities and she's an E! red carpet reporter. And, when she's not working on the yearbook committee, attending workout classes at the Y, volunteering, or going to private chem and calc lessons, she works on her YouTube videos. Even to someone like me, who's never going to attempt milkmaid braids or perfect a cat eye, they're awesome—though the "popular" girls don't seem to think she's pretty and put-together enough to fit in with them. I've tried explaining to Jenni that her inability to be insta-besties with Caroline and Pia probably just means that she's, you know, a *nice person*. But Jenni still, more than anything, just wants to be accepted.

The best thing about not having to go to school is that I'm free to do whatever I want as long as I'm sort of paying attention—which is why Mom installed Focustime, an app that limits the time I spend on non-approved "school appropriate" sites, on both my computer and my phone. My minutes tick down as I scroll through my Instagram feed—a cat picture from my cousin, a baby picture from my other cousin, a picture Lincoln took of his new Alfred Hitchcock poster, a selfie Jenni snapped at breakfast, a selfie Jenni posted at her locker—while Mr. Parker passes out the handouts explaining our huge physics project, due at the end of the marking period.

"Mallory," he says, looking right at me—or, I guess, the computer—"I'll be e-mailing you the handout, so be sure to check for it."

"Okay," I say. Mr. Parker isn't exactly up-to-date on technology—the last time he tried to e-mail me a handout, he forwarded me a lasagna recipe from his mom. He repeats himself no fewer than four times to "make sure that I heard." Juniper Brieze, a girl whose parents presumably named her after a Bath & Body Works spray, giggles like she's in the front row of a Comedy Central special.

When he's finally moved on from making sure I heard, Mr. Parker announces that we get to pick our own partners—thank God—and Jenni turns around and mouths, "Duh." Luckily, partner selection rarely adds to my anxiety.

Once the flurry of partner choosing calms down, Mr. Parker says, "For those of you looking to avoid the midterm, there is an incentive to excelling on this project. The pair who receives the highest grade when they turn their projects in will be exempt from the midterm."

Caroline, who I can just see on the edge of my screen, snaps her head around so fast that she almost falls out of her seat. Jenni's sleek black ponytail bounces around as she bobs excitedly in hers. Brad high-fives Cliff, even though I think it's about something else entirely. Monica seems to have fallen asleep. The best and brightest, right here at Reardon.

But now I'm paying attention, too. The terms of my at-home schooling clearly stipulate that I must take midterms at the school if the teachers want me to. No one is taking advantage of this except for, of course, Mr. Parker.

"Yes, Pia?" Mr. Parker asks as Pia raises her hand.

"That's the Monday after the homecoming dance," Pia says. "Don't you think that's, like, unfair to us on the homecoming court? I mean . . . unfair to the people who will be on the homecoming court."

I'm afraid my classmates might actually be able to hear my eyes rolling.

"Physics," Mr. Parker intones, "waits for no man. Or dance. You and your partner must create a project that captures how physics can make your everyday life more interesting. You will track your progress in a journal. Remember, results are not everything. In science, just as in life, you learn even more from your failures than you do from your successes."

Only Mr. Parker would make this a physics lesson *and* a life lesson. Luckily, Jenni is just as organized about her schoolwork as she is about her school-celebrity stalking and her nail polish collection, so I know we have this one in the bag.

When the bell rings, I log off and take out my notebook to start brainstorming.

How *does* physics affect my everyday life, I wonder as I tap my pencil on my paper. Mr. Parker probably doesn't consider a marathon of *Doctor Who* or old *Quantum Leap* reruns an A$^+$ example of how physics makes my life more interesting. A couple of weeks ago, he gave a huge lecture about ramps, and I can easily find plenty of those. There's even a skate park two blocks away, and taking a picture of a skater would be a perfect journal entry.

Two blocks away. I start feeling my anxiety creep in, the familiar panic that starts in my chest and swells to include every part of my body—curling my toes, blurring my vision, shortening my breath.

I snap my notebook shut. Jenni can help with collecting information, and I'll just do something else to contribute. Maybe I should look at Mr. Parker's handout for some inspiration.

I have one e-mail in my inbox, but it isn't from Mr. Parker. My stomach somersaults. It's a Google Alert for the name "Robert F. Sullivan."

My father.

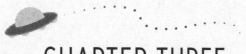

CHAPTER THREE

E-MAIL ALERT. THE ONE I signed up for months ago but completely forgot about—until now. It's a link to the Bird-Watcher's Association website, whose dull gray background and barrage of ads for field guides and festivals are ingrained in my memory. My dad's been a member for so long he used to act like he invented it. I've already checked their site about five hundred times hoping for some kind of explanation of where he is.

I scroll around for his name. There's a newsletter marked with today's date and *boom,* jackpot. Under a photo of a gray-and-yellow bird on a tree branch, the caption, "Cedar Waxwing. Photo credit: Robert F. Sullivan."

Holding my breath, I open the folder where I store all my dad's photos. Because he was "allergic to technology"—he doesn't even have a *cell phone*—I was the one he tasked to save and catalog all his photos, which are all still in one folder on my laptop. The cedar waxwing photo is *definitely* not in this folder—meaning it must be new.

I'm hoping Google will tell me that the cedar waxwing is found only within a five-mile radius of our town. But according to allaboutbirds.com, the cedar waxwing is found just about everywhere in the continental US. So much for narrowing it down.

I click on the bio he has up on the Bird-Watcher's Association site, but it's the same as it's been the other five hundred times I've read it. *Robert F. Sullivan has been a member of the Bird-Watcher's Association for twenty-three years. Robert F. Sullivan has loved birding since he was a small child.*

Robert F. Sullivan, apparently, didn't think to mention his family in his profile.

I swallow the lump in my throat and look through the newsletter one more time. There has to be something else. I stare at the photo of the cedar waxwing like it's a Magic Eye and my dad's whereabouts are the secret hidden picture. Then I see it: a tiny little announcement beside the photo.

> The annual Bird-Watcher's Association excursion will take place from November 13 to 18. Details given upon registration.

Of course. The excursion. It's a big deal and it's shrouded in secrecy, or at least as much secrecy as a bird-related trip can have. The board doesn't reveal where they're going except to those who register, and they've traveled all around the country to look at the rarest, most beautiful birds. I know my dad's been dying to go on one of these trips again; he organized one years ago when I was a toddler. But when Mom went into labor with Lincoln, he had to give his space on the trip to some other fervent birder, and since then, there's always been something that's kept him from going.

There's no way he's not going on this excursion. He's probably even in charge of it. If I could just find out where it's taking place, I could find him.

That is, *if* I could leave the house.

But this is it. I nod my head resolutely as I stare at the screen. This is the motivation I need to finally step off the porch and get back into my life. I used to leave the house pre–Cheesecake Factory Incident, and there's no reason to think I can't do it again if I have a reward more powerful than visiting the hallowed halls of Reardon High.

I see the cost and feel my heart sink into my stomach.

Five hundred dollars.

Since I currently have about twenty dollars to my name, this presents a problem. I quit my job at Sub Stop when I stopped going outside. I can't ask my mom to spot me, and Lincoln's out, too—he changes the subject every time I bring Dad up. Besides, he spends all of his tiny salary from Nickel and Dime, the local thrift store, on foreign films.

Short of rooting through my mom's purse or collecting change between couch cushions, how am I supposed to make money at home? I exhale, pushing my bangs off my forehead. I scroll through the job listings on Craigslist, but unless I'm willing to write SEO-optimized posts about penis-enlargement pills, I'm out of luck when it comes to at-home job opportunities.

I'm in a state of Craigslist-induced desperation when I see that Jenni texted me. Five times.

We're at lunch!

Where are you?

FACETIME ME. PLS. IT'S IMPORTANT.

Mallorrryyyyyyy. If you don't call me I'm ending our friendship, effective immediately.

Where are you?? Linc is doing his impression
of you . . .

I sigh. Jenni and I have very different ideas of what's
"important." I'm sure she's just going to tell me that Pia or
Caroline changed eyeliner brands, but I call her anyway.

"Mal! You made it!" Jenni speaks in exclamation points.
Even in the shitty cafeteria light, her skin glows. "I was worried
you were going to miss the homecoming court announcement!"

Of course. Jenni's acting like we're at a red carpet premiere
and Jennifer Lawrence just showed up. But today I can't even
humor her. "That's great, but I have something I need to—"

Before I can finish, Lincoln grabs the phone and his flushed
cheeks take up the screen. "Mal, you will not believe who's
sitting behind me in homeroom. Scott Lawson. You know—*Hot*
Scott," he says, tugging impatiently at the lock of hair that always
stubbornly curls out behind his ear.

"Linc."

"And let me assure you, the nickname is well deserved."

"LINC!"

He stops. "What?"

I take a deep breath, trying to act natural. "Hey, I have a
question for you. . . ."

Lincoln narrows his eyes. An unfortunate side effect of
growing up together is that he can almost always tell when I'm
trying to bullshit him.

"This had better be about Scott," he mutters.

"I found the pair of toilet paper tube binoculars Dad made

us when we were little, and then I started thinking about that crazy secret birding trip that used to happen every year; remember how Dad always talked about that?" I say in one breath. Hopefully, he won't be able to see how forced my smile is on the phone screen.

Lincoln purses his lips. "You know, we should change the direction of this conve—"

"Do you know how to find out where this year's excursion is?" I blurt out, abandoning all hope of being subtle.

"Good God, Mallory. No, I don't know, and frankly I don't *care* where some weird-ass gathering of bird freaks is happening." He takes my defeated silence as an opportunity to barrel forward in his discussion of Scott. "Listen, have you even *seen* Scott lately? I swear to God, his eyes are like . . . you know that shade of blue Mom painted the guest bathroom?"

There's no point in pushing my line of inquiry. He's got his *Don't* face on.

"You're saying his eyes look like a bathroom?"

"No, I am not saying the cutest guy in school has eyes like a bathroom."

"Brad Kirkpatrick is the cutest guy in school," Jenni corrects him, off camera.

"I'm just *saying* Scott's eyes are a deep—"

"—Cerulean," Jenni's voice cuts in again.

Lincoln snaps his fingers. "Exactly. Thank you. Cerulean."

"Cerulean Iris," I muse. "I'm pretty sure that's the exact shade Mom used."

As Lincoln shouts, "Scott's eyes do not look like a bathroom!" Caroline Fairchild's unmistakable golden princess curls come into view behind him. She struts into the cafeteria with all the confidence of one of the ponies I'm sure she shows on weekends.

Once, in third grade, Caroline pulled down my pants while we were waiting in line for the water fountain. Just because she thought it was funny. Frankly, I think that's all the evidence I need to conclude she's a psychopath. She's also one of the most popular girls in school, which just figures. And Jenni, in her never-ending optimism, always insists on sitting at the lunch table directly next to Caroline's usual. You know, just in case Caroline deigns to pay attention to her.

I try to tamp down my simmering bitterness only because Jenni's dying to be her friend. And because I have bigger things to worry about. Case in point: figuring out the Dad mystery.

Lincoln moves on from Scott's eyes to the shape of his nose ("Roman but not too Roman"). Ten feet away, Caroline shoots a look at him while leaning over to say something to her friends. All of them crack up.

For once, my hands aren't trembling from panic; they're dying to throw a sloppy joe right at Caroline's perfectly powdered face. There aren't many times I wish I were in school, but this is definitely one of them. Lincoln only came out last year, and it kills me that I can't be there to make sure no one's bothering him.

"There are so many cute guys you're missing." *Just Jenni* is as oblivious to meanness as ever. She scooches her face into the screen with Linc and lowers her voice. "Like Eric Brown. He's stopped wearing jorts. Big improvement. And Max, the guy who looks like a sixteen-year-old baby? He grew a beard and it's really helping that whole situation. And Brad Kirkpatrick is just as hot as he's been since second grade—"

I butt in. "Please don't tell me you're lusting after Brad Kirkpatrick as a second grader."

"I'm worried you're going to forget how to think boys are

cute. The only guys you see are your brother—no offense, Lincoln—and David Delaney."

"Duchovny," I mutter, regretting ever telling her about my *X-Files* obsession. "And he *is* cute, he's just . . ."

"An actor playing a fictional character and, like, a hundred years old." She raises her perfectly plucked and penciled eyebrows.

I sigh, then Lincoln sighs harder, and Jenni laughs at his impression of me before filling me in about some band kids who got caught making out in the tuba closet.

"That's disgusting." Lincoln waves a hand through the air. "I wouldn't want to make out near anything that has a spit valve."

Maybe Lincoln isn't interested in helping me figure out where Dad is, and for once, I don't want to listen to band gossip, so I change the subject. "Listen, I know this isn't as interesting as the spit-related activities of tuba players, but have you been thinking about our physics project? Maybe you can come over after school today and—"

Jenni cuts me off with a dramatic "Shhhhh!" as Principal Lu's voice booms over the loudspeaker.

"Good afternoon, Reardon High!"

I didn't think that it was possible for a crowd to cheer sarcastically, but that's what happens in the cafeteria.

"This is it!" Jenni hisses. "She's about to announce the court!"

"Woo-hoo!" I say, but Jenni's too preoccupied staring at the loudspeaker to notice.

My computer pings, so I balance my phone in my left hand as I use my right hand to open We Are Not Alone on my laptop. I have no interest in the homecoming announcement when I'm so close to figuring out where my dad went, so I might as well enjoy some quality WANA time. There are plenty of replies on my latest post, mostly from BeamMeUp. I snort. Why won't he or she just accept that I'm right?

I hear some whoops and cheers as Principal Lu gives her routine "we're role models at Reardon so let's keep it that way" preamble. Jenni helpfully (but unnecessarily) pans the phone around the cafeteria. I groan. "Jenni, do I have to stay on the line for this?" I can't imagine anything more boring than watching three girls get the dubious honor of running for homecoming queen. But Jenni keeps panning; she's even more excited for homecoming than last year, because homecoming court is nominated entirely from the junior class. Seniors get prom—our school is small enough that having separate proms for the juniors and seniors would just be kind of pathetic.

"The nominees are . . . Caroline Fairchild!" Principal Lu booms.

Jenni gasps as Caroline stands up, doing her best "Taylor Swift at an award show" impression.

"Pia Lubeck!"

Jenni keeps holding the phone up as Pia, who is of course sitting right next to Caroline, stands up and pretends to be embarrassed. For all the clapping and cheering, you'd think she won the Nobel Peace Prize.

"This is ridiculous," I mutter.

"And the last junior girl on Reardon's homecoming court is . . . Mallory Sullivan!"

The cafeteria that was just abuzz with cheers, claps, and shouts becomes eerily silent.

"Let's all give our sincere congratulations to Caroline, Pia, and Mallory!"

"What?" I whisper.

Jenni's phone is still aimed right at Caroline and Pia, and I see them look at each other, smiles playing on their faces. And then I hear it: laughter.

This is a *joke*.

Jenni's face appears on-screen. "Do you want to stand up?"

My mouth opens, but the *no no no* doesn't come out. Of course I don't want to stand up. But suddenly I'm looking down on my classmates, and I can tell that Jenni is standing up, brandishing her phone as if this is a totally normal occurrence.

Caroline looks right at me and says something to Pia, who tips her head back in laughter.

My body feels like ice that's melting; even sitting in my chair, my legs start to tremble. They voted me onto homecoming court as a joke. As if it's not embarrassing enough to be The Girl Who Attends Class on a Computer, now I'm also cast in a remake of *Carrie*, except that I don't have telekinetic powers . . . and I'm not even at school to do anything about it.

With the sound of my classmates' laughter ringing in my ears, I hang up.

CHAPTER FOUR

Migration can be extremely dangerous for birds, and many don't make it back to their starting point.

—*Audubon* magazine, 2012

I WRITE MYSELF AN imaginary doctor's note for my afternoon French and history classes. *Mallory Sullivan is under debilitating stress due to all the total jerks she goes to school with. Also, she still hasn't figured out a way to raise five hundred dollars. Please excuse her from all classes.*

I shove my phone under my mountain of pillows, trying to forget about the laughter in the cafeteria. I try to distract myself as I scroll through a We Are Not Alone thread about one woman's passionate affair with a Martian. But even 50 Shades of Extraterrestrial can't take my mind off what happened, and I have the masochistic desire to know what people are saying about me.

I bounce around online but don't find much. Someone shared a photo of Caroline and Pia making ridiculous kissy faces with the caption, "CONGRATS, BITCHES!" Other than a few generic "Can't wait till September 26!" statuses, there's nothing of interest. For a few minutes, I think people have just totally forgotten me.

Then I see the post that makes my heart stop. I always thought people were exaggerating when they said that—obviously your heart didn't really stop or you'd be dead, dummy. But I actually put my hand on my chest to make sure my heart is still beating.

It's a tweet from Marco Beveridge, a douche bag whose claim to fame last year was showing everyone the X-rated photos he had of Emma Finnerman on his phone.

> Nominations today were totally epic! Can't wait to see if the freak shows up at the dance! #stayathomecoming

My breath gets shorter and shorter. I clutch the edge of my desk with both hands until my knuckles are white. This is Marco, I remind myself. He's known for a sexting scandal, not for his incisive commentary. Probably no one's even noticed this.

I should just shut my laptop. I should go eat lunch and forget all about this. But the part of me that's full of sick curiosity searches Twitter for #stayathomecoming.

"Oh my God," I wail as I scroll through all forty-seven results.

> Can't believe what happened at lunch! #stayathomecoming

> This is definitely the most interesting court we've ever had haha #stayathomecoming

> Whose idea of a joke was that? LOL #stayathomecoming

Blinking tears out of my eyes, I close my laptop before flopping onto my bed. The silly glow-in-the-dark stars that have been up on my ceiling since I was seven stare back at me, creating a fake sky for me now that I almost never leave the house to see the real one.

How did this happen?

I always sort of assumed I was just a Reardon nobody, not a freak or a loser to them. Someone they barely even thought about except to theorize why I wasn't there anymore.

Clearly, that isn't the case.

I'm the butt of the whole school's joke. I was an idiot to think that my classmates would accept that I was home for "personal reasons."

My dad's gone, I'm broke, and someone conspired to make me a school-wide circus act. I don't want to think about any of this right now, so I pull my laptop into bed and try to numb my thoughts with my favorite *X-Files* episode, "Monday." It's about a girl who's stuck living the same day over and over. I want to do this—live a day over and over again, changing my decisions until I get it all right with just one small action.

I wonder, as I watch the main character walk into that bank for the millionth time, what could have stopped Dad from leaving. A cup of coffee from Mom? Tripping over the rug? One less sarcastic remark from me?

If I could live it over again, could I fix it and avoid all this?

I wish I could be like Lincoln—his reaction was the exact opposite of mine. While I shrunk further into myself, Lincoln seemed to grow two inches overnight. He got more extroverted, he smiled more, he laughed all the time. It's almost like he was *relieved*. He just says I need to move on, like Dad has.

But how am I supposed to move on without an answer? Isn't

it normal to be concerned when one of your parents disappears without a trace?

I'm not the weird one here, am I?

My phone buzzes from inside its pillow prison. "Crap," I say when I realize that it's time for my weekly appointment with Dr. Dinah. The last thing I want to do, besides explain hashtags to my therapist, is relive anything that happened today. But last time I didn't answer her call, my mom threatened to take away all my Internet time.

"Hello, Mallory!" she chirps, and I wonder again how her voice can simultaneously communicate warmth and the ability to cut me if I cross her. "What's going on with you?" she asks.

"Well . . ." *I'm still not leaving my house, I spend about 95 percent of my time wondering where the hell my dad went, I need five hundred dollars to register for a top secret bird-watching trip . . . oh yeah . . . and I just got nominated to homecoming court as a joke. Things are swell.*

"Same old, same old," I say.

Dr. Dinah doesn't miss a beat. "Let's get into more detail. What's your progress like on the action item we discussed last session?"

"Expanding your comfort zone and meeting new people?" I *do* have something to tell Dr. Dinah. "BeamMeUp!" I say.

After a long pause, Dr. Dinah says, "I'm sorry?"

"No, I mean . . . that wasn't a command. That's who I've been talking to—er, *engaging with*—on We Are Not Alone."

Dr. Dinah is already well versed in the intricacies of We Are Not Alone. I spent an entire session assuring her that WANA's moderators check that all users have a verified high school or college e-mail address—those who don't or "age out" move up to WANA's sister site, GalaxyFest. Since I don't like to talk about my dad or not leaving the house, there's not much else I *can* share with her. Five minutes later and I'm still just getting into my Air America argument and why it was so ridiculous for BeamMeUp to even attempt to argue with me when she cuts me off.

"Mallory, this is all great to hear. I'm glad you care about something so much—enthusiasm is important. But I have to ask . . . We Are Not Alone doesn't require you to leave the house, does it?"

Technically, We Are Not Alone doesn't even require me to leave my bed. "Well . . ."

That's when Dr. Dinah puts on her "business voice," the one that I know means she's going to make me do something I don't want to do.

"If you remember, our 'action item,'" she says, even her voice implying air quotes, "was to literally expand your comfort zone by taking at least one trip outside."

Biting my lip, I realize I have a death grip on my *X-Files* box set. The phone is hot against my cheek.

"There are no literal locks and chains keeping you inside," she continues. "The only locks and chains are in your mind."

Dr. Dinah must have a PhD in awkward silences, because she waits a solid thirty seconds before continuing.

"So what I'm going to need you to do is to try your best to open those locks and break those chains. I know you can't do it all in one day. Maybe you'll just jiggle the metaphorical door-knob. I want you to step outside—"

"Step outside of the prison of my metaphorical heart?" I say, clearly without thinking.

"No, Mal." Her voice goes stern. She's definitely a mom, or the owner of a very well-behaved dog. "You need to literally step outside today."

"But the thing is, it's sort of hot today, and I—I don't want to risk heatstroke . . . ," I stammer.

"For five minutes. You don't even have to leave your porch if you don't want to, okay? And I'll wait right here on the line for you to come back."

I swallow hard. "I'm just not really *feeling* outside today, you know?"

"Tomorrow is always one day away, Mallory. Today, you're going outside."

Damn, Dr. Dinah. The woman is tough. But the thing that really sucks is that she's right—how will I ever go on this birding trip if I can't even go in the backyard? Leaving the house today is the first step toward getting things back to normal.

"Fine," I say, standing up. "Are you sure you—"

"Just put the phone down and go outside."

"Can I take you with me?" My voice is small, and I know her answer before she says it.

"What do we say, Mal?"

I swallow. "I am safe, I am secure, I am capable."

"I couldn't quite hear that," Dr. Dinah says, and I curse her sick sense of humor. She is always trying to get me to say—believe—this dumb mantra, and nothing could make me feel more like a self-help book reader than actually saying it out loud.

"I am safe. I am secure. I am capable." I over-enunciate each word for her benefit.

"The more you say it, the truer it gets," Dr. Dinah reassures me. "Now, go on."

"Okay, okay. I'm going." Maybe getting a break from the aphorisms will be worth the pinpricks of hot and cold that will shoot through my body when I step onto the porch. Taking the stairs lightly, my breathing gets heavier. "I'm just putting the phone on the stand in our entryway, okay? But I'm going to be right back. So . . ."

"Mallory. It's okay."

I set the phone down next to a bowl of keys and walk toward the front door.

Then I take a deep breath and open it.

My heart starts beating so hard that I'm a little concerned it might pop out of my chest altogether. My palms prickle as I curl my fingers around the door frame. Slowly, I move one foot out like I'm trying to test the water temperature in a pool before stepping onto the coral tile with both bare feet. I have to really think about breathing; it's like I forget how to do it in real time.

I try to focus on how pretty it is out here. My mom spent a lot of time on our porch and the plants in our front yard. The outcroppings of cacti stand out against outdoor furniture spray-painted bright teal and yellow and, of course, multiple bird-houses hang from the trees. She's great at making things look good from the outside.

I take another deep breath. All I have to do is focus on one thing; I choose the tree house my dad built. The sound of my feet on the porch as I walk across to the railing smacks in my ears. Narrowing my focus makes it a tiny bit easier to forget that I'm outside.

My gaze fixed on the tree house, I close my eyes and try to imagine what's inside as my heart slows down from "jack-hammer speed" to "frantic hammering speed." Another one of Dr. Dinah's tricks. I inhale slowly as I think about the faded and creaky wood, the old toys we never bothered to clean out, the crayon-drawing "art" Lincoln and I tacked onto the walls, the view of the night sky out the window, the birding maps where Dad pointed out all the places he hoped to go someday. . . .

I breathe in sharply, and for once it's not because I'm panicking—my hands want those maps, to see the highlighted spots where he'd pointed out his favorite birding areas while I leaned over his shoulder.

To see, maybe, where he would have planned a top secret birding excursion.

Before I can talk myself out of it, I step off the porch and walk across the yard. Pebbles and rocks poke at my bare feet and the sun beating down on my face feels foreign, but I keep going, keep focusing on the tree house.

"You can do this," I whisper as I put my foot on the first old wooden "step" of the ladder. The explosion of sound in my ears, like someone turned the dial on "outdoor" noises to at least one thousand decibels, is scary—but familiar. The wood cracks loudly under my feet and I imagine plummeting to my death and confirming all my fears about leaving the house.

But I press my body up one more foot.

A door creaks. I look up and across into the neighbor's yard to see Brad Kirkpatrick sitting on a lawn chair—except Brad *definitely* doesn't have the tattoos that peek out of this guy's sleeves. He must be Brad's half-brother, Jake, the one who went to the same fancy celebrity rehab as Lindsay Lohan and then turned his back on a life of crime with a vicious New York City street gang to live with his dad.

Okay, so *all* of those rumors can't be true. But one of them has to be, right? Tattooed, rugged guys don't just move home to live with their parents for no reason.

I haven't seen a human being other than my mom, Lincoln, Jenni, and the mail woman in months. My feet are literally itching to jump off the ladder and run inside, so much so that I check to see if I've set off a nest of fire ants.

I wonder what Dr. Dinah will think when I tell her that my first time outside in months has given me foot splinters and a great view of a probable ex-con. Jake cracks open a can of beer and takes a swig. Day-drinking on a Thursday afternoon?

"Gross," I say before I can help myself.

He looks up—right at me. I freeze, but he simply offers a brief, guy-style raised-hand wave.

Panic swells in my chest. I kick my foot up, and the step I'm on splits right down the middle.

"Shit!" I shout, and grab for the tree house. My fingers just reach it, but instead of hanging on, I only manage to pull a bunch of old toys out of it as I tumble to the ground. The plastic dump truck, Barbies, and Lincoln's old xylophone do nothing to cushion my fall.

My mind screams at me to get up and run inside, but my yelping tailbone stops me from moving. Just as my breath is starting to come back, something blocks the sun.

The guy who might be Jake Kirkpatrick stares down at me.

"Are you okay?" he asks, a note of genuine worry in his voice. His knees crack when he crouches down.

"Um, yes," I say, trying not to hyperventilate as I slowly stand. "I only fell, like, a few feet."

"Are you sure?" he asks. I focus on his face. Instead of Brad's blond hair and green eyes, he has dark hair, deep blue eyes, and a sharp nose. In the right light, he might even bear a passing resemblance to a young Fox Mulder. You know, if you were imaginative.

He looks at me expectantly, and I realize he's still waiting for an answer. "I'm fine. I promise," I say, standing and taking an eager step toward the house.

"Because if you're hurt, I can call 911."

"Oh no!" I shout, then try to rein it in, red coursing to my cheeks as I realize he's probably joking. "I mean, oh . . . no need! I'm seriously fine, so I'm just going to go back inside."

Jake picks up a Barbie who happens to be wearing only a skirt. He's silent, but there's a question on his face.

I am 100 percent not going to explain my entire life situation to this guy. "Oh yeah, I was just getting these for my little brother," I squeak, grabbing the topless Barbie and pointing to her lack of shirt. My hands are so sweaty the Barbie almost slips out of my grip. "I need to talk to him about this, it's super inappropriate. So you can just go back home and enjoy your beer."

Shut up, I think to myself. Just get back to the house. Now.

Jake ignores Topless Barbie. "You're clearly having trouble breathing."

I place my Topless-Barbie-holding hand over my heart. It's beating even faster than my short, labored breaths. "I'm fine," I wheeze, taking two more tiny backward steps away from him. I'm calculating the seconds it'll take me to cross the yard. He bends down to pick up the box that I pulled down, and I take the opportunity to bolt for my front door.

"Wait," he calls after me. "Do you need this?" Jake's brandishing the box. A dirty, rolled-up piece of paper sticks out of it—I instantly realize that it's my dad's map. I basically run back and lunge at him, plucking it right from the box.

"Thanks," I say, sprinting back to the house before he can ask me any more questions.

"Hey!" Jake shouts as I grab the doorknob. I turn around to see him holding up the can. "This is root beer. I'm nineteen. Don't believe everything you hear."

But I'm already halfway inside. A cool wall of air hits me;

my house has never felt so good. I clutch the map to my chest like a prize, proof that I can do this.

As soon as my breathing has slowed to something resembling a normal speed, I grab the phone off the entryway stand. "Dr. Dinah?"

"How did it go?" she asks immediately.

"I fell out of my tree house and ran away from my neighbor. Talk to you next week!"

I hang up.

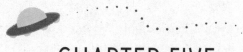

CHAPTER FIVE

THE BIGGEST PROBLEM WITH never leaving your house is that people always know where to find you.

Before I can "process" what just happened, Lincoln and Jenni burst through the door with awkward, totally transparent smiles pasted on their faces. I clutch Topless Barbie a little bit harder and slip the map under my bed.

"Are you enjoying your time in your cave?" Lincoln asks, grabbing Topless Barbie from me. I just shrug.

"Come look what we brought!" Jenni practically sings. She grabs my hand and pulls me downstairs into the kitchen, where there's a bakery box sitting on the island. Twelve delicious-looking cupcakes, all covered in piped pink frosting and topped with delicate gold crowns, peek out of the box.

"You went to Sweet Nothings?" I frown. A full dozen? She normally only lets me have half. Jenni must know how bad the whole homecoming thing is.

Lincoln nudges me with a bony elbow. "When have you ever hesitated in front of a cupcake?"

He has a point, so I mutter a "Thank you" and grab one.

"So." Jenni throws a quick glance at Lincoln. "We wanted to talk to you about today."

Even though my mouth is still full of sweet, sweet frosting, I say, "We definitely need to work out a schedule for the physics project."

"Mal—"

"Because Mr. Parker is right. We need to get started ASAP if we want to get the best grade in the cl—"

"We want to talk about home—"

"Let me go get my physics notebook," I say, brushing crumbs off my shirt.

"Mal!" Lincoln grabs me by my shoulders and plants me firmly on a horrifically flowered kitchen chair. "You are so incredibly annoying."

I shoot him a glare. He's the king of avoidance, so what would he know?

"We have a plan," says Jenni, directing my attention back to her. "Because you know what? You deserve to be homecoming queen."

"You are so much more fun than anyone else who was nominated," Lincoln continues. "Caroline Fairchild? Barf. She *looks* good, but she is literally so boring."

"She pulled my pants down that one time." I nod.

"In third grade!" Jenni cries.

"Jen," Lincoln says. "Not helping."

She holds up her hands. "Okay! But listen. Regardless of my personal feelings about Caroline, I think we all know that you're the best candidate. You're so fun, you're unique, you're nice to everyone. . . ."

"If by 'nice to everyone' you mean I just make fun of them behind their backs, then sure."

Lincoln crosses his arms over his maroon polo shirt. "You don't do it to their faces, and that's what counts. But mostly, I *know* you want to rub it in everyone's faces by beating those jerks."

I think about it for a second. "You're right, I do have a barely contained desire for revenge. But," I continue, looking at Jenni, "I honestly find it hard to believe that you want anything to do with showing up the popular kids. How will you ever get in with them if you're organizing a radical overthrow of their rule?"

I'm being sarcastic, but I regret the words as soon as I see Jenni's shoulders drop. "It's not like I'm going to ever date one of them or be friends with them anyway," she says in a little voice.

"But," my brother says, swinging an arm around Jenni's shoulders. "Just imagine what life would be like for you as best friend of the homecoming queen! You'd get a front row seat to every bit of drama and gossip and . . . style tips and stuff."

Jenni sits up a little straighter. "I *do* need to keep *Just Jenni* relevant. A beauty-and-style vlogger has to be on top of trends."

"And speaking of gossip," Lincoln says, crossing the room to the small window above the sink. The faint sounds of laughter and a ball bouncing float in through the window. "Did you hear that football practice got canceled this afternoon? Someone vandalized the practice field."

Usually nothing would bore me more than sports talk, but I'm thankful that some drama might have drawn some attention away from #stayathomecoming.

"Who would do such a thing?" I say in mock horror.

"They're pretty sure it was someone from Mayfield High, since they burned the words 'Mayfield High Rules' into the grass."

"Clever," I say, peering over Lincoln's shoulder. Brad—real

Brad—and all his teammates are in his driveway, playing basketball. Even through the closed window I hear them yelling profane insults at one another. Jake seems to have retreated inside.

"They do know they're playing the wrong sport, right?" I ask.

"Cross-training, Mal," Lincoln says, but the way he's staring at them doesn't suggest he's thinking about their athletic prowess.

"Gross." I wrinkle my nose. "Those guys are terrible."

"Not all of them," Jenni says. I sit back down next to her and pop one of the cupcakes' candy crowns into my mouth. "I know you like to pretend that every single popular kid is horrible, but some of them are actually nice. If you get to know them."

"Have you seen the hashtag?" I ask.

Jenni widens her eyes innocently. "Hashtag?"

"Nice try."

She twists her ponytail. "Promise me you won't look at that again."

"Seriously," Lincoln adds. "Only the dregs of humanity would take part in a hashtag bullying campaign."

I hold up my hands in surrender. "Fine! I promise."

"Hashtag aside," Jenni continues, "it would be so great if you really tried to do this—to win. We've been working on an awesome, foolproof plan aaaaall day."

"It was more like five minutes," Lincoln says without looking away from the window.

Anxiety shoots up as quickly as a dandelion in my chest. I unwrap another cupcake. "Foolproof, huh?" I ask, trying to sound as skeptical as possible.

Jenni sits up impeccably straight and, clearly already

planning her next vlog on how sugar causes breakouts, folds her hands on her lap. "Totally. Guaranteed victory."

I cross my arms. "Against my better judgment, I want you to tell me about it."

Jenni claps her hands together. "Okay, so you really only need one thing to get that crown . . ." She pauses for dramatic effect. "A popular date."

I laugh so hard that some frosting flies out of my mouth and hits the table.

"So let me get this straight . . . your 'plan' just involves getting someone 'popular' to be my date?"

Jenni nods, looking proud. "If you can get a super-hot, super-popular guy to be your date, you can totally win," she continues.

"You're my friend and I love you, but that isn't a plan."

Jenni opens her mouth to speak, but I cut her off. "I mean, I was considering calling my grandpa and asking if any of his friends would like to attend a high school homecoming, but now you're telling me I should invite a young, good-looking boy? This is revolutionary."

"I told you she'd be like this." Linc breaks his eye contact with the moving sculptures outside for the first time and makes a face at Jenni.

"There's something else," Jenni continues. "Remember how last year Liza Baker's mom complained that homecoming was just another patriarchal beauty pageant that existed solely to lower girls' self-esteem?"

"How could anyone forget?" I snorted. "She's the only person in the history of ever to have launched a one-person anti-homecoming protest outside the homecoming game, complete with a bullhorn."

"Well, I guess she wouldn't stop calling Principal Lu about it and it got super annoying, so now we have a homecoming committee and spirit points."

"Spirit points?" I ask. "Like . . . rah-rah, pom-pom school spirit?"

Jenni's ponytail bobs as she nods. "The committee is made up of teachers and students, but no one knows who they are. They're awarding spirit points to candidates who show school spirit in the next three weeks."

"Each spirit point is worth *fifteen* votes," Lincoln says. "Which means you could get a low popular vote and still win—as long as you get enough spirit points."

"There are, like, a million ways to get spirit points," Jenni says, counting them off on her fingers. "Going to football games, participating in the pep rally, helping out the team. So let's say you get a super-hot date on the football team. Instant spirit points! And popular votes!"

I shake my head. On top of everything else that happened today, this plan makes me want to crawl back into bed. "Guys . . . you do know that most of those would require me to leave the house, right? And I don't do that anymore?"

Jenni nods vigorously. "Which only makes you *more* attractive to guys! Guys love a chase and they love a mysterious woman. No one even sees you anymore, so you're *super* mysterious."

Lincoln grabs my wrist and yanks me to the window. "Jenni's right. You don't even have to leave the house. We'll just find you a date close to home."

I laugh. "And how are you going to swing that one? The only guy who lives nearby is . . ."

I trail off as I follow Lincoln's gaze out the window to the

Kirkpatricks' driveway, where Brad is effortlessly making shot after shot.

"Are you insane? Brad's lived next door for two whole years, and he hasn't even said anything but hi to me."

Lincoln turns to me, pushing his swooping, dark blond hair out of his eyes. "You should do this because we love you and you want to get the ultimate revenge. But you also deserve this."

"Yeah . . . ," I say. Jenni's cheeks tighten into a huge smile just before I finish. "No."

The dribbling next door sounds like a machine gun. Then silence, then a cheer and the slap of high fives.

Lincoln crosses his arms. "Okay, Jenni. Tell her the thing we haven't told her yet."

Jenni pipes up. "They're not giving out gift cards to Fat Boy's Pizza this year. The winner gets five hundred dollars. Which could buy an entire semester's worth of textbooks, which I've heard are *really* expensive . . ."

Lincoln's turned to the window again like what Jenni's saying is no big deal, but I can't even speak. Five hundred dollars? As in, enough money to register for the birding excursion?

"Think of what you could do with that money," Lincoln says. "Buy all the junk food you want, shower your wonderful brother with gifts . . ."

"Lincoln," Jenni scolds. "The average freshman spends that on just one class."

"Jenni, Mal has a *year* before she even starts her applications. . . ."

In my head, a million scenarios play out as my heart beats overtime. This could lead to massive-scale humiliation, like teen-movie-style, pig's-blood-dumping, life-ruining embarrassment.

And even if I do get the money, it could lead to the Cheesecake Factory Incident Version 2.0.

But if it worked—if I *actually* win that five hundred dollars and go on the excursion—it would be worth it. So, so worth it.

I could fix everything, and we could go back to normal.

"Okay," I say quietly.

Linc's mouth literally falls open. "What did you say?"

"I said . . . okay." I throw my hands up in surrender. "Let's do this. It's on."

CHAPTER SIX

With the right eyeliner, lipstick, and brow pencil, you can transform yourself into anyone you want to be. I mean, just look at the Kardashians.

—*Just Jenni*, 2015

I WAKE UP THE next morning to a text from Jenni. It's just a long string of heart and crown emojis that I *think* is supposed to be encouraging. I follow up by sending her the wad of cash with wings on it. A tiny pebble of guilt lodges in my stomach, but I ignore it. After all, I'm not lying, exactly, just creatively withholding a bit of information about why I want that five hundred dollars.

After a night of whooping and leaping and talking about who will play us in the romcom version of my triumphant homecoming story, Jenni left me with a schedule. In her words, "We only have three weeks to turn you into the most spirited girl in—er, out—of school." My first "assignment" for this morning is to leave a flattering comment on something Brad's posted online.

Upstairs, I sit down on my bed with my stuffed black bear,

Bananas, and my laptop until I realize that I have no clue how to start.

Scrolling through Brad's Facebook page doesn't help. He shared a clip of Jimmy Fallon on *The Tonight Show* a few nights ago and a link to a football fund-raiser last week. Not exactly illuminating stuff. After ten minutes, it starts to feel pathetic. I mean, what does Jenni think is going to happen?

Oh hey, Brad, that video of Dwayne "The Rock" Johnson lip-synching is so cool.

Wow, Mal, you think so? I can't believe we both love a charming former wrestler; we should go to homecoming together!

Doubtful.

I click over to We Are Not Alone—one of the only places that I never feel discouraged—and see that my latest half-finished response to BeamMeUp is still there. Yesterday, when I abandoned it, already feels like a lifetime ago. I add a few words and post it.

BeamMeUp: I thought you backed down.

I can't help but smile at the immediate response. At least I'm not the *only* person spending my Saturday on the computer. My interest in the Air America crash is running out, but I *am* all too eager to avoid my fruitless Brad-stalking a little longer.

AlienHuntress: So what makes you such an expert on aliens?

BeamMeUp: I wouldn't say I'm an expert, but I've spent way more time than any normal teenage guy researching this stuff. Two years ago, I entered this huge science competition for high school seniors with a project on the potential for the terraforming of Mars. I ended up spending pretty much every weekend going down Internet rabbit holes and even sent a weather balloon into space.

I figured BeamMeUp was just another bored college kid who'd rather binge on sci-fi novels than do homework—but he's some sort of genius. And, apparently, a guy.

Before I can ask him how his project turned out, he responds.

BeamMeUp: Obviously, I won.

I roll my eyes. Of course he's the worst kind of genius—the kind who knows he's a genius.

AlienHuntress: So what are you doing wasting your time on We Are Not Alone? Shouldn't you be out trying to change the world or something?

Another comment pops up on the thread from another user.

SoullyIsMyGirlfriend: Stop wasting our time. Why don't you two get a room?

"Real mature," I mutter, but about five seconds later a message pops up.

BeamMeUp: Well, it looks like we managed to become outcasts even on We Are Not Alone. That's either really impressive or really sad.

I've never used the chat function in We Are Not Alone because . . . well, as much as I love these glorious alien-obsessed freaks, I've never felt the need to take any of our conversations to a private level.

This conversation is infinitely easier than leaving Brad a comment, so I might as well keep it going.

> **AlienHuntress:** I say it's impressive—but then again, you're the genius, so you can decide. So obviously I know where you stand on the Air America debate (firmly on the wrong side). But what do you think about ghosts?

I hit "SEND" and lean back against my headboard. The typing icon, a little gray alien head, pops up, followed by a satisfying *ping*.

> **BeamMeUp:** Full disclosure: I don't really care that much about Air America. I just like to argue with people who are smart and know how to debate. It's like my form of competitive sports.

It's embarrassing that an Internet stranger telling me I'm great at arguing makes me feel good about myself, but after yesterday's combo homecoming–tree house disaster, I'll take what I can get.

> **BeamMeUp:** But re: ghosts. No way. I don't want to live in a world where I can be haunted by anyone, let alone creepy children or people who can walk through walls. Your turn: what's your position on time travel?

> **AlienHuntress:** Good answer. As for time travel, yes. I fully believe it's possible, if only because I really want to try it.

BeamMeUp: Okay, so we actually agree on a few things. I'm shocked. What about this one: Are aliens responsible for Stonehenge?

AlienHuntress: Obvs. How could humans lift those huge stones? And, more importantly, why the hell would they want to? It's clearly the work of aliens who have aesthetic standards we couldn't possibly understand.

The Facebook tab on my browser is blinking, but I ignore it.

BeamMeUp: Um, speak for yourself. I have a Stonehenge theme in my home and it's very attractive.

I actually laugh out loud.

BeamMeUp: So . . . time travel. How would you use it?

Maybe he expects me to give some silly answer, like that I'd want to go back to the day *The X-Files* premiered on television, or get serious and say I'd prevent some national tragedy. But I know there's only one thing I want to do.

My fingers hover over the keyboard, practically buzzing with the feeling that I might be able to be honest without being judged, when my mom pushes the bedroom door open.

"Uh, teenager here?" I say, throwing my hands in the air. "What if I needed time to hide my secret boyfriend in the closet?"

Mom rolls her eyes. Clearly, I get it from her. "Do you want anything from the store? I'm about to go get some things for Book Club tomorrow."

My face twists at the mention of "Book Club," but her eyes are too busy darting between the tower of papers on my dresser and the lump of unmatched socks on my floor to notice. "I'm good," I say. Instead of leaving, she gingerly steps over a pile of clothes like it's a hornet's nest and sits down on the edge of my bed.

"What was so funny? I heard you laughing."

"Um . . . you're probably not going to think it's as funny as I do."

She shrugs. "Try me." She's staring at me with her eyebrows raised and a half smile on her face like she expects this to be some *moment* between us, so what am I supposed to do? I scroll through my conversation with BeamMeUp.

"Okay," I say slowly. "So I'm talking to a friend, and he says . . ."

Mom narrows her eyes. "A friend? And it's a he?"

Rookie mistake. Now she's going to pry at me with a crowbar until I pop open. Even though she won't share *anything* with me.

"Yeah, Mom," I say, focusing on my computer.

She shifts on the bed. "Do I know him? Is he from school?"

I pause and look at her, considering how much I should tell. I'm definitely not going to explain We Are Not Alone to her again, or mention that I only know this guy through the power of the Internet. Technically, BeamMeUp is a guy who went to *a* school.

"Uh, yeah," I say brightly. "You don't know him, but he's from school." The white lies are really piling up today.

Her eyes twitch with the effort it takes her not to ask me more about BeamMeUp. She slowly smooths her hand over my quilt, handmade by Grandma Barb, and I know she's about to ask me something that I'm *definitely* not going to like.

"So, are things getting better?"

I don't know if Mom thinks she's being subtle, but we both know that "are things getting better?" is code for "when are you going to stop being such a total basket case?"

"Things are fab," I say, giving her a huge, fake smile before turning back to my laptop.

"I just read an article on the *Huffington Post* that said people who spend at least an hour outside each day are seventy-five percent happier," she says offhandedly, as if this is a fact she suddenly remembered.

I tilt my head without pulling my eyes from the screen. "That's weird. I just read an article on CNN that said moms who cite statistics to try to get their daughters to do things are a hundred percent obvious."

Mom presses her lips into a smile so thin I can practically *hear* the frustration in it. "I'd ground you for the back talk, but where would that get me?"

I feel a familiar prick of hurt and frustration in my chest, but I shrug like her comment doesn't sting. Slowly, I close my laptop. If this conversation is going where I think it's going, I'm going to need plenty of Internet time to "untwist my emotions," as Dr. Dinah would say.

Mom continues, still in the perky, pushy Realtor Voice she uses to convince people that they never *really* needed that open floor plan anyway. "You know, Mrs. Goodwin's coming over for Book Club. . . ."

I stiffen. The prick of frustration is back, turning into anger. "Maura's mom?"

"Yeah. Maura *loves* Yale. She spent her senior year volunteering at People for Pets, playing in the jazz band, and editing Reardon's literary journal."

Perfect-angel-former-valedictorian Maura *would*. "Dr. Dinah would say that Maura needs to clear the clutter from the closet of her mind."

Mom exhales heavily and looks at the ceiling before her professional mask drops. "All I'm saying is . . . listen, I know what a normal high school experience looks like. And it isn't spending every single moment in your house."

"I'm sorry I'm not more normal like *Maura Goodwin*," I say, snarling her name like it's a curse word. "But I guess you're pretty much the poster mom for a 'normal' life, right? Since you work around the clock and pretend nothing ever happened?"

"I do not work around the clock." She stands up and crosses her arms.

"That's not the point!" I shout. "The point is, Dad's gone! He left! And you won't tell me why!"

She pinches her nose and closes her eyes, exhaling heavily. "I wish I could give you a reason, honey, I really do, but I don't have one, either. Your dad wanted to leave, so he did."

"But that doesn't even make sense!" I say, praying that Lincoln can't hear this. Our shouting drives him nuts. "People don't just leave their families with no warning or reason."

My mom looks down at me. "I hate to break this to you, Mal, but sometimes they do." She turns and walks out of my room, shutting the door softly behind her.

Boiling, I slam my face into my pillow. My eyes sting, but I don't want to cry. I put my pillow behind me and fluff it up. I lean back, inhale, raise my hands above my head and bring them to a prayer pose in front of my chest. Jenni keeps telling me I need to use yoga to calm my brain, and while I'm way more interested in hearing her stories about the people who fart in yoga class than the poses, I remember this one.

After one more deep breath in and out, I'm calm enough to open my laptop and make the most of my remaining minutes. BeamMeUp is Out of This World, which is WANA-speak for "logged off." A lonely feeling pools in my stomach.

Okay, Mal, you shouldn't be spilling your guts to Internet strangers anyway.

My phone rattles on my nightstand. It's a text from Jenni:

Progress report?

Her photo ID is one of those mall photo booth strips, from about two years ago. In one frame we're making kissy faces at the camera, in the next we have our eyes closed and mouths open like we're screaming, and in the third we have our cheeks inflated and our eyes crossed. But the last frame is my favorite: We have our arms around each other and our faces smashed together, and we're smiling like everything in our lives will always go perfectly.

The look in my eyes in that picture is one I don't even recognize. I feel a familiar twinge of guilt. Jenni would never say it, but I know how disappointed she must be that I've turned out to be a Class A recluse. "This will be our year, when we become social butterflies and get boyfriends *and* straight As," she said to me on the phone the night before our first day as juniors, while anxiety was churning in my stomach on the other end. I didn't have the heart to tell her that my summer "staycation" didn't look like it was going to be over anytime soon.

I run my fingers through my hair. So maybe I still can't leave my house, but that doesn't mean I should just give up and spend all my time arguing with Mom and venting to alien-obsessed strangers.

It's time to do my homecoming work.

Brad's feed has a number of gems. There's a photo of him and Pia Lubeck, head cheerleader and one of Jenni's top fantasy friends. Almost all of her tweets are about reality show stars or Drake. I make a mental note to tell Jenni, as if she needs any encouragement to listen to more Drake.

And there Brad is in the football team picture. He's the only one in the whole picture who's smiling, which makes me less totally terrified of him—until the next picture, in which he's literally holding a cheerleader on each shoulder. Several more pictures indicate that every girl in school is in love with him. And in the pictures of him and his friends, it looks like every *guy* in school is in love with him, too. Everyone looks crazy happy just to be in Brad's presence.

A Focustime warning pops up, letting me know that I have thirty seconds. So much for coming up with a witty comment. At this point, I'll settle for "not insane." But I scroll so fast the photos can't load fast enough. Just before my Internet clicks off, I quickly write "Awesome!!!!" on the picture of Brad that happens to be up on my screen. My window freezes just when I realize it's a shirtless gym pic.

Thirty seconds later, Lincoln's in my room, brandishing his phone at me.

"Really?"

I groan and throw myself against my pile of pillows.

Lincoln throws his hands in the air. "You could've written anything on any of his photos. You could've liked the photo where he was volunteering at the food pantry. And you picked the one picture he's shirtless in?"

"I technically fulfilled my assignment!"

"Jenni should never have left this up to you. She should've

told you exactly what to say and where." Lincoln shakes his head, scrolling through his phone. "Now you look like a creepy perv who favorites random shirtless pics."

"Hey!" I shout. "I take offense to that!"

Lincoln shrugs and holds up his phone. "The record shows it."

"Can we at least revisit my failure over breakfast?"

Downstairs, my mom is emptying the dishwasher with an intensity that suggests she's still upset about our conversation. Lincoln grabs an apple out of the bowl on the island and widens his eyes at me. Mom snaps the dishwasher shut and breezes by both of us, grabbing her purse on the way out.

"Back soon!" she calls.

I furrow my brows. It's not even noon and I've already been called a perv by one relative and almost completely ignored by the other. I'm thinking that Sullivan family dynamics couldn't possibly be any weirder when I hear three even knocks on the door.

Mom would be totally screwed if I ever left the house. The woman can sell a three-bedroom ranch like nobody's business, but she can't ever remember her keys. I pad out of the kitchen and to the front door, feeling smug.

"Seriously, you should just wear your key around your neck."

But it definitely isn't my mom staring back at me. It's Brad Kirkpatrick.

CHAPTER SEVEN

ALL I CAN DO is blink as I stare at Brad—neighbor, football player, most popular guy in school. My homecoming date-to-be. A guy who looks like he could be in a boy band, with his blond hair and his green eyes and his defined jaw. He'd be the heart-throb, the one everyone is in love with, the one every single girl hangs a poster of in her room. And he's on my front porch.

I'd be less surprised to see the president. I'd even be less surprised to see the reanimated corpse of a former president.

I blurt out the first words that come to mind.

"Why are you here?"

Brad takes a step back. "Um, hi?"

"I—I just . . . wasn't expecting you," I stammer.

Brad tilts his beautiful head in what I think is either confusion or concern for my mental health. "Our project?" he says slowly, pulling his worn copy of *Physics in the Modern World* out of his backpack. "Didn't Jenni tell you?"

He points to his right and I poke my head out the door to

see Jenni, who is suddenly *very* interested in inspecting one of our birdhouses.

"Yes. Of course." *No way.* "How could I forget? Go ahead and sit down." I gesture to the kitchen behind me, then I do something that looks like a curtsy.

I poke my head out the door and whisper-yell, "Jenni Agrawal!" until she prances over. She's wearing a tiny pleated skirt, tights printed with little hearts, and a bright yellow cardigan. It's hard to be mad when you're talking to someone who's disgustingly cute.

"Okay," she whispers. "I can see that you're mad, but I can explain . . ."

"Mad? What would give you that impression?"

"I got Mr. Parker to swap our partners! Brad's doing terrible in physics and he could really use the help of the smartest person in class, which works out *perfectly* for our plan."

"It's nice how that worked out," I mutter, retreating from the doorway as much as I can while making sure Jenni has a full view of the angry daggers shooting from my eyes.

"This gives you and Brad alone time," Jenni says, nudging me with her elbow and stepping inside. "Which means he'll be able to fall for your natural charm." She gives me the once-over. "But maybe your natural charm should consider a change of clothes."

She grabs a compact from her baby-blue crossbody bag and thrusts it in my face. My hair is in a messy bun, there's a huge zit on my chin, and my T-shirt says THE TRUTH IS OUT THERE.

"Brad!" Lincoln's voice floats into my ears. Jenni's at my heels while I walk to the kitchen. Lincoln leans against the fridge, one hand on his hip and the other hand holding a bag of coffee. "I can't believe Reardon High's number one football player is right here at my table!"

I glare at Lincoln, but Brad is positively beaming. "Well, thanks, man. I'm here to work on a physics project with your sister."

"Fascinating," Lincoln says, smiling at me. I *deeply* want to murder him.

Jenni asks Brad a question about the assignment. *Someone* placed my physics book and notebook on the counter. I walk to the other side of the island and pull Lincoln into the den. "What are you thinking?" I whisper.

"This is what it takes, Mal," he says, in as close to a whisper as he can manage. "We're going to make sure you win."

I open my mouth to keep whisper-yelling at him but quickly stop myself. I need that money.

"You're right." I shrug.

Lincoln actually gasps and drops the bag of coffee on the floor. It lands with a thump and coffee grains explode up, showering the white sheepskin rug with brown specks. Mom's going to kill us. Lincoln's eyes are wide with disbelief.

"I'm just . . . I don't think you've ever backed down so quickly. Even when we were little and you tried to convince me that I was adopted, which I *knew* wasn't true, you maintained your position for *years*."

"There are hardly any baby pictures of you! But that's not the point," I say, leaning back into the kitchen to make sure Brad and Jenni are still talking. "I need money for the trip."

"Trip?" Lincoln asks.

Shit. Obviously I can't tell Lincoln about the birding excursion. He would stop helping me. He'd *probably* stop talking to me.

"For . . . the trip," I repeat myself stupidly as Lincoln stares at me with confusion.

"The Europe trip?" he asks slowly.

"Yes!" I pounce on it even though the rational part of my brain is screaming at me to stop. "I want to go to Europe. With my classmates. And I need to pay the deposit."

Lincoln crosses his lightly freckled arms. "I cannot believe this." I think he's chastising me for lying, and I'm about to sputter an apology, but then his face breaks into a gigantic, gloriously white-toothed smile. "I am *so* proud of you. This is a huge step. A transatlantic step."

"But can you promise not to tell Mom or Jenni? I want it to be a surprise." My relief instantly curdles into guilt in my stomach.

"Of course! Now, why don't you get back in there?" Lincoln nods toward the kitchen.

"No!" I grab his arm. "Come with me!"

"No can do," Lincoln says. "I'm not being your third wheel. Jenni! Coffee run!"

She whips her head toward us, her ponytail slicing through the air. "Great idea. Sorry we have to run!"

"Pretty sure there's still plenty of coffee in the bag," I say through my teeth.

"I don't like that kind." Lincoln breezes past me and hooks arms with Jenni. "Brad, it's been a pleasure."

Brad nods a genial farewell as I weakly say, "You guys sure you don't want to stay—?" But the door slams before I finish. Brad's sitting at the table with his physics book open. He looks back at me. In my head, Dr. Dinah is saying something like, *Jump into the full yes, Mallory.* I sit down at the table across from him.

"All right. To be honest, I need to kick some ass on this project," he says, tracing his pencil along the swirls of the marble counter. "The only class I'm doing okay in is history, and that's only because Mrs. Johnson is . . ."

"A barely functioning alcoholic," I finish.

"Not a very good teacher," Brad says at the same time.

I shrug. "I guess your version is nicer."

He smiles a bit. "My grades are pretty much terrible. If I have to take that midterm, I might fail physics. And if I fail, my GPA won't be high enough for me to be on the team."

I snort. "Don't teachers just fudge football players' grades so they can stay on the team? I've seen *Friday Night Lights*."

Brad pushes his hair back. "Seriously? That definitely doesn't happen. I'm in charge of raising my GPA from 'awful' to 'sort of okay' all on my own."

Great, I've already managed to insult him. "Maybe it will make you feel better to know I want to have the best project in the class just as much as you do. I need to avoid that midterm because, well . . ."

I trail off. It's not like I need to tell him that I don't come into school. As this week showed me, he's already well aware.

Brad lets the silence hang in the air as he nods. "I get it," he says, though it sounds like a question. I'm pretty sure there's no way he could understand, but I'm grateful for the reprieve.

"So," he exhales, looking at his notebook. "Examples of physics in our everyday life." He runs a hand through his hair again. "Jenni left us directions."

"Of course she did." The instructions are handwritten on personalized stationery. I pluck them from Brad, whose eyes and twisted mouth look overwhelmed at the sight of them, and read out loud. " 'Create an experiment that illustrates a physics concept we discussed in class. You must keep a journal as a way to show your progress *and* show that you understand the other concepts discussed in class.' "

Brad looks disappointed. "A journal? I hate writing."

"Leave the writing part to me," I say, seizing a task I know I can do. "It's going to be way harder to figure out this experiment. Do you have your notes?"

"Well, yeah . . . but yours are probably better."

"I don't really take notes," I say, reaching for his notebook.

"You don't take notes, either?"

"I keep it all up here," I say, pointing to my head. "Ol' Steel Trap Sullivan."

Now Brad's really looking at me like I'm crazy. I wonder if he noticed my comment on the shirtless pic.

"I usually just remember things," I clarify. "But it would be helpful if I could actually look through your notes."

Brad shrugs. "Go for it!"

There are pages and pages of what seem, at first glance, to be physics notes but on closer inspection are borderline incomprehensible. Formulas are half finished, sentences taper off, and one page just contains the word PHYSICS, circled at least a few hundred times.

I hold it up. "Were you afraid you'd forget?"

Brad leans back in his chair and looks at the ceiling. "You were warned, okay?"

He rubs the back of his neck. "Hey, I'm sorry, but I'm so hungry I'm having a hard time concentrating. I burned, like, five thousand calories at practice this morning, and now I'm starving. Can I grab a snack?"

"Sure." There are a few notes in a loopy hand in the margins stamped with Pia's initials. If I tear them out, maybe Jenni will just pay me five hundred dollars for them. "My mom ran out for groceries, but you're welcome to look through the fridge," I say without looking up. No way am I telling him about the Little Debbie supply under my bed.

As I cross out what I'm pretty sure are football plays, I hear the clink of pots and pans and a knife chopping. The sizzle of something cooking fills the kitchen.

"Um, no offense," I say, watching Brad as he moves around the kitchen. "But what the hell are you doing?"

"You had some roasted sweet potatoes and vegetables in the fridge, so I made a hash and put a fried egg on top. Want some?" He's moving the spatula around in the pan like he's trying to squash a bug, and in one fell swoop there's a mountain of delicious-looking food on a plate in front of me.

Brad Kirkpatrick is cooking for me.

I'm about to take a bite of food *Brad Kirkpatrick* made from leftovers in my fridge.

Pulling my phone out of my pocket under the table, I text Jenni:

> Does feeding our high school football star get me spirit points?

Though he's not looking right at me, I can feel Brad waiting for me to take a bite, so I grab my fork and scoop some into my mouth.

"Oh my God," I say with my mouth full. "This is incredible."

"Thanks!" Brad smiles and shoves the contents of the pan into his mouth in three bites.

My phone buzzes with a text from Jenni.

> WHAT????

"I used Rosemary. Don't tell Sage." He laughs at his own corny joke, and it's somehow a handsome laugh, and even the way his skin folds around his eyes is handsome, and my heart suddenly feels like it's going to explode.

But it doesn't, so I try to focus on eating the rest of my food as I finish looking through Brad's notes. They're incomplete and sometimes just flat-out wrong, but he does capture some stuff I didn't get. And I can't help but smirk at the little doodles of footballs and goalposts he does in the margins.

My head jerks up when I hear the microwave door slam. "Dude," I say as Brad punches the microwave keys. "I wish Mr. Parker would give us an A for cooking my mom's leftovers."

He waves me over. "We're going to use this chocolate I'm melting to measure the speed of light," he says.

I eye him warily but join him in front of the microwave.

After a second, I say, "I'm sorry, Brad, but I think you *may* have suffered some serious head trauma in your football career."

He laughs. "You're funny, you know that?"

Against my better judgment, I can feel myself inflating with pride, like a bird fluffing up its feathers. "Don't change the subject. You just want to eat chocolate."

"Trust me. My brother and his girlfriend used to do weird stuff like this all the time."

I start to scowl at the mention of Jake—after all, he did witness one of my *America's Funniest Home Videos*–caliber embarrassing moments—but I try to keep my face neutral for Brad. There's something about him that suppresses my urge to roll my eyes. I get out my phone and start filming.

"So first I put nine Hershey's Kisses on the plate—" he narrates.

"That you found in my cupboard," I interrupt.

Brad shoots me a look that clearly says, *Shut up, we're filming.*

"And I microwaved them for twenty seconds," he continues.

He pulls the plate out of the microwave. "Take a look at this. See how this one is almost completely melted, and this one sort of melted on the top? I'll just take a ruler . . . oh, I found this ruler in a drawer. I hope that's okay."

"Oh, sure. Please just go through everything in my home," I answer, trying to sound sarcastic.

"So then we just measure this distance, multiply this by two, and then multiply *that* by the frequency in hertz. And that's it! The speed of light!"

I tap the OFF button. "That was really cool," I say, not bothering to hide my surprise.

"Gee, thanks," Brad says, but he's smiling. "I may be God-awful at physics, but there are *some* perks to having me as a partner." He grabs a strawberry, which he must have found in our fridge, off the counter and swirls it in the Hershey's Kiss that's mostly melted. "Open up!"

Wait. Is Brad Kirkpatrick going to feed me chocolate-covered fruit like we're on some sort of romantic picnic or an episode of *The Bachelor*? I open my mouth and close my eyes like I'm about to be executed.

As Brad basically tosses the strawberry into my mouth (he has good aim), I hear a tiny giggle behind me. I whirl around to see Jenni and Lincoln standing in the doorway. Jenni's holding up her phone.

"Adorable pic!" she squeals.

"When did you guys become my personal paparazzi?" I self-consciously wipe my face.

"I'm on yearbook staff!" Jenni says, intently staring at her phone. "It's so important to get pictures of students who are dedicated to extracurriculars."

"Plus," Lincoln says. "It's showing so much school spirit."

"Spirit points!" Brad whoops as he throws his arm around me. "Take another one, then!"

Spirit points, I remind myself as I try to relax into Brad's very, very muscled arm. Jenni snaps another photo. "So cute," she declares, then looks at her phone and starts muttering to herself about Instagram filters. Brad's arm lingers on my shoulder, and he squeezes gently before letting go. My heart's palpitating when the doorbell chimes. Everyone I know is already here—who could it possibly be?

"Probably Tyler Perkins selling Girl Scout cookies again," Lincoln says. "She is ruthless."

"She's seven years old!" I yell as I walk past Jenni to the door, eager to have an excuse to stop leering at Brad while hoping he's never going to bring up my so-called pervy comment on his picture.

I pull open the heavy oak door to find Jake Kirkpatrick bouncing up and down on the other side, his dark hair looking rumpled and slept-on. Before I can even react with my trademark Sullivan charm and whip out another witty remark like, "Why are you here?" Jake says, "I know you don't really know me, but I just locked myself out of the house and I really have to pee. Really."

"Through the living room, past—" I say, but Jake's already running through the house.

I close the door and walk back into the kitchen. "Your brother's in my bathroom," I tell Brad, who's in deep discussion with Jenni and Lincoln about Friday's game, which I know for a fact Lincoln doesn't care about.

"Hey, Jake!" Brad yells without blinking. I wonder for a second what it must be like to be him, so confident and good-natured and accepting that you're not even confused when your brother shows up to use the toilet at a virtual stranger's house.

"Yeah, so, we probably hit a high point with that chocolate

thing," I say. The pinpricks of nerves up and down my skin warn me that if he stays any longer, chaos is sure to hit. I'm surprised at how hesitant my voice sounds. It was sort of—I can't believe I'm saying this—fun.

Brad slings his backpack over his shoulder and the four of us meet up with Jake, who's standing in the hallway and looking at family photos on the wall like he's inspecting our house for suspicious activity. He points to one of Lincoln and me at Halloween when we were little. I'm an alien, with green face paint, antennas, and a black cape.

"Good look for you." Jake points.

This guy already witnessed my literal fall from grace, and now he's making fun of my awkward childhood photos. Come on.

"Jenni, Lincoln, this is Jake," I say, getting the introductions out of the way as quickly as possible. Lincoln reaches out to shake his hand (as usual, being the much less awkward Sullivan) and Jenni offers a wave and a genuinely warm smile.

"So what brings you to Reardon?" she asks. She's far too nice to outright mention all the rumors about his past, but an appetite for gossip gleams in her eyes.

Jake coughs into his hand and I can't shake the feeling, for some reason, that he's making fun of her, or me, or maybe all of us. "Just enjoying the stimulating Reardon culture," he quips.

Jenni nods politely, and Lincoln shoots me a look that says, *What's this guy's deal?*

Ignoring him and looking straight at Brad, I say, "Next time, we really have to figure out what we're doing with this project. At least we got some stuff for our progress journal, though."

Brad nods. "Yeah—if we're gonna get the best grade in the class, we'd better nail something down soon."

"The best grade in the class?" Jake asks, looking skeptical.

"Sorry, but refresh my memory . . . what did you get last year in chemistry?"

Brad points at him. "A C−, which is passing."

Jake nods. "Passing, sure. Maybe not 'best grade in the class' material."

Jenni frowns and crosses her arms.

Eager to make Jake shut up, I blurt out the first thing that comes to mind. "Well, we're going to send a camera into space."

Brad lets out a soft *whoa*, while Jake raises his eyebrows. "Ambitious. And how, exactly, are you two going to swing that one?"

"Thanks for asking," I say, tucking my hair behind my ears. "I actually have a friend who did this project before."

Okay, so my "friend" is BeamMeUp, whose accolades have apparently made their way into my subconscious, but Jake doesn't have to know that.

Jake smiles a slow grin and gestures toward my face, then nods toward the small mirror on the wall behind me. Confused, I follow his nod—only to see the giant smear of chocolate that's been on my face this entire time.

"Think you can handle a project you can't eat?" he asks.

"We'll figure it out," I say, furiously wiping my cheek. I'm so mad that I'm strongly considering chasing this ass-hat into oncoming traffic, which is a big deal when you don't leave the house.

Brad laughs, shaking his head as he somehow avoids picking up on any tension. He claps me on the back and I almost fall over. "Awesome, Mal. Later, Jenni. Linc."

Jake shakes his head. Just when I think he's about to leave, he stops right in front of me. "Better learn to climb a ladder before you send something into space," he whispers.

"Rude!" I call out, but only to his back as he trudges home. As soon as I slam the door shut, Lincoln says, "That guy's even weirder than everyone thinks. *Stimulating Reardon culture?* What's that supposed to mean?"

"Ugh, yeah, total weirdo." I smack Jenni on the arm. "A yearbook photo? What was that about?"

"We have to create buzz!" Jenni says, smacking me back. She pulls out her phone, on which Brad is throwing the strawberry in my mouth for all of Instagram to behold.

"You look like a cranky baby," Lincoln snorts, but I don't even care what I look like. All I can see is that there are already 87 "likes" and three comments that are some variation of "aaaawwww so cute!!!!!" and a few that say "SPIRIT POINTS!"

Maybe this plan isn't as dumb as I thought.

BeamMeUp: Can I tell you something embarrassing? You have to promise not to tell anyone else on WANA.

AlienHuntress: I'm sure that will be hard, since I'm close, personal friends with all of them.

AlienHuntress: Okay, spill. What is it?

BeamMeUp: I've never seen Star Wars.

AlienHuntress: Wait. I'm sorry. I think there might be a problem with your keyboard. It looks like you just said you've never seen Star Wars.

BeamMeUp: That's right. Every time someone makes a Darth Vader joke or does that Chewbacca noise, I just laugh like I know what they're talking about. But I don't. At all.

AlienHuntress: Listen, I'm sorry, but as a card-carrying nerd I have to report you.

BeamMeUp: YOU PROMISED.

CHAPTER EIGHT

Newton's Law of Universal Gravitation: Any object exerts
a gravitational force on any other object.

—*Physics in the Modern World*, 2013

THE SUN EXPLODING THROUGH my blinds on Sunday
morning punishes me for staying up until 2:00 a.m. to chat
with BeamMeUp. I get more Internet time at exactly midnight every night—predictably, WANA users are most active
at night, BeamMeUp included. He sent me links to at least eighteen different camera-into-space supply lists, which I compiled
and e-mailed to Brad.

Today promises to be full of what Dr. Dinah refers to as
"positive interaction." Brad's coming over for another physics
session (one that hopefully won't be interrupted by his impossibly rude bathroom-seeking brother) and Mom's stupid book
club is meeting this afternoon, which means I'll be stuck in my
room while they tipsily discuss whatever book they could find
seven copies of at the library.

For the thousandth time, I remind myself why I'm doing

this. I grab the heavy, plastic, black frame of last year's family photo from my desk and study my dad's face. Sometimes I think it helps, but pictures are stale and static—all posed smiles and fake moments. In my head, my dad is present and in motion; he's holding his binoculars in front of his glasses, sitting on the armchair in the living room with a book in his hand and clumsily clicking through bird photos on the computer.

Linc's familiar, annoyingly cheerful morning-person whistle is coming down the hallway to my room at the very end of the hall (conveniently, the farthest room from the front door). He's fond of saying that Dad left during a Book Club meeting because he couldn't take one more afternoon of a bunch of drunk moms gushing over Nicholas Sparks in his living room. I slip the photo under one of my NOT ALONE T-shirts just as Lincoln opens my door.

"Uh . . . ," he says, slowly stepping in. "You're still in bed."

"I'm just resting up for Book Club."

Lincoln groans and flops down on my bed. "Mom's in the kitchen singing along to Katy Perry right now. It's, like, please don't tell me Book Club is the highlight of your month. Because that would be seriously depressing." He pulls out a sock from under the pillow, tosses it aside, and makes one of his "I can't believe you're my sister" faces at me.

"I bet she's making that cookie dough dip," I say, sitting down beside him.

Lincoln sits up against my wall of multicolored throw pillows and takes his phone out of his pocket. "Mrs. Potter better not eat all of it."

"Pretty sure cookie dough isn't alcoholic, so I think you're safe."

Lincoln doesn't respond—he's too busy staring deeply into his phone.

"Um, hello?" I say, waving my hands. "Offensive jokes about Mrs. Potter?" When Lincoln still doesn't respond, I reach over and try to yank his phone out of his hands.

"No!" Lincoln shouts, rolling away from me. I manage to grab the phone.

"Oh my God!" I squeal as my eyes focus and I see who he's having a conversation with. *"Hot Scott?!"*

"Give that back!" Lincoln lunges at me and grabs his phone, then walks across the room and leans against the window frame as if he's afraid I'll take it again.

"What's going on?" I ask, throwing Bananas the Bear at him.

"God, you are so embarrassing," Linc says, throwing Bananas back at me before covering his face with one hand.

"Are you *blushing*?" I ask. Lincoln has always been annoyingly embarrassment-proof (unless you count being embarrassed on my behalf), so this is unprecedented. The realization hits me like a pillow to the chest. "You're *so* into this guy!"

Lincoln looks everywhere in the room except at me. "I told you he was cute!"

"Yeah, but you also think the FedEx guy is cute, and you don't have a crush on him."

"Haven't I told you? FedEx and I are talking about marriage."

I roll my eyes. "Don't change the subject."

Lincoln crosses his arms and looks at his feet. "Scott's just . . . different. We've been texting a lot, and he's funny, and weird, and he even likes the same movies I do. His favorite director is Ingmar Bergman, and literally no other guy at Reardon even knows who he is."

Lincoln typically talks about his interests until I'm begging him to stop. "And?"

He sighs. "So, yeah, you got me, Mal. I like him a lot. And I think he likes me, but . . ."

"There's no but!" I say, raising my arms. "You like him, he likes you. Don't make it any more complicated! You guys can just be nerdy film obsessives together."

Lincoln pulls at the neck of his T-shirt, one of his rare nervous habits. "I know. It's just . . . I've never dated a guy before, you know?"

"You've never dated a girl before, either," I remind him.

"Um, Amber Martinez in fifth grade totally counts. We held hands at the roller rink!"

"Don't be dumb. You guys like each other, okay? It'll all work out."

Lincoln makes a little noise that's in between a scoff and a snort. "It'll all work out. Sure. Because that's what always happens for Reardon High's Big Gay Freak."

I pat him on the shoulder. "Don't be so hard on yourself. You're more like a *Little* Gay Freak."

Lincoln groans but immediately looks more comfortable, making me glad that I adhered to the Sullivan family motto: Why Be Serious When You Can Be Sarcastic? If any one of us gets too close to sharing a genuine emotion, another Sullivan is always there to pull us back from the edge.

Still, Lincoln's comment lodges in my brain. Is that how he thinks of himself? Sure, he hangs out with mostly the Tortured Artist kids, the ones who would way rather stand out than fit in. But then there are the kids who voted me onto homecoming court. The ones who started #stayathome-coming. Thinking about Lincoln being made fun of for something as basic as who he gets a crush on makes my heart physically hurt.

"I'm proud of you, you know? For being yourself."

"Oh, gross." Lincoln squirms. "Feelings! Stop!"

I laugh. The Sullivan family motto at work.

"I guess, if I'm being totally honest and, you know, 'sincere,'" Lincoln says, making air quotes while rolling his eyes, "I'd say that I'm proud of you, too. For the whole Europe thing. I know it's a really big deal for you."

A thousand tiny guilt rocks rattle in my stomach, so I do the only thing I can think of. I jump forward and put him in a headlock.

"A noogie?" Lincoln yells as I grind my knuckles into his scalp. "What are you, ten?!"

He pulls away from me and smooths his hair back into place, shaking his head. I laugh as he mutters, "You're a crazy person. And I think my scalp is permanently damaged."

I promise myself I'll tell him tomorrow. Or never.

When the doorbell rings at 2:45, I answer and am relieved to find Brad holding a backpack with no sign of his pompous brother in sight—I don't need to be reminded that we might be in over our heads.

"Rocket supplies!" he says in lieu of hello.

"Actually," I say, cringing at how nerdy I sound, "it's more like a weather balloon."

Brad shrugs. "But rocket sounds way cooler. Should we set up in the garage? I don't want to make a mess in your house."

"No," I say quickly. Not only is our garage brimming with

even more embarrassing Sullivan family artifacts than the tree house, it's also one step farther away from the safety of the house. After my experience in the backyard ended in physical pain and an unfortunate Jake encounter, I'm cool with just staying inside.

"How about the kitchen?" I suggest.

"You're the boss!" Brad says cheerfully while handing me supplies from his bag. We dump it out on the counter and start sorting through everything when he suddenly pipes up again. "Mallory, I'm really glad we're partners."

I drop the bag of zip ties I'm holding. They scatter across the marble counter like uncooked spaghetti. Brad flicks his eyes up at me. If he notices the red in my cheeks, he doesn't let on.

"It's just, if the team makes it to State, which, not to be cocky, but I think we will . . ."

"You totally will!" Like I have *any* idea how the football team's doing.

". . . I'll have no time to study for the midterm. You're really smart, and I want to get this done right."

"I hear you," I say, slowly collecting the spilled zip ties. "We turn in the best project in the class, we don't have to take that stupid midterm."

I'm still trying to process the revelation that Brad is excited to be my partner when the doorbell rings. Before I can even think about answering it, Mom runs down the stairs, muttering, "Shit, shit, shit."

She stops in her tracks when she sees Brad and me at the counter.

"Physics," I say, pointing at our supplies.

"Actually, it's Brad." He steps toward my mom and shakes her hand.

"Oh, honey, I know you. You came over and helped me with the lawn mower a few weeks ago!"

"Wait, what?" I ask, my eyes darting between Brad and Mom.

"No big deal," Brad says. Turning to me, he continues, "Your mom was having a hard time getting the mower started, so I just came over and helped."

"It was very sweet," Mom says, and—oh my God, is she blushing? Is the charm of Brad Kirkpatrick even getting through to my forty-three-year-old mother?

The doorbell rings again. I can hear the eager mom behind it.

"I fell asleep reading and didn't get a chance to set up for Book Club," Mom says, rushing to open the giant silver fridge. *"I'm coming!"* She frantically grabs trays of fruit and veggies. Brad takes one from her and carries it to the table. "Well, thank you, Brad!" she practically sings. When he's not looking, she gives me a wide-eyed *"What a guy!"* look.

I puff out my cheeks, but a part of me can't help feeling happy that, for once, our mother-daughter relationship is working the right way. Like every single girl in the history of the world, I'm embarrassed by my mom, instead of my mom being embarrassed by my general houseboundness. After Mom puts the cookie dough dip on the table, she runs to the door.

"We need to get out of here," I say, scooping the supplies into Brad's backpack. "Literally anywhere other than this kitchen. Prison camp. The surface of the sun. *Anywhere*, because this is about to turn into a wine-fueled, gossipy hell."

"To the garage, then!" he says as I push the backpack into his arms.

Too late. Mrs. Potter's in the entryway, saying, "I know you always have plenty, but I brought a few bottles of red anyway."

"Oh God, oh God, oh God," I mutter, pushing Brad toward

the back entrance to the kitchen, the one that heads to the garage.

"Well, what do we have here?"

I look over my shoulder and see Mrs. Potter and Mrs. De La Cruz, another neighborhood mom.

"Brad Kirkpatrick," Mrs. Potter says, setting two huge bottles of red wine on the table without looking away from us, "right here in the kitchen with our little Mallory!"

I stifle the urge to tell Mrs. Potter that I don't belong to her, but Brad is already shaking hands and "Hello, ma'am"-ing her and everyone who's spilling into my kitchen. If this football thing doesn't work out, he should consider a career in politics.

"So what are you doing over here, Brad?" Mrs. De La Cruz asks, flashing a huge smile. "Joining the book club?"

They all laugh uproariously. Maybe they've already dipped into the wine stash.

"Mallory and I are working on a physics project, ma'am. We're going to launch a camera—"

"Congratulations on being nominated for homecoming court," interrupts Mrs. Lubeck, mom of Pia "Heinous" Lubeck. "Was that a big surprise, Mallory?" she asks too casually, raising a newly poured glass of wine to her mouth.

"Um . . . ," I stammer, looking for my mom in the sea of other moms. She's standing in the back with an unreadable look on her face. I realize, my heart pounding, that we still haven't had a conversation about my nomination.

"Lincoln told me," she says softly, focusing on the pita chip she's holding.

Seven pairs of mom-eyes are trained on me. My legs feel a familiar itch to run, anywhere but here. I step back on my heel, feeling like I'm physically shrinking.

"It's not a surprise at all," Brad says, hooking one practically bronzed, definitely strong arm around my shoulders. "Mallory has just as much of a chance at winning as anyone else." He gives me a tiny, encouraging smile. I smile back, hoping that he can translate the gesture to read, *Thanks for trying to make me look good in front of a hungry mom-mob.*

As I look at the straight line of his teeth, the Hollywood-leading-man cut of his jaw, the way his blond hair isn't too shaggy or too gelled or too short like most of the guys at school, I think about what Jenni said. Not *all* of the popular kids are awful monsters.

"Well, isn't that great," says Mrs. Potter, giving us a grin so big it borders on manic. "And aren't you two just—"

"We have to go to the garage now. Excuse us, ladies," Brad says, sweeping me in front of him, around the island, and through the moms like I'm a giant football, right into the garage.

Before I can thank him for being my personal hero, Brad is pressing the button to open the garage door.

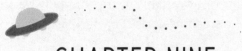

CHAPTER NINE

"DON'T!" I SHOUT, BUT it's too late. The door lumbers and squeaks open.

"It's a nice afternoon," Brad says.

With my hand clutching one of the many metal storage racks, I tell myself that this isn't a big deal. The open garage door is just like a big window, and technically, I'm still in my house. I can try—*try*—to feel okay in the garage.

"Iamsafelamsecurelamcapable," I mutter quickly, focusing on Brad's shoulders as he digs through his backpack.

"What was that?" he asks without looking up.

"Nothing!" I take a deep breath. The flowery smell floating in from outside mixes with the scent of old motor oil.

"Hey!" Brad picks up a football off the rack I'm clinging to for dear life.

Laughing in spite of the not-at-all safe, secure, or capable way my contracting rib cage feels, I gesture to the shelves full of tools and Christmas decorations. "How did you manage to find the football among all this junk?"

"Instinct," he says, then fakes a throw at me. I cover my face and he laughs.

I laugh weakly, grabbing the ball from him, which gives me an idea. "Are you thinking what I'm thinking?"

Brad looks at me thoughtfully. "That . . . you're annoyed with me?" he asks.

"No! What? No way." My face might really be on fire. "I was thinking that we can use this! For our project, to record parabolic motion!"

Brad's eyes brighten. "Oh, awesome! Good one, Mal! Let's do some throws."

I beam. Then I realize he's waiting for me to step out of the garage.

"After you," he says. Damn it, why does he have to be such a perfect gentleman?

You went in the backyard the other day, I remind myself. *And it was fine! Other than the falling and the embarrassment. You didn't die. You didn't stop breathing. No cars skipped the sidewalk and hit you. No rabid dogs ran into the yard and bit you. No virus-carrying birds pooped on you. Well, that you know of. Other than Jake, no one even saw you.*

It's not like I have to go to school. It's not like I have to go to the mall. I'm even on my own property. *It's the driveway, Mal. Just do it.* If I'm ever going to make it to the birding excursion in who-knows-where, I have to make it through this.

I take a deep breath and step onto the driveway, feeling the cracked pavement through my sneakers. I slowly come out of the shadow and into sunlight. Out where anything could happen. I close my eyes and inhale through my nose.

Am I safe? Am I secure? Am I capable? I'm not sure.

"All right, let's do this!" Brad says, and I exhale through my mouth and throw the football with all my might toward the sound of his voice.

"Ow!"

I open my eyes and see Jake Kirkpatrick hunched over the hood of his car in his driveway. He stands up and rubs his arm.

"What the hell?" He puts down a wrench and picks up the football. Then he throws it right at me.

"No!" I cover my head and duck, but the football flies into the garage, knocking over an empty trash can. I think Brad says something like "Whoa, Mal!" but I can't really tell because he's laughing so hard. And, apparently, can't stop.

I cross my arms and stare at him. "You done?"

He wipes his eyes. "Your arm is really strong. And your aim is terrible."

"Shut up," I groan.

"And you know you're supposed to catch the ball, right? Not just try to stay out of the way?"

"Not all of us can be sports stars, okay? I have physics, you have football!"

"*Do* you have physics?" Jake wonders out loud, definitely not to himself. Any regret I feel at hitting him with the football evaporates.

Brad smiles. "As QB, I can't allow this disrespect of a football to happen on my street. *Please* just let me show you how to throw and catch."

"Please don't," Jake calls from his driveway.

I glare at Brad, my arms still crossed.

"I'll give you one tip right now," he offers. "It doesn't involve screaming or hiding from the ball."

I shake my head. "You are the literal worst."

I got hit in the head with a volleyball three times during

freshman-year gym, and only two of those times happened when I was on the court. So my fear of catastrophe striking at every moment isn't *totally* irrational.

I'm about to ask Brad if we can just get back to our project, but I think about the "assignment" text Jenni sent me this morning along with approximately fifty heart emojis:

> Initiate physical contact with Brad. Innocently touch his arm! Brush an eyelash off his face! Something that requires you to touch him!

I would seriously rather die than brush an eyelash off Brad's face, but football seems like a relatively non-embarrassing opportunity to complete the assignment. And besides, I'm outside right now. Who's to say I can't become Reardon High's first female football star?

I throw my hands up in surrender. "Against my better judgment, okay!"

Brad actually fist pumps and then holds up both hands for a double five. I can't believe I'm hanging out with this ridiculously hot, upbeat weirdo. I roll my eyes but smack my palms against his.

"I can help record your trial throws."

I look away from Brad and see that Jake is no longer on the other side of the waist-high shrubbery that separates my house from the Kirkpatricks'. He weaves his way through all the moms' cars that line the street and joins us in the driveway.

"Oh, sweet," Brad says. "Thanks!"

"Aren't you busy with your car?" I ask.

Jake looks straight at me as he shakes his head. "It can wait."

Brad trots into the garage to pick up the football, and in a low voice I ask Jake, "What, are you stalking us or something?"

He leans in close to my face. There's a distinct toothpaste smell on his breath. "Just making sure you don't hurt yourself again."

I scoff. "Oh, shut up. You're—"

But Brad's back, holding up the ball and looking eager to get started. "Let's go over here in the side yard."

I hesitate at the edge of the driveway. I inhale, hold it, and exhale, trying desperately to think of a reason why I need to go back inside. My fists clench involuntarily and the back of my neck starts to sweat—God, the last thing I need to deal with right now is sweat stains. "Do you need any water or anything?" I call weakly.

"Nope!" Brad shouts, faking a few throws.

"Just don't get too close to the tree house," Jake says. "I hear it's dangerous."

I give Jake the finger when Brad turns his back to us. He grins at me, evidently enjoying this way too much.

"Don't worry, we'll stay away from it," Brad calls over his shoulder, innocent as ever.

Every cell in my body is screaming to run back into the house, get back in bed, and pull the blankets over my head. *The plan*, I think. *Jenni's assignment.* You can do this. The sun beating down on me makes me feel dizzy and weak, but I walk across the grass anyway. If I'm shaking, the boys don't notice.

Brad gestures me over. "Okay, so let's just get you comfortable with the football before we try to record anything, okay? You're right-handed, right?"

"Yeah," I say shakily, my tongue heavy and dry in my mouth.

"Okay, so stand a little bit to the right. . . ."

I mirror everything Brad does.

"Hold the football up and put your thumb underneath. . . ."

"Like . . . this?" I ask. The football seems way too big for my hand.

"Almost. Just put your arm more like . . . can I?" Brad asks, stepping behind me. I can feel his breath on the back of my neck as he adjusts my arm and my hand, and suddenly, I'm panicking, but in a totally different way. My own breath slows down and becomes a little less shallow. Having someone basically hugging me makes being outside a little easier.

That must be it.

Jake coughs. "You gonna throw the ball, or should I just come back next week?"

"Okay," Brad says. "So you just pull your arm back like this, and let 'er rip."

I nod, and Brad runs about twenty-five feet away from me, narrowly avoiding the hostas my mom planted alongside the garage. This time I keep my eyes open as I throw the ball toward him.

"Awesome!" Brad shouts, throwing his hands up in victory. "Wanna try again?"

I do. I throw the ball over and over, until I don't need Brad to adjust my arm anymore.

"I'm not saying you're good," Jake says after about twenty throws, "but you're getting better."

"High praise," I say, then fake-curtsy as Brad claps. Jake coughs "show-off" into his hand.

I'm not only out of the house for one of the first times in months, but I'm A) with two dudes I barely knew a week ago and B) sort of having fun. Have I slipped into a universe where Mallory Sullivan is a breezy, fun, normal girl instead of an anxiety-ridden weirdo?

My introspection is interrupted when Lincoln appears, running around Mom's prized rock garden.

"Oh God, you're outside!" he says at an embarrassing volume.

Seeing Linc snaps me out of my fantasy world. My palms start to tingle. *You've got this*, I think to myself. *You're in the yard. Nothing bad can happen.*

"Please don't alert the media," I say, trying to tell him to stop making a big deal of it with my eyes. "What's going on in there?"

Lincoln takes the hint. "I saw you guys playing from my window, and I wanted to be part of this momentous occasion." He puts his hands over his heart and looks at me. "My big sister, playing a sport."

I exhale a sigh of relief and give Lincoln a tiny smile, hoping my gratitude is transmitting via our shared Sullivan brain waves.

"I don't know if you guys know this," Lincoln continues, giving Brad a pointed look, "but I used to be a football star, too."

"In seventh grade, until you quit because you hated it," I remind him.

"My total apathy for team sports does not overshadow my raw talent. Also, the moms just put on Michael Bublé, and Ms. Wilson keeps trying to engage me in a conversation about how handsome George Clooney is."

"Uh-oh," I say. My mom's Michael Bublé playlist usually only comes out when they're several drinks in.

"Exactly. I mean, George Clooney *is* basically the Clark Gable of his generation and maybe the last truly classically attractive leading man in film for a long time, but I've always found the edgier aesthetic more—"

"So how about a little game?" I interrupt. I love Linc's enthusiasm, but if I let him keep going, he'll share his thoughts on Jon Hamm, and there's no way I can stay outside long enough for that.

Wait, what did I say?

"All right!" Brad shouts.

Jake crosses his arms and looks to the sky, sighing heavily, like he expects to find an excuse to ditch us written in the clouds.

"That's a yes," Lincoln says. "I call Brad!"

"Not fair," Jake protests. "You get the star player and I get Mallory? No offense."

"Plenty of offense!" I yell back.

"Yeah, offense is super important!" Brad adds, not even ironically.

"I'm sorry, what exactly does this have to do with your physics project?" Jake asks, and I stick my tongue out at him in response.

Lincoln jogs over, grabs the ball out of Brad's hands, and tosses it to Jake. "Start us off, dude."

Jake looks at me. "You got this?"

"Just throw it!" I shout.

"You sure?" He backs up a few steps and draws his arm back.

"Good God, Jake!" I call as he throws the ball toward me. While it floats through the air in a perfect arc, Lincoln whispers, "Play dead, okay?"

"Um, what?" I ask as my fingers reach up and curl around the ball.

"You're going down!" Lincoln shouts. I shriek as he throws all his weight on me and I slam into the ground.

CHAPTER TEN

"PRETEND YOU'RE REALLY HURT," he whispers in my ear as I lie on the ground, the dry grass scratching at my neck.

I want to yell at him that I really *am* hurt, but all that escapes from my lips is a tortured moan. This is why I don't leave the house. No one's tackled me to the ground while I'm in my room on my laptop. Well, except for the one time Jenni got too excited about the premiere of *Pretty Little Liars*.

To my mortification, a few tears sneak out of my eyes. I wipe them away as Lincoln leans over me. "This is all going according to plan. You're doing great!"

"My *ankle* doesn't feel great," I snap. Lincoln having a plan is never a good thing. Evidence: this homecoming plan. He says something about ice and runs inside.

"Are you okay?" Brad takes Lincoln's place beside me. He looks at me like I'm dying.

I wave him off and try to stand up. *Get inside, Mal*, my brain is basically screaming at me. "I'm totally fine, I prom—oh no."

Brad catches me with hardly any effort when I collapse. "Don't try to walk on it, okay? Just let me help you to the porch."

This was Lincoln's stupid plan? There has to be a way to get close to Brad that doesn't involve personal injury. I sigh. "Sure."

I don't expect him to pick me up, but he does, carrying me over to the front porch like I'm a heavy load of firewood. He smells exactly what he should smell like: cedar deodorant, pine, a little sweat. I finally stop smelling him and look over his shoulder. Jake's trailing behind us.

"If you had been focusing on physics, this wouldn't have happened," he says.

My heart starts to pound, and I clench my eyes shut as if that will stop it. Brad sits me down on the porch swing and rolls my jeans up above my ankle. I'm thankful I shaved my legs recently. You never know when a pickup football game will lead to the class's resident Hot Dude inspecting your ankle.

"I know it hurts, but I think you're okay," he says after gingerly touching my ankle. "I don't think it's sprained—you probably just landed funny. We'll keep it iced and see how it looks tomorrow."

I have a *tomorrow* with Brad Kirkpatrick. "Thanks, Doctor." I try to smile.

He smiles back. "I've had a million injuries. Cracked collarbone, fractured wrist, at least seven broken toes . . ."

I hold up a hand to stop him. Hearing about injuries makes me feel like passing out.

"And I had a tooth knocked out." Brad points to the inside of his mouth. "See this one? It's fake!"

"Dude," Jake says. "Stop showing off. I broke my finger once; you don't hear me bragging about it."

Brad leans toward me. "He slammed it in a car door. Not really the same thing."

Lincoln swings the front door open, ice in hand. Also, he changed his shirt. He places the ice on my ankle, and I inhale sharply.

"Thanks," I tell him sarcastically. "You know, for everything."

He smiles back at me. "You're *very* welcome."

"Who's that?" Jake asks, gesturing toward the Kirkpatricks' driveway. We all turn to see a red Lexus. The door opens and Pia Lubeck herself gets out, looks at the darkened windows of the Kirkpatricks' brick house, then looks around until she sees us.

"Brad!" she shouts, brushing her long, perfectly wavy hair out of her face as she flashes a smile that's angry and flirtatious at the same time. "Come on! We're already late!"

Brad turns to me with a grimace. "We're volunteering at the children's hospital. It's part of Principal Lu's thing about strengthening relationships between the community and Reardon."

"Right." That Pia is so crafty. She must be getting crazy spirit points for representing the high school at a *children's hospital*. Pia climbs back into the car and honks the horn in three sharp bursts.

"Dude," Jake says. "What are you doing at the children's hospital? And tell your girlfriend to cool it with the horn."

"We're setting up for tomorrow morning—it's Breakfast with the Team," Brad says, unfolding his height as he stands up. "And she's not my girlfriend."

My face gets hot. Am I imagining it, or did he say that just for my benefit?

"Do you want me to walk you inside?" Brad asks.

"You probably should," Lincoln says.

I shoot Linc a death glare as Pia holds down the horn. "It's okay. Lincoln's here to help me . . . and we don't want to deal with the Book Club moms again." Brad and I smile at each other, and it feels sort of nice and warm to be sharing an inside joke with him. Pia honks again and he looks toward his house.

"Well, a promise is a promise. I can't let everybody at the hospital down." He waves at all of us, then runs down the porch stairs. A second later, he runs right back up.

"Wait—you should get some spirit points out of this!" he says, pulling his phone out of his pocket with one hand and tossing me the football with the other. He puts his arm around me and snaps a quick selfie. Jake snorts a laugh that we're clearly supposed to hear.

"After all." Brad pulls away, nodding to the football I'm clutching. "You *were* helping the quarterback practice for the homecoming game."

"If by helping, you mean doing a few wobbly throws and falling down," Jake clarifies.

Brad turns around. "Watch it," he says, sounding almost angry for the first time in . . . well, at least as long as I've known him. Jake holds his hands up in a "sorry, bro" gesture. Lincoln looks back and forth between them, as entranced as if he were watching the original *Jaws*.

This is my chance. "Can we take another picture? That one didn't . . . show my good side."

"Okay!" Brad says. He crouches beside me and holds out his phone, which looks tiny in his huge hand. I try to mimic the poses I've seen Caroline, Pia, and all the other girls doing on Instagram. With physical contact, initiated by me. I lean my head into Brad's until our temples touch lightly. Then he presses his cheek against mine, which sends a cascade of hot and cold waves down my spine.

"Great!" he says. "I'll post it right now." He touches my shoulder and his hand lingers there for just a second longer than it has to. "You should have a fighting chance. You deserve it."

I smile. "Thanks."

Then he leaves for real, bounding across the yard and into Pia's Lexus. She peels off down the street.

Jake, who I'd kind of forgotten was even still here, says, "How nice that you and Mr. Perfect are getting along so well." He jogs down the porch steps, back toward his yard.

In the honk- and Jake-free silence, Lincoln stares toward the road with his mouth open. "What. Was. That." Then he turns to me, gesturing for me to stand up. "The game's over."

I glare at him. "You think I'm faking this?"

Lincoln's eyes widen in horror. "Wait, you're really hurt? Shit." He looks at Jake's retreating back and calls to him. "Can you help us out?"

Jake stops, turns, and walks over to us very, very slowly. "Only because I have nothing better to do," he says when he reaches us.

"Gee, thanks," I say, but Lincoln shushes me.

"I'm just going to do some recon work and make sure the moms are securely contained before you go upstairs. I'm sure you don't want to answer ten million questions about your ankle and what you and Brad may or may not have been doing when you injured it. Jake, wait with her and make sure she keeps icing it."

Jake drags one of our teal metal porch chairs over to me and sits down heavily. We both stare at my ankle, which currently feels like it's on fire *and* trapped in a vise. But it's more comfortable for me to focus on the pain than it is to think about how long I've been outside. A warm breeze gently rocks the porch swing and feels so unfamiliar against my skin that I get a sharp burst of panic in my chest. I'm okay, I remind myself, thinking of how far I've come tonight. I'm outside. And safe and secure and capable, or whatever. I got hurt, but I'm still here. I can't wait to tell Dr. Dinah about this.

There's a sentence I never thought I'd ever say.

Jake is sitting so close to me that we almost touch every time the swing rocks, but he's just staring off into space. He really does look a lot like Brad—just taller and thinner, like someone grabbed Brad and stretched him out. He has almost-black hair and eyes that are the kind of blue that I didn't know existed— like, when people describe eyes as looking like oceans or rivers I never really knew what they meant, but Jake's eyes do look like water. Blue and gray and moving, like there's something under the surface.

He looks at me and I get a straight-on view of them.

"What?" he asks, annoyed. "Why are you staring at me?"

"You're not very much like your brother," I say, adjusting the ice on my ankle.

"Really? You're the first one to mention that." He shifts uncomfortably in his chair.

God, Mal. How many awkward moments am I going to have with Kirkpatricks today? I need to say something fast to break the silence.

"Tattoo," I blurt out.

Jake blinks. "Um, what?"

I shake my head, like I'm knocking all the stupid thoughts out of my brain. I point to the tattoo that's half hidden by his T-shirt sleeve. "That's a cool tattoo."

"Oh," Jake says, surprised. "Thanks. I wouldn't have guessed you'd be into tattoos."

"I'm full of mystery," I say, which makes him laugh. "What's the deal with it?"

"The deal?"

"Yeah, I mean . . . no one just gets a tattoo for no reason. You have some story behind it, right? Like maybe you got it while you were in prison?"

Jake looks at me with raised eyebrows. "Yeah. I got it in prison."

"Seriously?"

His laugh comes out as a throaty chuckle. "No!"

The front door swings open and Lincoln waves us inside. I stand up slowly (which is sort of hard, since I'm in a porch swing) and start to hop on one foot toward the door.

"This is ridiculous," Jake says, and in one easy gesture he picks me up and swings me over his shoulder.

"How did you get so strong?" I ask, trying not to think about how my butt is basically at his eye level.

"Must've been all those workouts in prison," he says, walking through the front door as Lincoln holds it open. He bumps my shoulder into the doorjamb and I yelp.

"So much for stealth," Lincoln mutters, shutting the door behind him as Jake carries me upstairs.

BeamMeUp: So what are you reading right now?

AlienHuntress: *Physics in the Modern World.* Maybe you've heard of it? It's a simply *fascinating* textbook.

BeamMeUp: Ha. So you're not a big reader.

AlienHuntress: Pff. What are you reading, Genius Boy?

BeamMeUp: *The Handmaid's Tale.* It's set in a future where women have basically no rights.

AlienHuntress: I thought you said you only read science fiction?

BeamMeUp: :/

CHAPTER ELEVEN

AS SOON AS JAKE is gone and Lincoln is safely watching a movie in his room, I text Jenni and ask for any spirit points updates, which I'm sure she's got the inside track on.

Between being outside, conversing with other people, being carried by not one but two Kirkpatricks, and injuring myself while attempting to play football of all things, the day was exhausting. And, while Dr. Dinah would no doubt say I've made some progress toward the whole "overcoming my anxiety and becoming a functional member of society" thing, I'm not sure I've made enough progress toward the *way* more important "win homecoming queen and find my dad" thing. I try not to think of how many points Pia and Brad are racking up at the children's hospital.

For now, though, it'll have to do, because I need to check updates on my favorite threads on We Are Not Alone. A message pops up in the chat box.

BeamMeUp: Thank God you're here! Roswell1947 is telling everyone about his latest abduction and this one's even crazier than the last one.

I smile and start typing.

AlienHuntress: Oooh! Fill me in! I need deets.

BeamMeUp recounts Roswell1947's story and we decide that it mirrors an episode of *The X-Files* a little too exactly. I'm enjoying the familiar rhythms of our conversation.

BeamMeUp: So, do anything exciting today? Slay any aliens?

I pause, my fingers hovering over the keyboard like a UFO hovering over the landscape of Texas in Roswell1947's story. What am I supposed to say? "Today I left the house, which is probably NBD to you but is monumental to me because I have severe anxiety. Oh, and I got tackled and took a picture with a cute guy and, as weird as it may seem to you, those are actually the most exciting things to happen to me in months."

AlienHuntress: I spent the whole day trying on homecoming dresses with my best friend.

This isn't *totally* a lie because Jenni *did* text me pictures all day of dresses she thinks I'd look cute in. So really, this is more of an almost-truth, right? But I figure I should add something that's completely true.

AlienHuntress: I'm on homecoming court.

BeamMeUp: Whoa. Sounds like a busy day. Congratulations, by the way.

I don't know what to say to that, so I just sit there for a minute. That's what I like about the Internet—I'm allowed to be silent, to think, to just *sit*. I don't have to worry about whether I have something in my teeth or if my bangs look greasy. My awkward conversational skills don't even matter, and I can be the best version of myself on-screen.

The thing is, I don't even know what I *can* say about homecoming. I haven't been able to talk to anyone about how I really feel. I have to be excited around Lincoln and Jenni and Brad, but I don't feel psyched about the whole thing. I bite my lip distractedly, then stop, remembering what Jenni always tells me about how lipstick will never look good on me unless I commit myself to maintaining smooth lips. I'm not about to tell BeamMeUp about my dad or my need for five hundred dollars, but it seems like a safe bet to tell him some of my real feelings. After all, we don't know each other, so who cares?

> **AlienHuntress:** I'm just sort of nervous about it. I mean, I want to win, but I'm not so sure I can. I'm not even sure I deserve to. It's like there's all this pressure to make people like me and convince them that I'm worth it, but how can I do that when I'm not even sure I can do it?

I click SEND and close my eyes. I can almost see my true feelings shooting out into cyberspace. BeamMeUp's response is so long that I have to scroll down to read it.

> **BeamMeUp:** I probably don't have to tell you this, but everything in the universe—that's everything, no matter how small—exerts a gravitational force on everything else. A pencil exhibits a force on the sun. A quarter on Jupiter. A scoop of chocolate chip cookie dough ice cream

on a scoop of chocolate ice cream. And that
means you exert force on the universe, too. You,
AlienHuntress, are a force to be reckoned with.
Don't count yourself out before you even start
the game.

I can't help but smile. Is this super cheesy? Sure. But do I
feel like I could star in my own action movie montage set to an
'80s song? Yes.

AlienHuntress: Thanks :)

AlienHuntress: Ugh, sorry about the smiley
face. I got caught up in my own empowerment.

BeamMeUp: You need to kick ass and take names,
not apologize.

Then the little alien blinks for almost a solid minute before
his next response pops up.

BeamMeUp: So have you heard about the WANA
convention?

Of course I know about WANACON. The annual convention
has been one of the hottest topics on We Are Not Alone for
months, not that I would ever actually go.

AlienHuntress: Who doesn't know about
WANACON? It's probably my only chance to hear
about Roswell1947's abduction in person.

BeamMeUp: While I'm definitely not discounting
the excitement of meeting up with Roswell1947,
I thought maybe we'd run into each other, too.
You know, if you're going.

I freeze and pull my hands into my lap as if the keyboard is going to bite my fingers off. Meet up? Me and BMU? The whole point of my Internet comfort zone is that it doesn't require me to leave the house or tell BMU the truth about my life. I stare at our chat box stupidly, like my mind's suddenly washed of all normal human functioning. Then the Focustime logo pops up on-screen, blinking to let me know that I have thirty seconds of Internetting left.

AlienHuntress: Hmm, not sure if I'm going yet! I have to go now, though. Thanks for the pep talk.

Slamming the laptop shut, I lean against my pillows and cover my face with my hands. BeamMeUp's question is making me freak out for reasons I don't entirely understand. So I focus on something concrete: Dad's birding excursion.

I reach for the map under my bed—it's a little crumpled and stuck to some pretty impressive dust bunnies. Legs crossed, I spread it out on the hardwood floor and trace my finger over the cities Dad marked. The expanse of US cities and states sprawls in front of me, and I wonder how the hell I'm ever going to find him.

I don't care how much force BeamMeUp says I exert on the universe. I'm not psychic and I still have no help. There are endless places in this big world that my dad could be, but here in my little world, the one that begins and ends with my house, I don't know how I'm ever supposed to get to him. I fold the map up and shove it back under my bed.

I tiptoe across my room and gently push the door open, listening for the telltale tunes of Maroon 5, glasses clinking, or Mrs. Potter's wheeze of a laugh. But the only sound I hear is the dishwasher running, which means everyone's gone. Mom's always had a knack for cleaning up a mess as soon as possible.

Fifteen minutes after a party, you'd never even know there was one. A few months after her husband left, you'd never even know he'd been there.

I head past her closed bedroom door and down the stairs. In the kitchen, I go straight for the fridge and grab the almost-empty bowl of cookie dough dip (along with a spoon) and sit down at the island. The dishwasher hums gently in the background.

Between bites, I think about the distance I covered today—both metaphorical and literal. I completed Jenni's assignment, injured myself in a football game, and spent time outside. And someone who's never even met me wants to hang out. All of that adds up to one big realization that hits me as I sit there in the dark: Maybe BeamMeUp is right. I exert a force. I have a chance of winning this thing and finding my dad. Sure, it's a *small* chance, but it's still a chance.

And for right now, a small chance is just enough.

CHAPTER TWELVE

"HEY," I TYPE, THEN delete.

"How's it hangin'?" Delete, delete, delete.

"What's shakin', bacon?" Oh God, help me.

I stare at the blinking cursor in the We Are Not Alone chat box, trying to decide how to open my convo with BeamMeUp. It's been three days since we've talked—ever since I blew off his WANACON invitation, it's been radio silence on his end.

It's not like I don't have other things going on—yesterday in physics, Brad even turned around and waved at me, and Jenni said Pia's expression could only be described as stank face. And Jenni's keeping me updated on the day-to-day fluctuations of spirit points by checking the ReardonsFutureQueen tumblr. But I already miss the cozy ritual of maxing out my allotted Internet time talking to BeamMeUp. Even my favorite threads aren't that interesting to me anymore, including the one dedicated to an *X-Files* fan fiction story that involves Mulder and Scully as a married couple who run a haunted bed-and-breakfast.

BeamMeUp was the comfort zone I didn't want to complicate. We don't even know each other's names. I imagine actually meeting him and having to introduce myself:

Hi, I'm Mal, the recluse.

'Allo, Mal here, a girl so awkward she can ruin meetings in a single bound.

Hello, I'm Mal, I throw up when I go outside.

No, it's easier to keep our relationship where it belongs—inside the computer.

My Internet exile is even worse because Lincoln has barely been home since the football incident. He and Scott have gone to every night of Brian de Palma week at the art house theater, and judging by the takeout containers that keep showing up in our fridge, they've sampled every Indian restaurant in town while I subsist on frozen Stouffer's lasagna. And when he's home, Linc spends about 95 percent of every day looking at his phone and chuckling quietly to himself.

But Lincoln isn't the only one who's being super confusing. When Brad came over two nights ago, he brought me a hazelnut latte, just the way I like it (half whipped cream). He even left a smiling emoji on a picture of Jenni and me on Instagram. Is it possible he could be into me? I'm not even sure how that thought makes me feel. I know I had fun when he spent an hour teaching me how to make crepes the other night instead of getting any work done on our project, but then again, I have fun anytime Nutella is involved.

I'm tired of waiting around for BeamMeUp. I'll message him myself—after all, Dana Scully would never sit around and wait for a guy to send her a message. That's because she's way too busy performing autopsies or trying to convince Mulder that the Loch Ness monster isn't real, but still, she's a woman of action. And I can be, too.

I skip the hellos.

AlienHuntress: Sorry I had to bail on our last conversation. I needed to go work on my project. Obviously, I would way rather be here talking about aliens and weirdos, but we're running into a major snag.

For a moment, I think he won't respond, but up pops the little flashing alien.

BeamMeUp: No problem.

I frown. That's it? Then the alien flashes again.

BeamMeUp: So, are you stuck?

That's more like it.

AlienHuntress: You know how I told you I was doing a physics project that was *loosely inspired* by you? Well, it turns out we can't even get the basic construction down.

A link to an online tutorial pops up.

BeamMeUp: I had a lot of trouble securing the parachute to the capsule, but this info helped.

AlienHuntress: Wow, thanks! With your help, we might even be able to create a project better than your original.

This time, his response shows up immediately.

BeamMeUp: Doubtful.

I smile. Typical. The doorbell rings and I glance at the clock. It's 5:30 already, meaning that Brad's done with football practice.

AlienHuntress: Gotta go! My homecoming date is here. We have to coordinate outfits and figure out which limo we're going to take and stuff. You know, exerting a force.

BeamMeUp: Cool. Have fun.

A strange knot twists in my stomach. I can't help feeling a twinge of disappointment that things are back to normal. It's not like I expected him to fly into a jealous rage, but I thought I'd at least get a jealous whimper.

I can't focus as Brad and I sit across from each other at the kitchen island. He's trying to assemble another parachute and I'm taking down some notes in our physics journal. But BeamMeUp's last message, *Have fun*, is ricocheting around my head. What would happen if I actually went to WANACON, I wonder as I chew on my pencil. What if we meet? What if he likes me? What if he doesn't like me? What if I don't like him? What if his identity has been a long con and he's really a grifter who only befriended me in hopes of convincing me to buy him super-rare *X-Files* memorabilia at WANACON that he can later sell for a major profit?

"Mallory?"

I drop my pencil. "What?"

Brad smiles and sighs at the same time, pushing a lock of perfectly unkempt hair away from his face. "I've been trying to get your attention! It's like you're on another planet."

I almost laugh. If only he knew. "Sorry."

"White chocolate macadamia nut cookie?" He pulls a bag out of his backpack.

"Um, yes, please," I say, holding out my hands.

As I eat and Brad works, I decide to, as Dr. Dinah would say, "live in the now." My mom's in the office, working, and Lincoln's out with Scott, so we have complete privacy. This might be the only chance I get to ask him about homecoming.

"Do you know who you're taking to homecoming?" I ask.

Brad's fingers stop moving around the parachute and, although he's still staring at the wrinkled fabric, I can tell he's not really looking at it.

"Um . . . ," he starts to say.

"I'm sorry!" I say, my momentary self-confidence totally evaporating. "Was that a weird question?"

Brad shuts the laptop so that we're looking right at each other. "I'm sorry. It's not your fault. It's just . . ." He sighs, drumming his fingers on his closed laptop. "Everyone's been asking me that. Being on court, being on the football team . . . those things are important to me, you know? But that's not all there is to my life. I mean, look at me." He gestures to the parts scattered across the island. "I'm working on a physics project."

I smile because I have literally no idea what else to do.

"I love playing football. And I love being at my house and hanging out with Jake now that he's back. But all my dad ever wants to talk about is football. I just need a break, you know? And working on this project, with you? It gives me a chance to chill out a little."

"I never thought I'd hear Brad Kirkpatrick say that he relaxes by doing physics."

Brad laughs. "And I never thought Mallory Sullivan would enjoy working on physics with a football player." He gives me another one of those perfect, knee-melting smiles and gets back to work on the parachute. I keep writing about our progress in the journal, letting embarrassment wash over me. Clearly, I made him uncomfortable. But buried in the embarrassment is a tiny victory: He doesn't have a homecoming date yet.

About an hour later, after I've made Brad help me illustrate the journal entry with some diagrams of what we hope our project will do, it's time for him to leave. I walk him to the door because . . . well, that's what you do with friends, right? I'm just about to give him another one of those high fives he's so fond of when he surprises me by leaning in for a hug.

"Thanks, Mallory," he says into my shoulder. "Thanks for letting me talk."

I pat him woodenly on the back. "No prob."

He gives me a wave as he trots down the stairs and I shut the door. Brad and I are turning into real friends . . . the kind who talk about feelings. Who hug. And I'm not sure what that means.

I don't mention the conversation or the hug to Jenni or Lincoln that night, or even the next day. I just need some time to mull it over, and anyway, I'd much rather discuss the situation with someone who can be objective. Someone I only know through the Internet.

Luckily, by the time I've finished classes, BeamMeUp is signed into We Are Not Alone and I have about twenty minutes of Internet time left. It takes us about 2.5 seconds to get deep into a conversation on *The X-Files*. He's rewatching the whole series chronologically on Netflix, and although I just hop around and rewatch my favorites whenever I feel like it, I still enjoy talking about each episode with him as he sees it.

AlienHuntress: Listen, I need an outside perspective on something, and WANA is about as outsider as it gets.

BeamMeUp: Agreed. Shoot.

AlienHuntress: So let's say you have a friend. Who's a girl. Would you hug her, or are hugs reserved for girls you want to be your *girlfriend*?

I wait a long, long time for a response, imagining my Internet minutes floating away into oblivion.

BeamMeUp: Personally, I'm not much of a hugger when it comes to friends. But that's just me. And anyway, if a guy really wants to show he likes you, he should come up with something better than a hug, which, FYI, is free and requires no forethought.

I nod at my screen. Good point.

AlienHuntress: In that case, I'll hold out for that bouquet of Twizzlers or an edible dough-nut arrangement.

BeamMeUp: Good for you. Don't settle for anything less than true, diabetes-causing romance.

He then immediately changes the subject back to the *X-Files* episode where Mulder and Scully create an entire compendium of cities that have reported alien sightings.

BeamMeUp: Here's what I can't stop thinking about. What is it about those places? What makes Roswell so special? Why would aliens come to Omaha or Detroit?

I think about my dad's birding map and look down. It's sticking out from underneath my bed.

AlienHuntress: Maybe there's nothing inherently special about those places. Maybe the aliens are just bored. I mean, who knows what's happening on their planet. Maybe they don't have Netflix or Snapchat.

BeamMeUp: I guess you're right. Maybe they're just like people . . . always looking for something else. Maybe it doesn't even matter where it is, specifically, as long as it's somewhere new.

BeamMeUp is right. Some people—and some extraterrestrials, apparently—just need to stretch their metaphorical wings. But aliens don't stick around here on Earth forever—they're sighted, they find new things, and then they leave. They go back home.

And isn't that what everyone does? You always go home eventually. You can't stay on vacation forever.

Focustime pops up with my thirty-second warning.

I tell BeamMeUp I have to go, then sign out without waiting for his response. If everyone, even aliens, goes home eventually, then what about people? Even those people who left their families to go on mysterious birding excursions? Mom's made it abundantly clear that she'd rather host a paintball game in the living room than answer my questions about Dad, but that doesn't mean I can't continue to try. I remind myself, again, of everything Dana Scully goes through on *The X-Files*; the least I can do is handle an awkward conversation.

I walk down the hall to Mom's office (which, by the way, is

bigger than my room). I can hear her on the phone in her adjoining bedroom, so I sit down in her office chair to wait. It's not that I'm trying to snoop, but her e-mail is open on her computer screen.

I should look away. I should go wait for her in my room. I *should* do a lot of things, but when I see Dr. Dinah's e-mail address, all of my respect for privacy flies out the energy-efficient windows Mom had installed last month. Dr. Dinah's e-mail simply says:

> *This may be an option we want to consider. Let's talk more about it on the phone.*

I scroll down and see the words *rehabilitation center*, *recuperate*, and *anxiety*.

"Oh my God," I mutter. My mom thinks I'm so messed up that I need to go to *rehab*. All the words on the screen blur together, and I let my head fall into my hands.

CHAPTER THIRTEEN

The most important thing with any look: Just act like you know what you're doing. Seriously, if you wear your look with confidence, people will accept it, no matter what. Just pretend you're Beyoncé at the Grammys, or Beyoncé at the Met Ball, or...actually, just pretend you're Beyoncé. It's a solid life philosophy.

—Just Jenni, 2015

THE SULLIVANS ARE ALREADY down one family member, and Mom still wants to get rid of me.

I start to panic. I can't leave. How will I win homecoming if I'm not here? And if I don't win, how am I supposed to get that five hundred dollars? I'm pretty sure they're not going to be giving out checks at a rehab center.

And then, an even worse thought occurs to me. What if Dad comes back and I'm gone?

There are about a thousand more what ifs running through my mind, each one more out-of-control awful than the last. I leap away from her computer.

"Mom! MOM!"

I push her door open without knocking. She turns to me and

puts one finger in the air, the universal "just a second" gesture. "I'd like to reduce closing costs and also consider—"

"Mom!" I shout again, then reach over and hang up her phone for her.

"Mallory!" She looks at me like I'm insane. Maybe I am, but at least I'm not the one considering sending my only daughter away. "That was a business call! You can't just—"

"I'm going to school tomorrow!"

I take a step back, shocked by the words that just popped out of my mouth.

My mom blinks, then sits down on her neatly made bed. "Really?"

I nod. "Yes!"

"Are you sure you don't want to just wait until Monday?"

I shake my head. If I have the whole weekend to think about it, chances are good that I'll totally back out. "I really want to go tomorrow."

"Hmm," Mom says with her head tilted, clearly still wondering what I'm up to. "Have you told Lincoln?"

The thought of telling one more person feels like a lead weight on my chest. "I kind of want to surprise Linc in the hallway."

"Well, that's your decision. You know how Lincoln feels about surprises."

I know Mom's just remembering the time that Lincoln peed his pants at his surprise eighth birthday party when we all jumped out from behind the couch, but I'm hoping my unexpected presence isn't going to make him wet himself now that he's in high school.

"Either way, I'll show up with a latte to get in his good graces."

Mom smiles at me, and then, taking us both by surprise, she reaches out and pulls me into a rough hug.

"Hey, kid," she murmurs into my hair. "I'm proud of you. I know you and Linc have been handling a lot of things yourselves lately, but work's going to slow down soon and I'll be home more, okay?"

I squirm a bit, wondering if it would be possible for her to make me feel guiltier if she tried. I know what she would say if I told her this was all part of a plan to figure out where Dad is. Or, rather, I know what she *wouldn't* say—anything at all.

"Have you grabbed the mail yet?" I ask, sliding out of her embrace.

"I was just about to," Mom says, patting me on the shoulders. "Why, are you expecting something?"

"No, I just thought . . . maybe I could go out and get it?"

Mom breaks into a smile so big that you'd think I told her we were going on a Pottery Barn shopping spree. "Go ahead!"

I run down the stairs, my steps getting shorter and slower the closer I get to the front door. I pause with my hand on the doorknob as I inspect the front yard through the screen.

Why did I think I could do this? If going outside is rough for me, why do I think there's even a minuscule chance I could actually make it to school tomorrow?

I spot the football sitting on the porch, right beside the swing where Brad must've left it after our impromptu game. I guess there are some good things that come from being outside. And some injury, too, but at least my ankle feels totally better now— and, okay, the sweet text Brad sent to check up on me didn't hurt, either.

Dr. Dinah keeps telling me that this will get easier; that each trip outside will get better. That five minutes on the porch will lead to five minutes in the yard will lead to leaving my property. And while I want her to be right, I'm just not sure. But I have to keep trying if I ever want to get that five hundred dollars and all the way to wherever the excursion is.

Our mailbox is beside the road, just a short walk away from our porch. It's not far, and I know I did just fine being outside the other day, but it's like each time I try, I have to push through the same feelings of fear. I challenge my thoughts, another "anxiety management technique" Dr. Dinah imparted to me.

I feel like something terrible will happen if I leave the house. *Nothing will happen. I'm just getting the mail.*

I feel like my heart is actually going to pop out of my chest. *Pretty sure that's not even possible.*

I feel like I'm going to stop breathing. *Not possible. My body won't let me suffocate, as Dr. Dinah has told me one million times.*

Nothing bad is going to happen. Just go just go just go.

And then, mentally cringing as I do it, I whisper, "I am safe. I am secure. I am capable."

I pull open the front door with gusto. I run across the porch, leap down the stairs (ouch—maybe my ankle wasn't quite as healed as I thought), reach the mailbox, pull out the mail, slam the box shut, and run back to the porch.

Panting, I look through the mail. A bill for Mom, another bill for Mom, a reminder from the dentist (I am, unsurprisingly, way behind on my appointments since Dr. Watson simply refuses to do dental house calls), and a copy of *Entertainment Weekly*. Jennifer Lawrence is on the cover, and I *am* really interested in her new movie where she plays a woman who almost single-handedly fights off an alien invasion while managing to look great in an evening gown. We Are Not Alone, of course, has multiple threads dedicated to it.

That's it. I'm going to stay out here to read her interview.

I sit down on the porch swing, looking around. No one is in sight; for once, there aren't even any stray Kirkpatricks wandering around. I force myself to breathe deeply, fighting the urge to take in shallow little bursts. In through my nose. Hold. Out through my mouth. I prop my feet up on the swing, tucking myself into a little ball, and—safely, strongly, and capably—I read all about how J. Law got in shape for the role.

By the time I finish the article, I know that she did a lot of Pilates *and* seventeen whole minutes have passed. My breathing becomes steadier as soon as I step into our slightly dim entryway.

Okay, so maybe most people don't record the amount of time they spend outside. And maybe most of them don't run to and from the mailbox. But this is progress. And if I'm making this much progress, who knows . . . maybe I *can* go to school tomorrow?

Mom gets so excited and freaked out about my sudden change of heart that she makes me have an emergency phone session with Dr. Dinah so we can discuss "coping mechanisms" and "anxiety management techniques" for my first day back at school.

As usual, Dr. Dinah doesn't waste time on pleasantries before launching into it.

"I hear you're going to school tomorrow."

"You heard right."

"And how do you feel about this?" she asks. Even though I've only seen her in a picture online, I imagine her sitting at a desk, pen poised in the air, ready to write down everything I say.

"Just *fan*tastic."

"Mallory," Dr. Dinah says, an edge of warning in her voice. "We can't make any progress unless you're willing to push past your defensive sarcasm."

Damn. I swallow hard. "Well . . . I'm kind of freaked out, for starters. Kind of afraid."

Dr. Dinah makes one of her generic noises; I can never tell if they're supposed to be sympathetic or frustrated. "We know you have difficulty leaving your comfort zone, correct?"

I nod, then realize she can't see me over the phone. "We do."

"It can be especially difficult to leave those comfort zones when you feel alone and exposed. Some people find it helps to leave the house with people they trust."

Sort of like a portable comfort zone. Maybe I should carry around my *X-Files* box set.

"It might be easier for you to leave the house if you do so with someone you trust. Perhaps you could go to school with Lincoln or Jenni tomorrow?"

"Perhaps," I say, accidentally lapsing into her speech patterns. I file Dr. Dinah's tip away for future use, but I have no plans to tell Lincoln or Jenni I'm trying to go to school tomorrow. The last thing I want is for another person to be disappointed in me if it doesn't work out.

I stay up late to confide in my #1 comfort zone compatriot: BeamMeUp.

AlienHuntress: Have you ever had to do something you really, really don't want to do?

BeamMeUp: You know you're describing the human condition, right?

AlienHuntress: I mean, something that makes you feel like you're going to puke? Something that makes you feel like your skin is going to crawl right off your body? Something that pushes you so far out of your comfort zone that you think maybe you might actually die?

I'm worried I just dumped a little too much Mallory melodrama onto BeamMeUp's screen, but he responds quickly.

BeamMeUp: I've been there. And, AlienHuntress, I'd venture every single person on WANA has been there, too.

I smirk as I type back.

AlienHuntress: You're probably right. I'm sure getting abducted by aliens took Roswell1947 pretty far out of his comfort zone.

BeamMeUp: Judging by the extremely detailed probes he explained, it seems like there was nothing comfortable about it.

AlienHuntress: I just wish I could stay inside talking about aliens and weirdos and TV all day, you know?

I wanted to add "with you," but let the words melt back into all the other things I shouldn't be saying to BeamMeUp. He doesn't respond right away, so I continue.

AlienHuntress: But, you know, without the erotic alien fiction. I could live without that.

Finally, BeamMeUp's reply pops up.

BeamMeUp: Sorry, but I have to go.

"Sure," I type, but he's already gone. I stare at the screen in silence as my comfort zone evaporates like a drop of water in the desert.

CHAPTER FOURTEEN

THE NEXT MORNING, I get up bright and much earlier than I normally do for Skype-school. BeamMeUp's not on WANA, which is half disappointment, half relief—I'm still trying to shake off the weird dream I just had about him building a Twizzler monument to me in the backyard.

I dig through the clothes on my floor to find something halfway suitable to wear and try to sculpt my hair into a style that doesn't just look like "girl who spends most of her time by herself." My dad's birding map sticking out from under my bed reminds me why I'm going through all this. I have to figure out how to leave the house without hyperventilating if I want something more than just a crinkled, scribbled-on map to remember my dad by.

"Do I look like a normal, functioning member of society?" I ask my mom as she crams a protein bar in her mouth in the kitchen.

My mom rushes across the kitchen—another one of those hugs—and says, "Don't forget your lunch, okay?"

"You packed my lunch?" I say into her shoulder.

"Don't get too excited. I bought you a Lunchable."

"A Lunchable?" I open the lunch bag she hands me.

"You used to love them!"

"When I was in second grade. Oh wait, you got the pizza kind?"

She gives me a self-satisfied smile. Neither of us says anything for a moment, and I realize that this is it—I have to leave the house now. Go to school, which I haven't done in months. The thought of walking into the cafeteria makes my knees buckle. But I can't back out now.

"Okay, I'm out of here!" I shout, running toward the door. Maybe if I do this with enough momentum, I can get to school without even realizing what's going on.

I run to the mailbox, just as far as I went yesterday. But today I have to keep going.

"Just walk," I mutter to myself. A few cars drive by. No one pays any attention to me.

That's a good thing, I tell myself. If no one notices me, I can blend right in and become ghost girl once again. Except that's not really possible anymore, is it? Not since I was nominated for homecoming as a joke. I put one sneaker out on the gray sidewalk, then the other. One step. Two steps. I try to count the blades of grass sticking up through the cracks in the cement. I breathe in shakily. This is okay. I'm just walking. Still, I can't stop sweating, even though it's a mild day. Visible pit stains are not cute, but I can't seem to stop.

I glance back, once, at my house. Mom's not staring out the window at me, but I know that soon, she'll get in her minivan and drive the opposite direction to work, confident that I'm happily on my way to school. I just have to prove her right.

A squirrel darts out of the bushes and runs across the

sidewalk. "Good Lord!" I shout, nearly jumping into the grass. My hands slam to my heart before I can stop myself.

A rodent will not deter me. And I'm pretty sure Reardon has never crowned a homecoming queen who was in rehab—I mean, Becky Paulson did develop that drug problem, but that wasn't until several years after she won. One foot in front of the other. Plus, avoiding every crack in the sidewalk, because why take any chances?

I reach the curb—the part where I cross the street. I'm only two blocks from the high school. I press my nails into my palms so hard that I'm sure I must be drawing blood. I look left, then right. I can do this.

With a loud, mechanical moan, a school bus putters by slowly, spewing out a cloud of gray exhaust. I start coughing, and then I can't get my breath, like there's suddenly a swarm of bees in my lungs. I bend over, dropping my lunch bag, and hack.

"I am safe. I am secure. I am capable." Wheezing now.

"Are you okay?" asks a middle-aged woman with a stroller. Where did she come from? She's holding the hand of a little blond boy with a backpack. "Can you breathe?" she asks, stepping toward me.

I think I'm going to barf, and the last place I want to barf is on this strange woman's feet.

I stand up, head swimming. "Yes! I'm fine!"

She reaches out to touch me, but the unfamiliar feeling of her hand on my arm is like a million needles poking my body. I pull away from her and take off toward my house.

This was the stupidest idea I've ever had, I think as my sneakers slap against the pavement. A horn honks and pulls me out of the moment, because now, the noise is deafening. I don't even recognize the deep blue car that drives by or the people inside it. The logical part of my brain tells me that they're kids from school, but their faces blur together into one giant blob of panic. I keep running. What made me think that playing a quick game of football or reading a magazine on the porch was anything like going to school? I need to curl back up in bed and Skype into physics. I need to get home. Now.

I skid to a stop in front of my house when I see my mom's minivan still parked in the driveway. She's almost always gone by now. If I go back inside, she'll know I'm nothing but a huge liar. So I duck under the windows and run into the backyard, positioning myself behind our trash and recycling cans and lean against the house, panting.

"You okay?"

Jake is in his backyard, holding a hose and looking at me like I'm crazy. I wave him off, which he takes as an invitation to turn off the hose and walk toward me.

"Go away!" I hiss. My vision's getting wavy. Not with panic, but with tears. Frustration, disappointment, fear of being dragged off to rehab—it all feels like a flood. I blink it back.

"What's going on?" he asks at a normal volume.

"Can you keep it down?" My voice is ragged. "What are you doing here?"

"I could ask the same thing of you," he whispers sarcastically.

"I'm taking out the trash."

"Whispering and looking over your shoulder. Do you need . . . help with something?"

Damn Jake Kirkpatrick. "We have a raccoon problem. They keep getting into the garbage, and I'm just staking out the scene so I can scare them away." Great save, Mal.

Jake narrows his eyes. "I didn't know raccoons were active during the day."

I nod vigorously. "These raccoons come out at all hours. They're relentless."

Jake runs a hand through his hair and part of it stays sticking straight up. He nods his head slowly in a way that doesn't at all make me think he's convinced. "And the whispering?"

"I don't want the raccoons to hear me. I'm going to scare them when they show up. You know, jump out from behind the cans, yell at them . . ."

"Tell them it's game over?" Jake asks.

"Yes. See, you get it. Are you telling me you guys don't have a raccoon problem?"

Jake crosses his arms over his wrinkled Harvard T-shirt. "Not so far. No."

"Well. You'd better hope they never show up. Because they will ruin your life."

Jake nods, giving me the tiniest smile. He so rarely smiles that, I have to admit, it would be sort of cute if he weren't such a jerk who devotes his life to bothering me.

"You might want to get out of here," I say. "Because of the raccoons."

"Right." He gives me another one of those brief guy waves and walks back into his yard. I let out a sigh of relief and slip around the corner . . . only to come face-to-face with my mom. She's deadly still, flanked by two of our yard's most intimidating cacti.

I swallow, hard. "I just forgot something, so I came back to get it."

"You forgot something in the trash?"

I don't say anything.

"Where's your lunch?"

I have a vague, hazy memory of dropping it on the ground by the lady's feet I almost threw up on.

"I think . . . I think I lost it," I say helplessly.

Mom shakes her head. "Mallory . . . you told me you were going to school today."

I nod. The sweat on my forehead is so thick I have to wipe it away.

"I know you and Lincoln have never met a situation you couldn't joke your way out of, but this isn't funny anymore. This is your education we're talking about. And your health."

My eyes burn again and I look away. How could she think I'm anywhere close to joking? I would give a million Lunchables for an interruption from Jake right now.

"Look at me."

I'm shocked to see tears in her eyes. I can count on one hand—maybe even one finger—the times I've seen my mom cry. It's something our family does even more rarely than hug.

"I am *worried* about you. I need you to show me that you're doing okay . . . and that you're improving. And if you can't . . . well, Mallory, we don't have any choice. Dr. Dinah knows a place that's made for people like you. . . ."

People like me. I shudder to even think about what that means.

"I'm doing okay!" I burst out.

Mom widens her eyes, flustered. "How is this okay? How is hiding in the garbage okay?"

"Technically, I wasn't *in* the garbage so much as *near* it. . . ." She presses her lips together, about to say my name. "But . . . you won't let me get better! I promise I'm trying."

"I want to believe that. I really do. But what's your end goal here? Are you going to stay in our house for the rest of your life?"

"Just give me two weeks, okay? Until after homecoming!"

She pulls a curl of her shoulder-length hair behind her ear. "Mallory, I don't believe that you are actually going."

"I am!" My voice is flat, choked. It feels like the sun's bearing down on me. I breathe in, close my eyes, think about Brad. "I'm going to win," I say with as much conviction as possible.

Mom's confusion and disbelief are written in big, bold letters all over her face, but I can tell that it's not about my chances of winning. It's that I *want* to win. As I study her face, I realize that I'm just as shocked as she is. I haven't been invested in anything since Dad left. The unfamiliar feeling blooms in my chest—*wanting*. Not being afraid. Not avoiding. Not hiding. But wanting, trying, doing.

It's scary and weird, but I missed this feeling. I don't want it—or me—to go away.

Mom purses her lips. "I want to believe you, so much. But . . ."

"Two weeks, Mom. Just make your decision after homecoming. Please."

Mom throws up her hands. Her bracelets clank against one another. "Okay. But if this is another attempt to—"

"I can do this," I say. "I'm going to the dance."

CHAPTER FIFTEEN

The great thing about lipstick is that it makes everyone think you're totally put together. You can be wearing a dirty T-shirt and cutoffs, but if you take a second to swipe on some MAC Ruby Woo, all of a sudden people are, like, "Whoa, this girl knows what she's doing."

—*Just Jenni*, 2015

IN MY ROOM, I pull my phone out of my pocket and text Jenni. *SOS.*

Jenni's practically glued to her phone because she's obsessed with checking her YouTube views and comments (even though her comments are always either from teenage girls who think she's their idol or creepy old men who say inappropriate things that, frankly, shouldn't be allowed on YouTube). Thirty seconds later, I get a call.

"What's going on?" she says as soon as I pick up.

A toilet flushes. "Are you in the bathroom?" I ask.

"Duh! You said SOS, so I had to go where teachers wouldn't see me making a call!"

I explain my whole ridiculous story to Jenni, raccoons and

Lunchables and near-puke included, and she confirms that it's pretty bad.

"We really need to take our plan to the next level," Jenni says. "I don't mean to be the bearer of bad news, but I just checked the ReardonsFutureQueen tumblr, and Pia and Brad are the highest in the polls."

"That stupid children's hospital," I mutter. This scheme has turned me into a monster.

"You need to get more points, Mallory."

"Oh really? Is that how I win? Here I was, thinking I needed to get fewer points."

"Your bad attitude isn't going to help you," Jenni says primly. "But, luckily for you, your best friend has a great idea. I'm afraid my little assignments are not going to cut it anymore."

"Another idea? You mean an idea like the time you thought we could get Justin Bieber to date us by writing poetry about him in his Instagram comments?"

"That would've worked if we weren't twelve and didn't have such limited vocabularies. And if *wiener* weren't the only thing we could think of that *kind of* rhymed with *Bieber*."

"The world just wasn't ready."

"This is a *much* better idea. I can't tell you about it now because I know you and you'd just complain about it. Just be ready tomorrow, okay?"

"Ready for what?" I ask, but all I hear is the sound of the hand dryer as Jenni hangs up.

When I stumble into my kitchen to make breakfast the next morning, someone shouts, "Wakey-wakey, eggs and bakey!"

I jump and hold up my laptop in front of me like a shield. But it's *Just Jenni* in a bright yellow dress and adorable frilly apron. Her hair, as always, is sleek and frizz-less. Because I'm so groggy that I still can't form words, I plop down at the counter. She walks over to me with a plate of pancakes, which I quickly grab from her.

"Shouldn't you be, like, at yoga, or debate practice, or yoga debate practice?"

"Debate is super not zen," Jenni says, beaming. "But that's not it. Remember my idea?"

I chew the delicious, fluffy pancake and nod.

"These pancakes are merely intended to butter you up," she says. "Pun intended." Jenni clears her throat, hands me a huge coffee mug, and does jazz hands. "Two words: Puppy Playtime."

I swallow. "Is this the thing where people pay to play with puppies?"

"You do listen! I've been planning the yearbook's annual Puppy Playtime fund-raiser for, like, months. People can play with a puppy for a dollar a minute. And they can adopt the puppies, so it's good for the yearbook *and* the shelter."

"I don't really understand where I come into this."

"Okay, well, we were going to have the fund-raiser on the practice field, but since Mayfield High defaced it, now the landscapers are working on it and it's out of commission. I thought we were going to have to cancel the fund-raiser, and I was *so* upset, because everyone always gets so excited about seeing the puppies and their little faces, and last year, there was this baby puggle . . ."

"Jenni!"

Jenni sighs, sits down next to me, and smooths her dress over her knees. "Mal, we're having the fund-raiser here—it's perfect. What could get you more spirit points than hosting a fund-raiser? This is so much better than a stupid children's hospital."

"Listen to yourself." I scowl. "You're defaming a children's hospital."

"Only in the name of victory! Now, come on!" She stands up and claps, making the rings on her hand *clink* softly together. "I already called the shelter and set everything up. Everyone will be here in two hours!"

"Two *hours*? Jenni, are you insane?"

"Nope," she says with a wide, completely insane-looking grin. "I'm just an awesome friend. You're going to be a fund-raising hero and the pictures are going to be all over Instagram. Nothing's ever as popular as puppy pictures. I mean, besides the time Kayla accidentally took that picture where her nipple was showing."

"Oh, I could only hope to attain the popularity levels of an illicit nipple," I say, feeling that familiar tightening in my chest.

"But you can get close," Jenni says, walking toward the sink full of dishes. She turns around to stare at me, and that's when I realize that the panicked noises I thought I'd been making internally are very external. "Are you okay?" she asks, her eyes wide.

"No!" I wail. "Jen, I can't handle this! There's a reason I don't go to school. I can't face all those people."

Jenni rushes back to me and sits down. She puts her arm around me and her dark hair spills over my shoulder. "You don't have to leave the house! Promise. You won't even have to go in the yard, okay?" Jenni says. "Do you think Beyoncé would hide out in her bedroom if she was feeling overwhelmed?"

I shrug. "Maybe?"

Jenni looks at me with a flicker of rage in her eyes. "No!

Beyoncé filmed a documentary, is raising the number one celebrity baby, and recorded a secret album. She would not stay in her room for Puppy Playtime. She would put on a leotard and blow everyone's minds." I turn to look at Jenni and focus on her brown eyes as the rest of the room spins. "You can do this. I know you can. Just put out some snacks—I know you have those—and make sure everything stays stocked. And if you're really overwhelmed, find me. I'll be here."

Jenni couldn't tell a lie if her life depended on it, so I know she must really believe that I can do this. My own mom thinks I need to be basically committed, but at least my best friend thinks I can be a functioning member of high school society.

"This will get you on everyone's radar and get you that much closer to winning."

And that much closer to five hundred dollars, I think to myself. "Okay," I say.

"Yaaaaaay!" She stands and hops up and down. "This is so exciting. Go get things set up in the kitchen and I'll put together an outfit fit for a homecoming queen, okay?"

"My mom okayed this? You know how she is about letting people mess up the yard."

Jenni waves me off. "Don't worry. I already cleared it with her and Linc."

At least this might help Mom see that I'm doing okay. After retrieving a few bags of chips and pretzels from the pantry in the basement and emptying them into big, colorful plastic bowls, I turn around to see Jenni sitting at my open computer.

"What are you doing?" I ask, running toward her and trying to shut my laptop.

"I don't think so!" she says, holding it open. "Who is this person you've been talking to?"

"That's just my nerdy alien forum. I told you about it."

"But you never mentioned . . . BeamMeUp? Is this a guy?"

"Yes, but that doesn't mean . . ."

"Um, what's this, where he says *you are a force to be reckoned with*?" She swivels around to look at me. "This guy is into you!"

"He is not!"

"These messages say otherwise. Trust me. I read a *lot* of advice columns." Jenni's eyes flick back to the screen. "Mal, guys don't just say this stuff unless they like you. You clearly don't know your own potential."

Thankfully, a *ping* from Jenni's phone interrupts us. She glances at it and her eyes go wide. "We're putting a pin in that. The yearbook committee is going to be here any minute. Let me do your makeup," Jenni says, clasping her hands under her chin.

"I thought you said we had two hours!" I try to squirm out of her reach.

"That's when everyone else is going to get here, but the committee's coming by to set up. Seriously, it's just a few people—Robby and Melodie. And José. And Sarah-Beth."

I sigh. Cool—maybe Sarah-Beth and I can talk about how she dropped me like an anxious hot potato once I stopped coming to school. "Fine. Just do my makeup."

Jenni exhales and closes her eyes slowly. "You have no idea how long I've been waiting to hear you say that."

Twenty minutes later, I have a delicate cat eye, my lips are hot pink, and I'm wearing blush that, according to Jenni, is really "defining" my cheekbones.

The doorbell rings. "I'll get it! Now you have to find something cute to wear," Jenni chirps.

In my room, I dig out a long blue-and-white maxi dress from the recesses of my closet and pull it on. The dull pound and clink of a hammer hitting something taps against my window. Outside, yearbook kids set up temporary puppy pens in the space between our house and the Kirkpatricks'. Jenni looks totally in her element directing people and, what's more, everyone on the yearbook staff seems to love her and listen to everything she says. I'm clearly not the only one who doesn't know my own potential.

My heart leaps when I see Brad walk into the yard. For a second, I let myself imagine he's holding a bag of Twizzlers behind his back with a note that says, *Homecoming?* But real-life Brad gives Robby one of those smack-on-the-back hugs that dudes give. Jake's tagging along with him. They're both wearing RHS football shirts—Jake must have borrowed one of Brad's, because I seriously doubt he has a secret stash of Reardon merch. They both look pretty good. I go downstairs and watch from the kitchen window. You know, for homecoming.

Jenni trots over to Brad with an impossibly fluffy golden retriever puppy in her arms and he lets it lick his face. Then she demands a dollar, which Jake gives her. I can't help but smile. Everyone outside is playing with Labs and Chihuahuas and border collies. I watch Lincoln pick up a puppy and cradle it like a baby. My bare feet bring me toward the side door.

I stop in my tracks as my total stupidity registers, toes tingling hot and cold. I can't go outside when all those people are out there. What if what happened yesterday happens today? And this time I almost barf on my classmates instead of just some random lady with a stroller? No garbage will shield me from that. I close my eyes and partake in my favorite pastime, thought-challenging, just like I did that day I went all the way to the mailbox.

Is anyone out there going to spit in my face or tell me I'm a loser? Doubtful.

And even if they did, would it be the end of the world? Okay, maybe not.

And why do I feel like someone's standing right behind me?

"Hey."

"How did you get in here?" I ask Jake, who's two feet deeper into my personal space than I'd like him to be.

He waves. "Good to see you, too."

I sigh and adjust the waist of my dress. *Be nice to Brad's brother.* "I didn't mean that—"

"You're having a fund-raiser at your house," he says, sitting down on one of the stools at the island.

"In the *yard*. People might be tempted to partake of my glorious snack selection, but Jenni said that everyone would be mostly staying outside."

He shrugs as he inspects the bowls on the counter, then grabs a handful of pretzels. "This is probably none of my business, but . . . there's this weird girl outside who keeps asking if anyone's seen you. And she wants to know if your house is haunted."

"Oh my God, was it . . . ?" I look out the window and come face-to-face with Monica Bergen herself. She has her hands cupped around her eyes and her whole face pressed up against the window.

"I'M ALIVE!" I shout, then pull the blinds shut.

"High school's gotten weirder in the months since I graduated," Jake says, shaking his head.

"That's Monica Bergen. She thinks I'm—" I stop myself before I spill anything to Jake. "You know what? It's really not worth explaining. Why aren't you out there with the puppies?"

"Well, everyone was kind of wondering where you were. But I know why you're not out there," Jake says, confidently popping a pretzel into his mouth.

"Yeah?" My voice is about twelve octaves higher than usual. Blood rushes to my head and my vision swims for a second. The last person I want confronting me about being housebound is Jake.

"Raccoon-induced rabies." His face is as serious and stony as Mount Rushmore.

I laugh, partly because it's so corny it's funny, partly from pure relief. "I held them off for another day, but you know how they are. They strike when you least expect them."

Jake doesn't smile. "Your mom seemed pretty upset," he says.

The smile instantly melts off my face. "What? You heard that?"

"Not much. But . . . you guys were being pretty loud."

"Were you spying on me?"

"You live next door. What do you want me to do, wear headphones every time I'm in my own yard so I won't hear you yelling about God knows what?"

My heart speeds up. I grip the counter. This is the last thing I want to deal with when I have a yard full of people . . . and puppies, who don't deserve to witness a full-blown panic attack.

"Maybe you should just mind your own business," I mutter.

"Mind my business?" Jake stands up so fast the stool skitters a few inches backward. "If I actually *did* care about butting into your life, I'd ask you what you're trying to prove here."

I shake my head, bewildered. "What's that supposed to mean?"

He gestures toward the yard. "There's a fund-raiser going on in your yard and you're hiding in the kitchen. Clearly you want nothing to do with it. So why are you faking it?"

"That's none of your—"

"Business?" Jake says, but I can tell he's not really asking. I open my mouth to respond, but the sound of the front door opening stops me.

"Hey, party people!" Lincoln shouts, walking into the kitchen. "Whoa, you look amazing! Not you, Jake. I mean, you look fine, but Mallory!"

"Thanks," I mutter. Out of the corner of my eye I can see that Jake's staring right at me. I'm so busy being pissed that I almost don't notice that Scott is right behind Lincoln, holding a trembling black puppy with floppy ears.

"I'm going to go see what Brad's up to," Jake says to Lincoln. "Nice to see you."

"What were you guys talking about?" Lincoln asks as soon as the door shuts. "He's skulking around like one of those glitter vampires in *Twilight*."

"Hi, I'm Mallory," I say to Scott. My hand's still shaking with anger at Jake.

Scott smiles. "I'm Scott. Lincoln's boyfriend. I'd shake your hand, but, you know . . ."

"You're holding a puppy. Common excuse," I say, but all I can think is, *Whoa, boyfriend already?* I sneak a glance at Lincoln, but he's intently studying the puppy in Scott's arms, who's currently trying to eat Scott's hand. How could Lincoln not tell me that he and Scott have a label? We used to tell each other everything—he even told me last year about his weird crush on Mr. Jordan, the PE teacher whom he swears looks sorta-kinda like Idris Elba (he doesn't).

Lincoln ignores my probing looks and says, "So Puppy Playtime is causing some Puppy Problems. This guy is not such a fan of crowds or the outdoors. Can he hang here with you?"

"Oh, I guess," I say, scooping the wiggling puppy out of

Scott's arms. "It's a rough job, but I'll take one for the team. What's his name?"

"Arthur," Scott says.

"Hey, Arthur," I coo. Arthur licks my cheek in response.

"Well, we're going back outside," Lincoln says. "Also, you now owe Jenni a dollar."

As soon as he finishes his sentence, a huge boom shakes the house, followed by shrieks from outside.

I peek through the blinds. The sky has opened up and is currently drenching our yard with rain. It doesn't storm often in Reardon, but when it does, it comes fast and furious. The yard is a blur of rain and teenagers hastily picking up puppies. Then I hear the front door whine open.

Jenni's power walking toward me, flinging water everywhere with her long hair. It's criminally unfair that even when her bangs are plastered to her forehead, she still looks cute. "We'removingthefund-raiserinsidenowokaythanksbye!" she shouts, then runs back to the door to help some kid I don't even recognize carry in a crate.

"What?" I shriek. Arthur's whimpers echo mine.

"It's okay," Lincoln says. "I know you haven't seen most of these people for months—"

"Yes, please remind me of all the reasons why this is freaking me out," I spit, not even caring that Scott is witnessing all of this. He might as well get used to my crazy family sooner rather than later if he and Lincoln are basically married already.

"Just give it a try! Maybe—"

A black-and-white puppy runs through the kitchen, barking, narrowly avoiding knocking over the very large orange tree my mom stuck in the corner of the room. He disappears through the back entrance and José comes running after him.

"You guys see a puppy? Half a foot tall, black and white, goes by Grover?"

Scott and Lincoln point toward the back hallway, but I'm already shaking. José waves and takes off. I'm not sure how long I can handle this. It feels like someone is jumping up and down on my chest and I'm struggling to breathe. I want to go to my room, but getting to the stairs means fighting my way through the crowd of people that has gathered in our entryway.

"Oh hey," says a familiar voice behind me. I turn to find myself face-to-face with my former friend Sarah-Beth's short blond bob.

"H-Hi," I stammer, running my fingers through Arthur's fur. I read somewhere that petting animals can be calming, but it doesn't seem to be holding true.

Sarah-Beth points to the wall. "You guys painted in here."

"Yeah, Mom redid the kitchen a couple months ago." Sarah-Beth and I used to stay up late to watch *SNL*, and now we're awkwardly discussing my mom's redecorating? My feet, fingers, hands, and face feel like they're on fire with nerves.

"So," she says, her eyes lighting up as she finally discovers a new topic. "I heard you know Brad's brother. What's his deal? Did he really kill somebody?"

I realize that I've been petting Arthur with such intensity that I might be causing fur loss. "It's been great, Sarah-Beth, but Arthur and I need a break," I say.

"Cool," she says, taking out her phone. "Glad to see you're still just as impossible to talk to as ever."

She turns away from me and I catch the sight of the tiny heart tattoo on her shoulder poking out from her tank top. She got it a year ago at The Rusty Squirrel, where no one cares if you have a convincing ID. Jenni and I waited for her by the front desk, making fun of all the potential tattoos on the wall and trying to figure out who would ever get one of zombie Tigger from *Winnie the Pooh*. That was only a year ago.

And just like that, my comfort zone implodes on me.

CHAPTER SIXTEEN

STILL CRADLING ARTHUR, I speed walk to the small table in the corner of the kitchen and squeeze under it. Trying to tune out the party only makes the laughter, barking, and occasional shouting louder, like a slow explosion. I wonder if Brad's here, and the thought kind of makes me want to smile and puke at the same time. I definitely don't want him to see me all anxious and panicked about the million and one classmates in my house.

And, I realize, I really don't want anyone to go in my room, where I have my computer open to We Are Not Alone and the collage of all my favorite movie stars and TV shows on my wall. It's hard enough feeling like I'm totally different from my class-mates; I definitely don't want to explain why I find David Duchovny more attractive than Channing Tatum.

I close my eyes and pull Arthur closer. He snuggles into my chest.

"Knock, knock," Lincoln says, lifting up a corner of the tablecloth.

"Is Scott with you?" I ask. My eyes are squeezed shut.

"He went to go help out. He can get along with anybody, so he doesn't mind."

With Linc here, my heart rate slows and the noise becomes a little less unbearable. "So . . . boyfriend, huh?"

"Nice try. We're talking about you right now."

"I'm only under the table because I care about Arthur's well-being. I don't want him to be scarred for life because of a traumatic socializing experience!"

"That's so kind of you, Mal, but why don't you just try to come out. No one's making you leave the house, okay? Just get up, say hi to a few people, and then go hang out in your room for the rest of the day like you always do."

"I don't always hang out in my room."

"Oh, my apologies . . . like you do *ninety percent of the time*."

I'm about to counter with another argument when my mother's voice carries over the sound of the crowd. "Look at this . . . party!" she says. I can tell by the measured quality of her voice that she's internally surveying the damage that muddy paws and sneakers have done to our carpet. "I'm so happy—I mean, *Mallory* is so happy to help out with the fund-raiser!"

The desire to stay comfortable and the desire to prove that I'm "better" battle it out in my head. Hanging out underneath the kitchen table isn't going to do anything to convince my mom that I'm feeling okay—in fact, it will probably do the opposite. Socially well-adjusted people, as a rule, do not spend parties under tables.

"I am safe. I am secure. I am capable," I mutter.

"What?" Lincoln asks.

I give Arthur one last snuggle before handing him off to

Lincoln. There's no reason he should suffer just because I have to prove a point.

I scoot out from under the table and right into the wall of people in my house. Holding my breath, I weave through the crowd, giving curt nods and the occasional "hihowareyou." I just have to make it to the stairs.

In the living room, a puppy is climbing on top of the coffee table, strangers are sitting on my couch, and . . . oh God, why is Monica Bergen even still here? Seeing all of these people I haven't seen in months makes my stomach flip over and over like a coin flying through the air. Everything I've been trying so hard to avoid has come to me. Even my house isn't a safe space anymore. The laughter and yelling pushes into my ears and into my stomach, where the handful of pretzels I just ate rolls around. My lungs seem to contract, taking in less and less air no matter how many deep breaths I take.

And that's when I know that I'm one hundred percent, definitely, actually going to barf.

I know I can't make it to the upstairs bathroom, so I run through the living room, lock myself in the bathroom by the laundry room, and hurl into a clothes hamper. With tears in my eyes, I slump down with my back against the door. Even though the house was full of chattering and barking just a few seconds ago, now all I can hear is the barking . . . which means that everyone who doesn't have four legs and isn't covered in fur was probably listening intently as I puked my guts up.

There are three tiny raps on the door. "Mallory?"

"Can you just make everyone leave, Jenni?" I ask weakly.

I can barely even hear the disappointment in her voice as she says, "Of course I can!"

She went out of her way to set up this fund-raiser so it would benefit *me*, and how did I repay her? By hiding under a table and then ending the whole thing with a poorly timed barf. I sigh and hold my head in my hands, wondering if they can take away spirit points.

After a few minutes and a lot of shuffling around and murmuring, Jenni knocks on the door again. "It's safe to come out!"

I open the door slowly and then throw my arms around her. "I'm sorry!"

"Don't worry about it," Jenni says. "A lot of people donated money because they felt sorry for us, what with the weather and then . . ."

"The barfing girl," I say flatly.

"You did good, Mal," Jenni says, so sincerely that a tear involuntarily sneaks out of my eye. Every last bit of my heart wants to believe her, but as I rest my forehead on her shoulder, I know that I'm doing the opposite of good right now.

After Jenni leaves, I watch a few episodes of *The X-Files* in bed and end up falling asleep. By the time I wake up, it's already dark and I feel like shit. I ruined a fund-raiser, threw away any chance at getting spirit points, probably scared Brad off, and definitely didn't convince my mom that I'm a functioning human being. And I'm not any closer to getting five hundred dollars.

I can't even be mad at my mom for doubting me, because right now, I have next to no faith in myself. Dr. Dinah says that this will get better in time. I thought I was getting better, after playing outside with the guys and hanging out on the porch. But is today what *better* looks like? My mantra isn't "I am safe. I am secure. I am nauseated."

I roll over and grab my phone, expecting a text from Jenni. There are three—full of exclamation points and emojis—but there's also one I didn't expect. From Brad.

> Hope ur feeling better. Can't have my physics partner getting sick! :)

Maybe this is doing better. I'm making friends—friends who care about me.

And are extremely hot. Not that it matters.

I turn on my lamp and open my computer. At least my unusual level of IRL activity today means I have tons of Internet minutes saved up. BeamMeUp messages me immediately.

> **BeamMeUp:** What do you think's up with those lights on the horizon?!!! Possible UFO?

As happy as I was about Brad's text, I'm ten thousand times gladder to get BeamMeUp's message. In BeamMeUp's eyes, I'm a cool, put-together girl, the kind who would *definitely* never ruin a fund-raiser with her anxiety. The kind of girl who doesn't barf at all, let alone in a clothes hamper.

And he used three exclamation points? That kind of irresponsible punctuation must mean something's up.

I walk over to my bedroom window, which faces east, and inspect the sky. It's clear—almost a liquid black—and I see the moon and some stars, but nothing else.

> **AlienHuntress:** What are you talking about? Where? I can't see any mysterious lights.

> **BeamMeUp:** You must not be looking in the right place. Are you inside? Go outside!

I scowl at my computer. Sure. Go outside. Because it's that easy.

But I've been on the porch. For seventeen whole minutes, even. And I played football. And I need to redeem myself after the puppy party disaster.

Is a tree branch going to snap off, falling and crushing me instantly? *Not likely*.

Am I going to lock myself outside and then be unable to get back in because Mom and Lincoln are sleeping and then I have to sleep outside and get eaten by coyote-wolf-bear hybrids overnight? *Probably not*.

Safe. Secure. And, laughing to myself as I think about my shitshow of a day, *totally capable*.

I step out of the front door into the dark, quiet night. I lean up against the railing, listening to the gentle noise of the crickets and inspect the sky. It's the same moon and stars that I saw from my bedroom window. And then, slowly moving across the sky, a blinking light . . . that is clearly an airplane.

I snort. *Very* mysterious. Maybe BeamMcUp isn't the scientific genius he thinks he is.

Still, I can't deny that the stars are a whole lot prettier when I'm under them instead of taking them in from the other side of my bedroom window. The airplane blinks its way across the blackness. The sky is full of people crisscrossing the world right now, and I think about my dad. He's out there, somewhere. I just have to figure out where.

A light snaps on in one of Brad's house's upstairs windows, making my chest thump a little—just a little. I sit down on the porch swing and draw my knees into my chest. Breathing in the scent of the post-rain air, I watch the plane until it disappears into the dark.

BeamMeUp: No way. Pizza demands to be eaten with hands. I can't believe you're a forker.

AlienHuntress: A forker?! Come on. Pizza is hot, it's greasy, and it's way easier to eat with a fork. Also I'm civilized.

BeamMeUp: Cute.

AlienHuntress: Did you just call me cute?

BeamMeUp: I called your pizza-eating style cute. Don't get too full of yourself.

AlienHuntress: What do you eat your pizza with, your massive ego?

BeamMeUp: Sounds like something a forker would say.

CHAPTER SEVENTEEN

"YOU'RE FREAKING OUT OVER nothing," Lincoln assures me. "Seriously, no one even cares."

Lincoln and Jenni are nice enough to Skype with me on Jenni's phone before class starts on Monday morning. They're in the hallway at school, so I hear a constant drone of lockers slamming and kids yelling.

"I planted a story that you have a serious dog allergy and all the fur in your house made you sick," Jenni says.

"You 'planted a story'?" I ask. "What did you do, call TMZ and give them an anonymous tip?"

Jenni looks at me like I'm being deliberately obtuse. "I talked about it on *Just Jenni*, of course! And I told Caroline about it, so that means . . ."

"The story's all around school because she told Pia and has absolutely no respect for other people's very serious fake allergies?"

Jenni beams. "Exactly! And here's the best part: The story

totally caught on, and now you have ten more spirit points than Pia does!"

"I *just* checked it last night. How do you even know that?"

"She has her phone set up to get notifications whenever the ReardonsFutureQueen tumblr updates," Lincoln says.

"Wow. I feel . . . sort of guilty?"

"But not guilty enough to set the record straight, right?" Lincoln says with one eyebrow raised.

"Nope. I just wish I hadn't ruined your party with my anxiety-induced nausea."

Jenni shakes her head. "I already told you a million times, it's fine! And," she whispers loudly, leaning in closer to the phone so the kids at the lockers behind her won't hear (even though, from what I can see, they're making out so intensely that I'm concerned the girl might swallow the guy's head), "Brad's being super sweet about it, isn't he? He told me he texted to check on you."

"When did you talk to Brad?" Jenni shouldn't be scheming more than she already is.

"He texted me to ask about you!" Jenni says quickly. "And I'm doing everything I can to make sure you get spirit points."

The first bell rings, which means there are five minutes to get to homeroom. We say our good-byes, and I'm alone until it's time to log in to physics class.

The deadline for the physics project (and homecoming) is getting closer, and Brad and I still have so much to do on that stupid project and our pointless journal. But it's a little hard to concentrate on physics when:

A) I want to be closer to winning, getting five hundred dollars, and finding my dad.

B) I still feel like an idiot for barfing when Brad was around.

C) I fought with Brad's brother again. I kind of doubt Brad and Jake sit around and talk about me, but what if they do compare notes about me and Brad starts to think I'm a jerk because I yell at his brother literally every time I see him?

Hours later, after I've suffered through physics class and sufficiently wasted most of my morning commenting about that Jennifer Lawrence movie on WANA (there's a new trailer and the forum members have taken the "offensively unrealistic" depiction of the aliens *very* personally), it's time to log in to my history class.

The doorbell rings and I pause with my fingers hovering over the keyboard. If watching *Dateline* on Friday nights has taught me anything, it's that answering the door when you're home alone is a one-way ticket to Getting Totally Murdered-ville. But Mom got super pissed when I didn't answer the doorbell a few weeks ago and the UPS guy couldn't deliver a box of her new business cards, so I reluctantly trudge down the stairs.

I open the door cautiously, only to come face-to-face with the only person worse than a murderer: Jake Kirkpatrick.

"I'm sorry, did you think of a prying question you forgot to ask me this weekend?"

Jake's looking everywhere but at my eyes. "I'm not here to talk about that, okay?" he says to the porch light.

"Do you need to use my bathroom again? It's out of order."

"No," he says to his feet. "I just noticed that . . . well, look."

He holds out his phone and I see what he's talking about. In the picture on his screen, the word *freak* is scrawled across . . .

"Oh my God, is that my front window?"

He finally looks at me and I barely even notice the crazy blueness of his eyes because all I can see is how awful he feels.

My stomach churns. *Freak.* The exact word Lincoln used when he was talking about things between him and Scott. Some asshole who was here yesterday must've just had a hard time holding in their disgusting feelings.

I clench my fist around the doorknob until my knuckles turn white. I wish I had gone to school so I could punch whoever did this in the face. I wish I could do a lot of things, but right now the only thing I can do is make sure Lincoln never, ever knows about this.

"I need to get this cleaned up before Lincoln gets home," I say, running to the kitchen for an empty bucket and some sponges. Jake follows me and watches while I fill the bucket with water and a random combination of cleaning supplies that I hope won't kill me.

"I think it's just cheap paint, so it should be easy to wash off."

"Thanks," I say, handing Jake a sponge. We carry the bucket outside. "Did you see who did this?" He just shakes his head.

The letters are huge and dark red, so washing them off takes a fair amount of elbow grease. As Jake and I work in silence, I'm sort of glad he's here. He may be a nosy, stuck-up jerk most of the time, but it would take me forever to do this myself.

"We adopted him," Jake says, scrubbing the *F*.

I focus on the *K*. Eventually, we're going to meet in the middle, like some sort of bizarro *Lady and the Tramp* situation, but I try not to think about it.

"Arthur?" I stop scrubbing and turn to look at Jake.

Jake nods.

"That's great!" I say as I get back to scrubbing the window. "Although you strike me as more of a cat person."

Now Jake stops scrubbing. "What's that supposed to mean?"

I shrug. "Cats don't really like to hang out, they like to spend time by themselves, they aren't very friendly . . ."

"They don't help you wash your windows when some d-bag writes on them," Jake says pointedly.

I'm doing one hell of a job of being nice to Brad's brother. When he goes home, Jake can tell him that I unfavorably compared him to a cat. "Sorry. I'll mind my own business," I mumble, trying to make my frustration as faint as possible.

We scrub in silence for a while, working on the *R* and the *A*.

"It just . . . I don't know, it kind of broke my heart to see how alone he was, you know?" He clears his throat. "All the other dogs were running around, having a great time . . ."

"Pooping behind the couch," I add.

"But he just seemed so out of place. I get that. And all I had to do was mention the idea to Brad and, well, you know how he is. Next thing I knew, we had a new puppy."

"Yeah, I know how he is." Of course Brad's the kind of person who would adopt a scared puppy without thinking twice about it. He probably wouldn't even be mad if he discovered that the dog pooped behind his couch.

Jake washes off the *E* before I can get to it, sparing us the conclusion of that *Lady and the Tramp* scene.

"Thanks for helping me," I say. "You didn't have to. And I know you didn't want to."

"Are you kidding? Washing insults off of windows is probably my number one hobby. I should be thanking you for letting me help. Otherwise, I would've been writing on my own windows just to have something to wash off."

I smile and shake my head. "Right. I'll see you later. Have fun . . . doing stuff."

"Mal, wait," Jake says, lightly grasping my elbow.

I make the mistake of looking up at him, which means I end up just staring into his eyes for a solid ten seconds before asking, "Yeah?"

"Your cheeks are sunburnt," he blurts. "You should wear sunscreen."

With that, Jake turns and jogs back to his house. Confused, I put my hand on my face and feel my burning cheeks. They're hot. From being out in the sun.

I realize I just spent at least thirty minutes in the front yard without freaking out at all. I didn't even notice. No sweating, no shaking, no trouble breathing, no panicking.

Whoa. I feel a little safe, a bit secure, and (despite my slightly sore biceps) pretty capable.

Maybe it really is getting easier. Maybe it was just my protective big-sister instincts kicking in and overriding my usual feelings. Or, maybe it has something to do with what Dr. Dinah told me . . . that it can be easier to leave the house if I do it with someone who makes me feel comfortable.

I can probably discount that theory, because if there's anything Jake Kirkpatrick makes me feel, it's definitely not comfortable.

Even after watching three episodes of *The X-Files* and eating an entire sleeve of Oreos (washing windows works up an appetite), I'm still waiting for Lincoln to get home after school. Mom comes home and, before she retreats to her office with her Lean

Cuisine, mentions something about Lincoln being out with Scott. She doesn't seem concerned, and I start to feel like *I'm* the parent waiting up for my kid to come home as I sit at the kitchen table. When Lincoln finally walks in the front door, he doesn't notice me at first.

"Hello, Lincoln."

He jumps and turns to look at me. "Good Lord, Mallory! What the hell are you doing?"

I cross my arms on the table. "Waiting."

"For what?" Lincoln asks, depositing his backpack on the table and sitting down across from me. "To murder me?" I guess watching too much *Dateline* is a family thing.

"I just wanted to talk to you about how things are going at school. And with Scott."

Lincoln crosses his long, freckled arms. "I told you. Scott's great."

"So everyone's cool with you guys dating?"

Lincoln narrows his eyes and tugs at his hair. "I haven't polled the student body yet, okay, weirdo? I'm gonna go watch TV. Join me when you're done playing *True Detective*."

Lincoln walks into the living room and, after a second, voices blare from the TV. I'm trying to think of a subtle way to bring up the window thing when I see a piece of paper poking out of his backpack.

My curiosity wins out over my respect for personal property as I pull the piece of paper out and uncrumple it. Scrawled across it in red ink, looking pretty much like what was on the front window this morning, is the word *freak*.

As my heart pounds in my chest, I march into the living room and stand in front of the TV. Lincoln throws his hands in the air from his position sprawled across the couch.

"I'm sorry, can a man not relax by enjoying a casual third rewatch of *Twin Peaks*?"

"What's this?" I hold up the paper.

His eyebrows smash together on his forehead. "Were you going through my backpack?"

"Lincoln!" I shout. "I'm your sister, okay? If kids at school are making your life hard, I want to know. It sucks that they're jerks, and I know they're hurting your feelings, but—"

"Can you just forget about it?" Lincoln mutters, turning his eyes to the floor.

"No!" I can feel the heat rising in my body. "It's not fair that the kids at school make your life hell just because they can."

"Mallory," Lincoln says with an edge to his voice. "I'm serious. Drop it."

"I can't. Just tell me who did this. I know I can't go to school and physically hurt anybody, but I can send a very strongly worded Facebook message. . . ."

Lincoln finally looks up, his eyes almost hidden behind the hair that sweeps across his forehead. "It wasn't for me."

"Oh. Scott?" I ask.

"No, Mal. It wasn't for Scott, either."

It takes a minute for what he's saying to sink in. If the sign in his backpack wasn't for him, then the bright red message on the window wasn't, either. And unless someone's very angry at my mom for grabbing the last clearance pencil skirt at Ann Taylor, there's only one person these messages could be for. I stop breathing.

Of course. Of course it's not for Linc.

"In the hallway right in front of the cafeteria they have the homecoming ballot boxes set up with everyone's picture taped on the wall," Lincoln says, staring at his hands. "And this morning I saw that sign by *your* picture. I wasn't even going to tell you, but it turns out you're a big snoop, so there you go."

Lincoln takes a giant breath. I collapse onto the lumpy chaise longue Mom loves so much.

"Because being out at Reardon isn't even that big of a deal. Yeah, there are a bunch of jerks at school, but what's new? I got made fun of more for being shitty in choir than I do for being gay. But you know what *is* hard, Mallory? Having a hermit for a sister. You don't know anything about what's going on in my life. You've met Scott . . . what, one time? I can't talk to you about him because you don't even know him."

"Maybe you can bring him over to the house sometime," I say quietly.

"No!" Lincoln says, looking exasperated. "Because not all of us just want to hang out in this house for the rest of our lives!" He angrily picks up the remote, shuts off the TV, then storms past me and up the stairs.

Lincoln might as well have just punched me in the stomach, because it feels like all the air has just left my body.

I fold into myself and lay my head on my lap when his door slams. When did this happen? Last year, Lincoln could barely even say the words "I'm gay," and now he's out and he has a boyfriend I barely know . . . and meanwhile, I've become a total freak.

I always thought of myself as Lincoln's protector, as the big, bad sister who would destroy anyone who dared to make fun of him. But Lincoln doesn't even need protecting. He's been growing up as I've been trying to avoid the world and everything awful that can happen in it.

Something bad could happen to me if I go out—but is that really any worse than what will happen if I stay here?

I run my fingers over the crumpled piece of paper on my lap. *Freak.* The masochistic part of me decides to make things worse, so I pull out my phone. I search for #stayathomecoming and press my finger too hard against the screen when I scroll through the results. There are a few, but one from an account called ReardonAnonymous stands out.

```
hey #reardonhigh who needs the gym? let's
have homecoming at the freak's house so she can
go, too. #stayathomecoming
```

This time, no tears push against my eyelids. My lips press together in a hard, tough line. I can't keep doing this. Observing Lincoln's life through a screen, being afraid to leave the yard, getting so upset by a tweet from a stupid anonymous Twitter account.

I toss my phone on the cushion, and it bounces with a quiet thump. Leaving it behind, I grab the car keys off the hook in the entryway. Before I know it, I'm knocking on Lincoln's door.

"I'm sorry about what I said," he says as he opens his door. "It was really mean, and . . ."

I hold the keys up and jingle them. He furrows his eyebrows at me.

"Wanna go for a ride?" I ask.

CHAPTER EIGHTEEN

An object at rest stays at rest, unless it's acted upon by
an external force.

—*Physics in the Modern World*, 2013

"ARE YOU SURE YOU want to do this?" Lincoln asks. The
click of my seat belt sounds too loud for my ears, but I fight the
urge to run back into the house.

"Yes," I say firmly, turning to look at him. "I have to. Dr. Dinah
said it will be easier for me to leave the house if I'm with someone I trust. And who do I trust more than my baby bro?"

I reach out to pinch Lincoln's cheek and he squirms. Conveniently, I leave out the part about how this is small potatoes
compared to the birding excursion.

"You are disgusting. We're doing this, but"—he looks in the
rearview mirror as we back out of the driveway—"please open
the door if you get sick, okay? I don't want to clean up your puke."

"Thanks for the concern."

We head down our street. Lincoln slows way down as he
drives over the speed bumps, which makes my stomach feel like

a balloon. But it's not so bad. We pass the corner where I frightened that lady with the stroller. This is now officially the farthest I've gone in months. The streetlights seem extra bright and every tree and street sign glows like a foreign object. An old, run-down house that Lincoln and I used to pretend was haunted is gone now, the wooden bones of a new house in its place.

I guess a part of me thought I'd see nothing but scorched earth, that the world around me stopped existing when I holed up at home. But life clearly went on without me.

"Let's go to Reardon," I decide. The familiarity is a small comfort. Very small. When Lincoln parks in the empty parking lot, I clutch my seat belt so hard that I think I destroy my fingerprints.

"You still sure?" Lincoln asks as he turns off the car, which sputters in response.

"Yes!" I say. It comes out sort of like a shriek, which earns me an unconvinced look from Lincoln.

Lincoln nods. "Just remember: No one's here but us. And you're with someone you trust."

"I know," I say, swallowing hard. I involuntarily reach toward my pocket, wishing I had brought my phone so BeamMeUp could be here with me, too.

I step out of the car, and a hot breeze flutters through my hair. Just feeling the parking lot asphalt under my sneakers is like walking on Mars, even without classmates around me or school buses idling by the doors. Lincoln follows me as I walk toward the huge, empty, green-and-white football field, and puts a gentle hand on my back when my steps get smaller and smaller. After what seems like an eternity, we reach the fifty-yard line and lie down. The grass is surprisingly cool against the bare skin of my arms and legs. I inhale deeply as the stars, which are easy to see since the only light around us is coming from a few weak security lights around the school, wink back at me. I wonder if Lincoln can hear my heart pounding.

Lincoln turns his head to me. "Remember how you used to make up constellations when we were kids?"

I laugh. "Oh God. I totally forgot about that."

"You'd be like, 'Can't you see it? Right there? It says *Mallory*. And over there is the Big Slice of Pizza. And the Little Scoop of Ice Cream.' I *totally* believed you."

"You know," I say, pointing at the sky, "there's the Northern Donkey right over there. . . ."

Lincoln slaps my hand. "I believed everything you said back then because I looked up to you."

"When did that change?" I try to say casually, but it comes out sounding a little bitter instead.

"Are you serious? I *still* look up to you!"

"Even though I haven't left the house in months?"

Lincoln holds his hands above his head. "Look around you! Are you in the house now?"

He's right. My house, in spite of Linc's *Friday Night Lights* phrase, does not have bleachers.

"This school year has been really hard for me, Mal. And not because of Dad—because of you. I *miss* you."

"I'm right here," I say quietly, clenching and unclenching my fists.

"Yeah, but you're not. You're not at school to talk to Scott and hang out at lunch. I mean, Jenni's great, but I can only have so many conversations about which MAC lipstick best flatters her complexion, especially when . . ."

"They all do," we say at the same time.

"And it's even tougher because soon you'll totally

abandon me for college. Unless you decide to be a recluse forever, that is."

I groan. I've been researching schools, a little. "I swear I've thought about it. But I have so much going on, with homecoming and therapy . . ."

Lincoln rolls over on his side to look at me. "You *are* going to college . . . you know that, right? Whatever you're doing with Dr. Dinah is working. And I know that your horizon is a whole lot bigger than the front porch."

I stare at the sky, knowing that if I look at Lincoln I'll start crying.

"And I know you're upset about Dad. I'm upset, too. But when he was here, I was always afraid of what he thought about everything I did. I didn't want to deal with his judgment about me dating guys or being into film or, frankly, not giving a shit about birds."

"Dad loves you."

He collapses back onto the grass and exhales loudly. "I know he did—or does, or whatever—in his own way. But now that he's gone, it's like . . . it's okay to be *me*. I know you're here for me no matter what, and Mom's pretty psycho, like, ninety-five percent of the time, but she loves us both. With Dad out of the picture, I feel like I can finally be the person I've always wanted to be. And I want that for you, too."

"When did you get so smart?" I'm crying now, for real. I close my eyes and let the tears make small rivers down the sides of my face until they run over my earlobes and into the grass.

There's a smile in Lincoln's voice. "I learned from the best."

I laugh, then swallow hard, letting his words sink in. He squeezes my hand. I'm starting to feel like I'm the crazy one for actually caring where my dad is. If there was ever a time to tell

Lincoln the truth about my plan and why I need that five hundred dollars so much, it would be now. I take a deep breath and open my mouth.

And that's when, out of the corner of my eye, I see something moving.

I bolt up. "Do you see that?" Familiar panic starts to tap at the inside of my chest. I mentally calculate how far away we are from the car.

"If it's Big Slice of Pizza again, sorry," Lincoln says. "Not buying it this time."

"There's someone else here!" I hiss.

Lincoln stands up and we both watch a shadowy figure run full speed toward the school.

From our vantage point on the field, we have a clear view of the school across the parking lot. The shadow struggles to open the back door of the school. It's locked, obviously, so the shadow turns its attention to the huge REARDON HIGH SCHOOL CLASS OF 2015 banner.

"Come on," I whisper, fighting the urge to run straight home. We creep silently across the football field and hide behind the marching band bleachers, channeling the badass spirit of Dana Scully. At least I am. Linc's more of a guest star who gets killed off in a mysterious fashion by the monster of the week.

"He looks like a young dude," I say softly. The shadow's only about forty feet away now. "Do you think he's from Mayfield?"

"Duh," Lincoln whispers back as he pulls out his iPhone and starts recording.

I know for a fact that the Reardon Spirit Club spends, like, a week on that dumb banner every year. It's covered in the names and pictures of all the seniors on the football team and, while I still would never say I care about football, I care about Brad. I'm not going to let some douche bag from Mayfield High tear down his banner.

"Give me the keys!" I demand.

"No way. We're not leaving now," Lincoln says without even looking at me.

"I'm not going. Make sure you video this. I have an idea."

Lincoln slides his hand into his pocket and carefully hands me the keys. I run on my tiptoes toward the car, which is parked about thirty feet away, and open the door as silently as I can. I slide the keys into the ignition, take a deep breath, and I flash the headlights, illuminating the no-longer-shadowy person. Then I start honking the horn like hell.

He turns around, giving us a perfect view of his pale, terrified face and purple Mayfield High T-shirt before running. I jump out of the car and chase him, yelling, "Halt, intruder!"

It turns out staying in your house without exercising for months on end isn't exactly great for your speed. By the time I finally round the corner of the school, he's nowhere in sight.

I walk back to Lincoln, panting, my T-shirt stuck to me with sweat. "I lost him."

"Just get in the car!" Lincoln shouts. "Maybe we can find him!"

After twenty minutes of driving around, I see the familiar terra-cotta of our house in the distance. My chest aches from being a badass, so I suggest we call it a night. "The kid's long gone, Lincoln. And all we've managed to do is really freak out that lady walking home from the grocery store."

"In my defense, she had the build of a seventeen-year-old boy," Lincoln says. A smile is plastered on his face, right between his huge dimples. "Although I'll admit that yelling, 'The buck stops here, scumbag!' may not have been my finest moment."

"But you have it all on video, right? And we had a clear shot of his face."

Lincoln waves his phone in the air. "All anyone's been talking about all month—besides homecoming, and that gross infection Brady Munroe got from his nose ring—is catching Mayfield High in the act. And we did it. *You* did it."

I lean back in the seat and look up through the sunroof, which frames the Little Dipper and probably a few made-up constellations, too. Lincoln was right. My heart beats fast and heavy in my chest, but for once, it doesn't freak me out. I don't feel like I can't breathe or even like I'm going to puke. My whole world just cracked open. I know I'm not magically "fixed," but it's all about taking steps. This feels like a big one.

"Just promise me something," Lincoln says, turning into our driveway. The tires make a comforting crackling noise as they roll over all the small pebbles on the pavement.

"Yeah?" I look at my not-so-little-anymore brother, his grown-up face illuminated by the streetlights.

"Never get a piercing at The Rusty Squirrel. Brady's entire nose is green. It's disgusting."

I crack up as we pull into the driveway and, for the first time in forever, I can't stop laughing.

AlienHuntress: Ultimate sci-fi hero?

BeamMeUp: Ripley from *Alien*. Obviously. She's like a feminist badass who fights through her fear.

AlienHuntress: And I'm sure your choice has nothing to do with that scene where she's in her underwear or your crush on Sigourney Weaver.

AlienHuntress: Hello? Am I right?

BeamMeUp: Shut up.

CHAPTER NINETEEN

AS SOON AS WE walk in the front door, Lincoln uploads the video to YouTube and posts links everywhere he can.

"And now, we wait," he says dramatically, sitting down at the kitchen table and staring at his phone.

"I'm going upstairs, okay?" I say. "I'll check on it in the morning."

But before I can even get into bed twenty minutes later, Lincoln bursts into my room.

"Does no one in this family knock?" I ask. But Lincoln just shoves his phone in my face.

The video already has hundreds of views. I read through comment after comment.

Mallory deserves to be homecoming queen!!!

Mayfield High is going down!

Mellissa Sullivan is the ultimate badass. #haltintruder

That last one got my name wrong, but this hashtag is *much* better than the last one I inspired.

"If this is what leaving the house feels like, I guess I should do it more often," I say, sitting down on my bed.

"Typically, it doesn't involve a foot chase, but I've been meaning to tell you—you *should* get out more," Lincoln says, eyes still searching his phone.

Throughout the night, he bursts into my room a couple more times to update me on views and comments. "Everyone on Twitter is saying that you'd better get five million spirit points from this," he says. He won't leave me alone until I threaten to tell Scott about his surprise party pee story. But still, I fall asleep with a smile on my face and spirit points in my dreams. I don't even check We Are Not Alone before bed because, for once, my real life is actually more exciting than my online one.

And, apparently, BeamMeUp thinks so, too, because when we talk on Wednesday, he breaks up with me. Well, as much as you can "break up" with a platonic Internet friend.

It's a pretty typical night for us—we're talking about how much we hate the second *X-Files* movie—when he asks me how my week's been going.

I decide to break my normal rules and tell BeamMeUp something about my real life.

AlienHuntress: I sort of apprehended a vandal.

BeamMeUp: Really? Is AlienHuntress living up to her name?

I tell him an abridged version of the story, leaving out any identifying details—but definitely leaving in the part about how I led a foot chase and coined a catchphrase.

BeamMeUp: Wow, AlienHuntress. You're basically a high school version of Dana Scully. What *can't* you do?

I snort, and before I even know what I'm doing, I tell more of the truth.

AlienHuntress: Everything except get the most popular guy in school to ask me out.

BeamMeUp is typing out a message, but when it pops up, it's not anything that I expected.

BeamMeUp: Listen, I've been busy lately, and it sounds like you have a lot on your plate with homecoming and everything, so maybe it's best if we just don't talk for a while.

My mouth falls open in shock just as my thirty-second warning pops up.

I start to type back, but all that greets me is the message "BeamMeUp Is Out of This World" before the screen flicks off.

Being rejected by BeamMeUp stings, but Jenni doesn't leave me any time to dwell. When I tell her about the whole pathetic situation, she insists that it's for the best.

"BeamMeUp only exists on the computer. You need to focus on what's in front of you, especially since we only have one school week until the dance."

So instead of moping, I help her sort out homecoming dresses by color, shape, and sparkle in my living room on

Saturday. Lincoln brought home a trash bag full of dresses from his part-time job at Nickel and Dime, the tiny thrift store on Main Street, which Jenni promptly ripped opened and scattered in piles all over the couch, chairs, and floor.

"Everyone else is going to look like a lemming in their boring-ass department store dresses—no offense, Jenni," Lincoln says.

"Whatever. I'm going to look like a disco ball," Jenni says breezily, flicking her hair away from her face.

"But *you*." Lincoln pulls a black feathered dress out of a pile. "*You're* going to be unique. Like *Pretty in Pink*, except that Brad is hotter than either of the dudes in that movie."

"You guys, I can't even remember the last time I got dressed up. Do I really have to do this?" As I paw through a pile of tulle and organza, I don't have Jenni's and Linc's confidence that Brad is going to ask me to homecoming—we're a week away and he hasn't done it yet.

"Well, you can't exactly wear a T-shirt and sweatpants," Jenni says, gesturing to my current outfit.

"And you have to look good, because we're all going together," Lincoln insists. "You're pretty much Reardon's hero right now, and I just want to bask in the glory of being related to the high school's golden girl."

He waves a gold-and-silver-sequined dress like it's a flag. I cover my nose against the mothball smell. From somewhere under the dress mountain in front of me, my phone starts to ring. I dig it out.

"Oh my God!" I shout, throwing it back into the dress pile. "It's Brad!"

Lincoln and Jenni shoot each other a look.

"Um . . . answer it?" Lincoln offers.

"Why is he *calling* me?"

"He must have seen the video!" Lincoln says. He grabs the phone, answers it, and throws it at me, leaving me no choice but to catch it. I dive into the kitchen.

"Hello?" My voice cracks.

"Mallory? It's Brad. What's up?"

"Good," I blurt out. "I mean . . . nothing. You?"

I rest the heel of my hand on my forehead. Brad says, "I just saw the video Lincoln posted. That's insane! You were a beast!"

I cringe. "Beast" doesn't necessarily translate into "girl I'd like to ask to homecoming."

"Thanks," I manage to say.

"I just wanted to ask you something. . . ."

I gulp. This is it—the moment Jenni and Lincoln were so sure was going to happen. A week's cutting it close, but better late than never, I guess.

"Do you have some time today to work on our project? Like, maybe in twenty minutes?"

Feeling like a rapidly deflating balloon, I peer into the living room and see that Jenni and Lincoln are standing right on the other side of the kitchen doorway, listening to every word of my conversation. Jenni's eyes are big with concern. I shoo both of them away.

"Yeah, that would be good! See you then!" We say our good-byes, then I stomp into the living room. Jenni and Lincoln are going through the dresses intently, like they've been there the whole time.

"(A) You guys are the worst, and (B) Brad's coming over in twenty minutes." I sit down between them.

"That means we have time for a fashion show!" Jenni shouts, throwing her arms above her head. She picks up a red sparkly dress and holds it against my shoulders while Lincoln tries to unzip a blue dress with a full skirt.

"You guys know this isn't going to be some eighties-movie makeover montage, right? The kind of thing where you put a dress on me and take off my glasses and all of a sudden I'm the hottest girl in school?"

"You don't need a makeover," Jenni says, unconcerned. "You just need to put on a dress. And maybe not put your hair in that weird braid."

I grab my hair, insulted. "I like this braid! It keeps my hair out of my face!"

"You kind of look like . . . you know, women in cults, how they wear those big prairie dresses? That's the look you have right now. Like you're in a plural marriage," Lincoln adds.

Jenni cracks up. "It's an easy fix, Mal," she assures me. "Just let me turn you from homebound to homecoming queen, okay?"

I try on five dresses. The only one that doesn't look terrible is covered in big red splotches that look like bloodstains.

"Do you honestly think I would wear that?" I ask, gesturing toward the sleek purple dress with a barely-school-dance-appropriate slit up the side. "I'd be a walking hepatitis risk."

Lincoln shrugs. "I guess there's a reason these were all shoved into the back room."

"Thank you so much for letting me have your thrift store's rejects, Linc."

"The one you have on looks nice!" Jenni says.

I look down at myself. "It's okay, but I'm not really feeling . . ."

"The va-va-voom," Jenni says, nodding sagely. "Homecoming is like a wedding. You only get one shot at queen, so you want to get the perfect dress. We'll keep looking."

She takes my hair out of its braid and creates an updo with the bobby pins that, no surprise, she carries around in her purse.

"Okay, so it won't be quite as messy when I do it for real, but here's a prototype. What do you think?" she asks, handing me the mirror she, no surprise again, also keeps in her purse.

It's messy, but still less messy than my apparently cultlike braid. Jenni left some waves loose around my face and the rest of my hair is pinned up in the back.

"You look like a candid photo of Vanessa Hudgens at Coachella," Jenni says admiringly.

"I love it," I say, just as the doorbell chimes. I run to answer it, and Jenni starts to shove the pile of dresses back into the bag.

"Should I have worn something different?" Brad asks, gesturing to his Reardon T-shirt and jeans.

I look down at my dress. "Crap! Sorry. Jenni, Lincoln, and I are trying on dresses . . . I mean, *I'm* trying on dresses, and Jenni and Lincoln are helping."

Brad steps inside, his eyes flicking down to my toes and back up. "You look really pretty."

I know he's just being polite, but I still can't help blushing. Over his shoulder, I can see Jenni and Lincoln watching us from the living room. Their tongues are practically hanging out of their mouths.

"It's too bad Jenni and Lincoln have to leave now," I say loudly enough for them to hear us.

"We're heading out for coffee!" Lincoln says. He stuffs the bag of dresses behind the couch.

"You guys get a lot of coffee," Brad says as Lincoln and Jenni walk between us.

"We are highly caffeinated individuals," Lincoln responds,

patting Brad on the back. Then he turns so only I can see him and pretends his hand is on fire.

"Have fun!" Jenni chirps, giving me a wink as they head out the door.

"Ready?" Brad asks, holding up his backpack.

"*So* ready. Just let me go change first."

When I come back downstairs, Brad has all of the parts, including his old cell phone that we're using for GPS tracking, set up on the table, along with a giant drawing on graph paper.

"Okay, here's the problem . . . ," he starts. "Pretty much everything is going according to plan. But what I don't get is how our parachute is going to stay attached," he says, pointing to the parachute and then to the drawing. "It doesn't look secure like it does in this plan. Or this one. Or . . . this one."

Looking back and forth between the drawing and the parachute, I realize that we may have gotten in a little bit over our heads. We're basically completely submerged at this point.

"Well . . . where did you get this blueprint?" It's a jumble of shapes and measurements, with what I think is a parachute at the center.

"Jake did this," Brad says like it's completely obvious.

I deflate faster than our defective parachute probably will. "Listen, I know Jake likes to work on his car, but that's not exactly the same thing as working on a physics project."

"I'll just get him to come help us," Brad says, pulling out his phone.

"No need to do that," I say, thinking about the weirdly nice but still definitely awkward window-washing interaction we had. My face flushes, like it's remembering the sunburn Jake pointed out.

"It's okay," Brad says, holding the phone up to his ear. "Pretty sure he's not doing anything important."

About twenty seconds later, the doorbell rings again.

"Having some trouble?" Jake asks, stepping past me and into the house.

"No, we just called because I really wanted to see you," I say drily.

Jake turns around and looks me up and down. "Nice hair," he says as he heads into the kitchen.

I self-consciously touch my hair and follow him.

After a few minutes of looking it over and Googling some things on Brad's laptop, Jake picks up our rocket, bringing it close to his face. "You guys have done a lot of work, but as it is, this thing is going to crap out and fall down somewhere around Reardon without even getting above the tree line. And the phone is going to fall right out," he says, shaking it to make a point. The phone falls out and clatters to the table.

"Well, that's bad," I say. "Because we kind of need it to go to space."

"Really?" Jake says, looking at me with his eyebrows raised. "You mean you don't want to look at the physics behind your project crash landing?"

I ignore his jab and ask, "So what are we supposed to do?"

"Short version: You need a couple more parts. Lucky for you, I'm pretty sure I have them. I'll just bring them when I see you guys tonight."

For a second, I think that I must have misheard him. But then Brad says, "I haven't technically told her yet."

"Told me what?"

He turns to me and, with a big, handsome smile, says, "I got us an awesome surprise for tonight. You know how you were so concerned that we didn't have enough examples of real-life physics for our physics journal?"

I nod.

"Well, we've got free, after-hours passes to Adventure's Peak!"

"The . . . amusement park?"

Brad nods. "Roller coasters are all about physics, right? I mean, centrifugal force, or something?"

"I—I guess . . . ," I stammer, already trying to think of ways to get out of this.

"I hope you're ready to ride the Canyon of Fury!"

I gulp and look at Jake. He's looking at the rocket in his hands, but I can see the tiniest smile form on his lips.

My insides start to do their own roller coaster loops.

CHAPTER TWENTY

As the coaster climbs up a hill, it builds a reservoir of potential energy. As the coaster falls down the hill, the potential energy is released as kinetic energy. Energy is all about position.

—Physics in the Modern World, 2013

SAFE. SECURE. CAPABLE, I remind myself as I pull out a kitchen chair and sit down shakily. Going to Adventure's Peak would've been unthinkable even a couple of weeks ago, but now it only throws me into a *mild* panic spiral.

"Wait . . . after hours?" I ask.

Brad nods. "Yep. No one's going to be there . . . except for us."

I trace the swirls on the marble counter, hoping if I just sit here long enough, the Kirkpatrick boys will just leave. This all seems weird, and maybe like the basis for a horror movie where teens are killed off one by one in increasingly gruesome ways, like being bludgeoned to death with the Whack-a-Mole hammer or run over by a roller coaster gone amok.

But on the other hand, a whole evening with Brad will give

him plenty of time to ask me to be his homecoming date. And getting farther away from the comfort zone of my bedroom will be great practice for the birding excursion and making my life normal again.

"Okay," I say, taking a deep breath. "But how are we getting in after hours?"

"You know Rusty Randall?"

Everyone in Reardon knows who Rusty Randall is. He's the owner of Adventure's Peak and his name has the word *rust* in it. It's not exactly a great sign of safety.

"His daughter, Clementine, and Jake have a . . . history together." Brad puts air quotes around *history*.

Jake snorts, tinkering with the project instead of looking at us. "That's one way of putting it."

"Who—" I start, but make sure the rest of that sentence stays lodged in my throat. But really—I'm genuinely surprised at the idea that Jake could tolerate anyone for more than an evening. Even though he's still tinkering on the rocket, Jake's cheeks flush pink, like he knew what I was going to say. "Who . . . who you used to measure the speed of light with."

"She's super nice," Brad pipes up. "We kept in touch after . . . well, after Jake, and she's always saying we should all go there some night and take advantage of no crowds and no lines. So why not now?"

No crowds. No lines. No people. Brad's speaking my language for sure, but I know this is a lot different than hanging out on the football field. For one thing, I won't be around Lincoln, whom I trust more than just about anyone. But I'll be with Brad, and I'm not really leaving my comfort zone if he *is* my comfort zone.

And then there's the small fact that I love roller coasters.

Thinking about my hair lifting up in the air as I plummet down a hill makes my stomach flip, but in a good way. Roller coasters let you get up close and personal with scary stuff, hurtling through the air while upside down, but you're strapped in—safe and secure.

"I'm in," I say, trying to look casual. Brad fist-pumps then high-fives Jake, who reluctantly joins in.

"This is going to be the most epic night ever," Brad says. A tiny part of me believes him.

I thought my mom might be against me leaving the house at 10:30 p.m. with two guys, but she gives me the smile she usually reserves for clients with tight deadlines and big wallets. And so at 10:43 p.m., Brad, Jake, and I pull into an almost entirely empty parking lot.

"You ready for this?" Brad asks.

"Yeah," I say, smiling in spite of myself.

"Oh!" Brad says, reaching into the backseat beside Jake. "I almost forgot. I have something for you."

My heart does jumping jacks. "For me?"

He hands me a blue shirt. "I wanted you to have this for the game on Friday. It's my practice jersey."

I hold it up by its shoulders in front of me. "Thanks?"

Jake snorts in the backseat. Brad brings his hand to the back of his neck and gives me a small, embarrassed smile. "I always forget you're not so into school spirit."

"No I love school spirit!" The last thing I need is Brad thinking I don't care. "Go, Reardon!"

His huge smile immediately lights up his face again. "So

during the ceremony at the game, everyone on court gets introduced to the crowd, and we're supposed to wear Reardon stuff. And since everyone on court is a football player or a cheerleader except for you . . ."

I clutch the jersey to my chest like an old-timey lady cherishing her fiancé's handkerchief. "You didn't want me to be left out. Thank you. I can't wait to wear it."

"So are we just gonna sit in the car all night?" Jake asks. I slowly fold the jersey and put it in my bag, then turn around to give him a dirty look. In the darkness he flashes me a small, smug smile. He must be excited to see Clementine. My stomach roils at the thought of being on a double date with the Kirkpatricks.

Clementine meets us at the front gate, waving both her hands in the air. She's wearing an Adventure's Peak T-shirt and cutoff denim shorts, and her platinum-blond hair is cropped into a pixie cut. She's one of those girls who can not only pull off a short haircut but who makes you consider getting one, too. Even if you're me, and Lincoln once told me I would look like "our weird uncle Mark" with short hair.

"I'm so happy you guys could make it!" she says, throwing her arms around Brad and giving him the kind of hug most people reserve for their nearest and dearest. He lifts her a few inches off the ground and gently sets her back down. I feel a ping of jealousy, but then she lunges at me and wraps me in the same intense hug. And then she moves on to Jake, cooing, "Jakey-Bakey! It's been forever!"

So, Clementine's just a hugger. And I guess I'm going to call Jake "Jakey-Bakey" every chance I get.

"The nightly fireworks show ended about an hour ago," she says, walking through the gate and gesturing for us to follow her.

"So it's just us, the nighttime cleaning crew, and a couple of Adventure Ambassadors who stayed on to show you guys a good time."

"Adventure Ambassadors?" I ask.

Clementine rolls her eyes. "Sorry. I've been using park doublespeak all day so I forget what English sounds like. Everyone who runs a ride or a game is called an Adventure Ambassador. It's hella cheesy, but . . ." She shrugs.

"Adventure Ambassador," Brad says. "I like it."

Clementine smiles at him, and I actually do start to feel jealous. Maybe she should leave some Kirkpatrick for the rest of us.

The giant, sleeping coasters rise over us like dinosaur skeletons. The silence is eerie, and every noise shivers up my back. I arch my neck to look up at the top of the Ferris wheel to our right. Lincoln and I used to demand to be at the top, nestled into the seat across from my mom and dad. Every time, Dad pointed toward the horizon and said, "Look, you can see our house from here!" I nodded even though everything just looked like tiny coral-colored dots.

The memory makes me feel warm and calm, even though I'm miles from home. Other than the woman in an Adventure's Peak T-shirt pushing a rumbling trash can down the boardwalk, there's nothing to be nervous about.

Clementine skips ahead in her white-and-pink Converse, beckoning Brad to skip alongside her. As she gestures wildly with her hands, talking a mile a minute, I fall in step with Jake. The sound of Brad's and Clementine's footfalls fade as they get farther from us.

"So . . . they're friends, huh?" I ask.

Jake rolls his eyes. "Brad's never met an enemy in his life."

"Is it weird for you?" I ask. His eyes follow Clementine, who easily jumps over the counter of one of the game booths and sets up some glass bottles for Brad to knock down.

"Why would it be?"

I look at him like he's insane. "Because your brother is practically BFFs with your ex-girlfriend?"

Jake crosses his arms. "Why, is it weird for you? Is it getting in the way of your romantic amusement park date night?"

I narrow my eyes. But a small thrill courses through me— if Jake thinks it's a date, maybe it is.

We walk across the boardwalk and sit on a bench that's right in front of the silent, darkened carousel. He leans his lanky frame all the way forward, putting his elbows on his knees. I follow his stare—Brad is coaching Clementine as she lobs a ball toward a pyramid of translucent green bottles. Jake seems to have forgotten I'm next to him. The look in his eyes feels intensely familiar, like I'm staring in the mirror; it's the look of someone who's always on the outside of things.

We both watch as Brad tosses the ball and easily knocks down the pyramid of bottles. Clementine shrieks with joy and throws her arms in the air . . . a huge contrast to the quiet, mostly grumpy guy sitting next to me. The silence—and the space—around us starts to settle on me, leaving trails of goose bumps on my arms. I shiver, trying to shake them off.

".Why are you here?" I ask suddenly, eager for a distraction. Jake's forehead is scrunched up like an accordion. No matter what he said, Jake clearly wants nothing less than to be watching his brother and ex-girlfriend shriek with joy while he's stuck with his weird neighbor girl on a crusty bench.

"I have no choice," he says. "You know I'm supposed to be in college?"

Oh. So he's talking about why he's in New Mexico, not just

why he's sitting on this particular bench in this particular park at this particular time.

"I mean, I guess?" I consider making a joke, but the way Jake's staring into the distance makes it seem like he's not in a joking mood right now. "I just . . . no one knows anything about you."

"I was never in prison. Or rehab. I couldn't even pick Lindsay Lohan out of a lineup." He leans back and spreads his arms out on the back of the bench, doing that typical dude thing of taking up as much space as possible. I'd be annoyed, but I'm too busy noticing that his hand is just lightly touching my shoulder.

"I doubt that very much. She has a distinctive look," I croak. My heart starts to thump.

"You didn't really believe all that stuff, did you?" he asks, pulling his gaze away from Clem and Brad.

I meet Jake's eyes and shake my head.

He looks back at Brad and Clementine, who've switched places so that Brad's stacking up the bottles. "I'm supposed to be at Harvard."

"Harvard? Like . . . the college?"

He gives me a look. "No, the *other* Harvard."

"So you don't even have to be in Reardon, the armpit of New Mexico? You could be at Harvard, hanging out with geniuses and doing whatever geniuses do and learning about . . ." I trail off, unsure what Jake even studied.

"Physics," he supplies.

Right. That would explain why he's so helpful with our project. "So . . . what happened?"

Jake crosses his arms behind his head. "*I* happened. I lived with my mom, in Indiana. . . ."

I nod, even though I didn't know that.

"Well, I drove all the way from Bloomington to Cambridge. And that's a long drive. But once I got there, I . . . I couldn't even get out of my car. I was the smartest kid in my high school. . . ."

"Brag much?" I mutter, but when Jake shakes his head at me I add, "Sorry."

"I had—have—a full scholarship. To Harvard. Which is huge."

"A lot of people would gladly murder you and assume your identity to get that."

"I know." Jake looks at me with his bewildered, wild blue eyes. "I mean, not the murder part. So many people wanted to be me. But I just . . . couldn't. I wanted one second to not be under pressure. I just wanted to get away . . . from the tests and the all-nighters and my mom obsessing over competitions and prizes."

My hand instinctively reaches toward Jake's knee, which is gently pressed against mine, but my brain catches up and yanks it back before I make contact. Jake doesn't seem to notice. "So . . . you came here," I say, prodding him to continue.

"Yep. I was able to defer and I came to Reardon, where no one knows me and no one in my house gives a shit about science."

"Brad gives many shits!"

Jake gives me a wry look. "Listen, he's always gonna be my brother, but Brad thinks astronomy means horoscopes."

I look at Brad, who's currently rifling through the stuffed-animal prizes, no doubt picking out something for Clementine. I wrinkle my nose.

"You and Clementine are good, right?" I ask, turning back to Jake. "Like, you talk to her about all of this?"

Jake laughs. "Not quite. She broke up with me."

"Really?" I try to sound disbelieving.

"Clementine has a lot of love to give, and when she dumped me, she even had *me* thinking that it was unfair to expect her to give all that love to one person."

I wince, but Jake says, "Ancient history. Water under the bridge. Some other dumb saying that will convince you I'm not a pathetic loser who's pining after an ex."

"Let the water of your past flow under the bridge of your present," I say sagely.

Jake tilts his head. A strand of dark hair falls into his eyes. "I'm sorry?"

"Sorry." I shake my head. "Sometimes my therapist's sayings turn themselves into earworms, and I have to inflict them on other people."

Jake holds a hand over his heart. "And you chose me? I'm touched."

I smile. Brad and Clementine call our names from across the boardwalk and turn back to finish off the last bottle tower. "Come on, Jakey-Bakey," I tell Jake as I get up to walk toward them, but he wraps his hand around my arm, pulling me back.

"Mal."

Even though I almost stumble into him, he doesn't let go. It's dark, but in the light of the rides, I can still see the slightly crooked tilt of his nose. "Yeah?"

He nods toward Brad and Clementine. "Do you like Brad?"

I open my mouth and try to say . . . what? My eyes search Jake's face, looking for an answer between his sharp nose and those stupid-blue eyes, but he just stares back, and all my thoughts slide out of my head and puddle around my feet.

Of course I like Brad. He's nice, and sweet, and he sticks up for me when I fake weird allergies. And he's, hands-down, the cutest guy in school and my ticket to a homecoming win.

But I stare at Jake, my mouth opening and closing like words should be coming out, even though I know it's just silence. Who cares what Jake thinks of me? This is Jake Kirkpatrick, the guy who tried to make me feel bad for lying to my mom, the guy who acts like he knows who I am more than I do.

The guy who sort of understands what it's like to hide from all your problems.

"Hey!" says Clementine. She's suddenly at our side, wiggling her eyebrows. "We interrupting something?"

I jerk my arm away from Jake's hand. "Nope!" I shout too loudly, backing up into a trash can and almost knocking it over.

"Did you win that for Clementine?" Eager to change the subject, I point toward the stuffed elephant Brad's holding.

Brad gives me a smile that illuminates the whole park. "This is for you!"

"Trust me," Clementine says as Brad hands it to me. "My dad's owned this park my whole life. At this point, the stuffed animals have overtaken my room *and* the hall."

"That's so nice," I say, suddenly desperate to make sure no silence passes between us. Words are spilling out of my mouth like popcorn. "*You're* so nice."

"No problem!" Brad says easily. "I'm just glad you could come with us!"

I smile, steadfastly avoiding looking at Jake, even though I can feel his eyes on me.

"This is all very adorable, but I'm gonna have to cut the lovefest short," Clementine says. "Rusty Jr.'s ready for us over at the Canyon of Fury."

"Rusty Jr.?" I ask.

"My older brother. Don't worry, he's a trained professional and he can operate any ride in the park. Except for Nightmare Mountain." She rolls her eyes. "Some moron fell out of it last year, broke every bone in his body, and sued us. Whatever. Come on!"

As we trot behind her, I whisper to Brad, "I thought we weren't going to die tonight."

Jake pipes up. "No, I said *Clementine* wouldn't be the one who killed us. Big difference."

As we snake our way through the dividers that normally control the line, I can't even believe I'm here. Out of the house. In what is increasingly becoming a dangerous situation, with two Kirkpatricks and a girl named after a fruit.

The weirdest part? I feel good, despite the memory of my conversation with Jake poking into my side like a giant thorn made out of confusion and anxiety. Even climbing the steps to the coaster, everything all lit up and glowing, makes me feel exhilarated. I haven't felt this much excitement in . . . well, in I can't even remember how long.

"Y'all ready?" asks a guy with a dirty blue Adventure's Peak baseball cap and a cigarette dangling out of his mouth as he peeks his head out of the operator's booth.

"Rusty Jr.!" Clementine shouts. "You know Dad would chop you up and feed you to the goats in the petting zoo if he saw you smoking that!"

Rusty shrugs. "I don't see anybody around who's gonna tell him about this. Do I?"

He looks at each of us slowly and we all shake our heads, me harder than the rest. No one wants to mess with Rusty II: The Reckoning.

"Fine. Make yourself smell terrible. See if I care." She turns to us, her voice instantly brighter. "You guys ready?"

Jake claps his hands together and I give her a thumbs-up. The harsh glow of the lights on the platform makes Brad's face look pale, like a really attractive ghost.

We sit down and Rusty Jr. pulls the harnesses down over our shoulders.

"Wait!" I shout, wiggling to reach into my pocket. I hand my phone to Jake. "Take our picture?"

He doesn't make eye contact with me as he grabs it. "Try to smile!" he calls out.

"I am smiling!" I yell through my teeth, but after Jake takes the picture and tosses me my phone, I realize he wasn't talking to me but to Brad.

"Are you okay?" I whisper. Clementine's and Jake's belts *click* behind us.

"Mallory," Brad asks, his voice quiet with fear. "Have I ever told you I'm afraid of heights? And being upside down? And dying on a roller coaster?"

"No!" I hiss. "You conveniently forgot to mention those things when you invited me to go to an amusement park with you!"

Rusty Jr.'s voice booms monotonously through the loud-speaker, and we lurch into motion. "Attention, riders. All four of you. Please keep your arms and legs inside the car at all times. Don't be a dumbass. Enjoy your thrilling descent into the Canyon of Fury."

As our car slowly ticks up the first hill, I try to get a good look at Brad's face. Even with our huge dirty orange shoulder harnesses partially blocking my view, I can see that his skin has none of the rugged, athletic glow that it normally does. His eyes are closed so tight that they make two jumbles of eyelashes on his face.

"Brad?"

I lean closer to hear what he's saying, but he's just muttering, "Oh no, oh no, oh no, oh no," in a steady stream.

"This is no big deal," I say quickly. "You're Brad Kirkpatrick. You regularly tackle huge dudes on the football field and you win every game you play. Trust me, you can handle this."

The car moves more slowly on the track as we get closer to the peak of the hill. Our backs are parallel to the ground, and my hair feels strangely heavy. Clementine laughs boldly behind us, and I wonder, briefly, what Jake is saying that's making her laugh so hard.

Then we're at the top, and the car grinds to a stop. I take in a quick view of the whole park. There are just a few lights sprinkled across blackness. But past the parking lot, the rest of Reardon is all lit up. One of those little specks of light is my house, just like Dad said, and I wonder if I could pick it out if I tried.

For that split second before I know we're going to drop, the reality of where I am hits me. I'm out of the house. On a roller coaster. Pride grows in my chest and I look over at Brad, eager to share this moment with him.

"Help," he whispers, and clutches my hand.

And then . . . nothing. Except for Brad's hand curled around mine. I give him a sideways glance—his eyes are still closed.

"Mallory?" he asks in a tiny voice. "What's happening?"

"We're just taking a little break," I say as calmly as possible. He grasps my hand even tighter.

"Rusty!" Clementine screeches. "Do you think this is funny?!"

"Oh, good Lord," Jake mutters before he starts laughing.

"If this is the end for me," Brad says seriously, without opening his eyes, "I just want you to know that you've been a good friend."

"Brad!" I say. "We're not going to die here on the Canyon of Fury."

It's weird to be in the position of comforting someone instead of the other way around. In fact, I'm channeling Dr. Dinah levels of calming sternness . . . which gives me an idea.

"Can you repeat after me?" I ask.

"Can you repeat after me?" Brad repeats. I smirk.

"I am safe."

"I am safe," Brad whispers.

"I am secure."

"I am secure." The coaster makes a tiny hiccup forward.

"I am capable!" I finish.

"I am capable!" Brad shrieks as we surge into motion and plunge down the hill, rattling in our seats. My head bumps against my harness so hard that I'm a little afraid I'm going to end up with a concussion. Each time we go over another hill or through a loop, Brad grips my hand harder, until I'm concerned that I might lose circulation in my fingers. But despite the various physical pains I'm experiencing, I scream in elation right along with Clementine.

Less than sixty seconds later, we're done. Clementine lets out a triumphant scream as the cars jolt to a stop. Rusty Jr. presses the button that unlocks our harnesses, and she leans forward between Brad and me. "You guys have fun?"

"Yeah!" I notice that my fingers are still tangled with Brad's. Clementine notices, too.

"There's something about these Kirkpatrick boys, huh?" she whispers before crawling out of her car.

"Are you okay?" I ask Brad, who's staring off into space.

Rusty Jr.'s voice comes over the loudspeaker, even though he's only about ten feet away from us. "Attention, riders. Ride's over. Get out."

"We'd better go." I take my hand away from his and push myself up, onto the walkway. Brad reaches a shaking arm toward me, which I pull until he's standing next to me. I can't help but notice he's covered in a sheen of sweat.

He stumbles to the railing and leans way over. We all quickly look away as he pukes.

"Are you serious?" Rusty Jr. asks, this time not over the loudspeaker.

"Shut your mouth," Clementine snaps, "or I'll tell Dad about what you've been doing with Katie the carousel operator on the Ferris wheel after hours."

Clementine leads us down the walkway and past a huge screen that shows a picture of every car on the coaster. I didn't even know our picture was being taken, but there, right next to a bunch of pictures of empty cars, is a shot of Brad and me. My mouth is wide open in pure excitement, and he looks like he's awaiting certain death.

And it's very, very clear that we're holding hands.

Maybe I should be a better friend. Maybe I should be more concerned that Brad's sick and that he faced one of his biggest fears tonight. But visions of spirit points dance in my head. I snap a picture of the screen and immediately share it on Instagram.

Brad and Clementine walk ahead, Clementine throwing her head back in laughter as she makes sweeping arm movements. Jake hangs back, waiting for me to catch up.

"You all set?" he asks as I walk up to him.

"Just had to make sure Rusty Jr.'s number was in my phone."

Jake nods, picking up on the joke right away. "I could sense some sparks between you two. I was, like, get a bumper car, guys."

I laugh, happy to sweep our earlier conversation into one of Adventure Peak's overflowing trash cans. "You're disgusting. He probably tastes like an ashtray filled with Mountain Dew and Cheetos."

"Hey, I don't want to hear about your weird fetishes. Keep that between the two of you."

"Shut up, Jakey-Bakey."

Jake sighs. "I didn't say Clementine was perfect for me, okay?" Ahead, I see that Brad and Clementine are waiting for us by a Dippin' Dots kiosk. "Are you glad you left the house tonight?"

Startled, I look at him, but his eyes don't betray anything. He just looks back at me, his face full of questions but no answers.

"Yeah," I say. "I'm so glad." And as an easy smile breaks over Jake's face, I realize that I'm not even lying.

AlienHuntress: Hi!

AlienHuntress: Hi?

AlienHuntress: Earth to BeamMeUp?

CHAPTER TWENTY-ONE

Not everyone understands makeup. They say things like, "I don't have the time," or "Guys don't like it," or "No one has naturally blue eyelids." And that's fine. But if all the world's a stage like Shakespeare said, then I want to make sure my cat eye is perfect when the spotlight's shining on me.

—*Just Jenni*, 2015

"STOP MOVING!"

For the millionth time, I try to hold still while Jenni swipes black eyeliner across my eyelid.

"You're going to be under some harsh lighting." She's filling in my brows with yet another pencil. "So I want to do some extra-dramatic makeup. You're going to look fantastic when Brad finally asks you to be his homecoming date."

She snaps open her blush, a palette of red and pinks. I'm trying to let the soft brush strokes calm me down, but it's not working. How could I have convinced myself that going to the homecoming game would be okay? I run my fingers over the hem of Brad's huge jersey, which I'm worried looks ridiculous on me. But Jenni assures me that I look "sporty cute."

An even bigger worry is ricocheting around in my head.

"Guys, it's the night before the dance. Brad's so polite, there's no way he'd ask anyone out this late." And there's no way I'll win, get that money, or find my dad, which means I'd better get ready for disappointment or start planning a bank robbery ASAP.

"Kind of a good point," Lincoln concedes without looking up from his phone.

Jenni shakes her head vigorously, and waves of flowery perfume hit me. "Didn't you hear that Pia asked him yesterday? He turned her down. Why would a red-blooded man turn down a beautiful woman like Pia unless there was someone else he had his eyes on?"

"Maybe because she's a megabitch?" I give Jenni an exaggerated shrug.

"Stop moving around and push your lips out a bit," Jenni says.

I obediently pout.

"We're going to use a rich berry shade to complement your coloring, and . . . voilà!" Jenni steps back and looks at me proudly, like I'm a kindergartner about to star in the class musical.

I focus on my breathing, just like Dr. Dinah says I should do when I get overwhelmed: slow in, slow out. I went to the football field. I went to Adventure's Peak. And now I'm going to the homecoming game.

Going to a football game full of people is something else entirely, especially when those people will be staring at me. I imagine standing under the bright lights with the stands full of people clapping, yelling, and cheering.

Or laughing.

After Jenni and Lincoln argue over who's going to drive us to the game—Lincoln doesn't want to listen to Jenni's Taylor Swift playlist, and Jenni doesn't want to listen to Lincoln's "whiny, sad stuff"—Lincoln wins out. We compromise by listening to the oldies station on the drive to Reardon High, which is shorter than the actual argument.

"So glad I can get pumped up by listening to this sweet Elton John jam," I say.

Lincoln gives me a sideways look. He's wearing his only Reardon T-shirt, left over from his junior high football days, and it's so tight he can barely move his arms. That's the thing about someone knowing you for literally his entire life—he understands that your sarcasm is just a front that's inefficiently hiding your raging nerves. Jenni puts her hand on my shoulder, and I turn around to see her giving me an encouraging smile from the backseat.

"You're going to kick so much ass tonight."

I smile a little.

"All you have to do," Lincoln says, "is go out on the field when your name is called. Stand there while they announce the rest of the court. And we'll be right there watching you the whole time, so anytime you get nervous, just look for us. And Principal Lu will talk about how this homecoming court is such a great representation of what Reardon High has to offer, blah blah blah, you'll princess-wave to everyone, and that's it. You're done. We'll go home."

I nod and swallow, hard. "Easy."

We pull into the school and Lincoln parks beside a van that has windows painted with charming sayings like, KICK MAY-FIELD'S ASS!

"You ready?" Lincoln asks, his hand resting on the door handle.

My fingers are trembling, so I compulsively clutch my knees to get them to stop. Students and parents carrying blankets and water bottles stream past our car, some with their faces painted bright blue. The longer I stare at them, the more they start to swirl.

I gulp and nod. "Totally ready."

Lincoln eyes me skeptically, but a text distracts him. "Holy crap. Scott says Mayfield stole our mascot costume."

"Artie the armadillo?" Jenni asks.

"God, those guys are jerks," I mutter. Even I know that Artie is the heart(ie) and soul of Reardon football. The mascot costume is an unexciting gray-brown, but whoever plays Artie always manages to clap, dance, and keep up everyone's spirit. And that can't be easy when you're wearing a huge costume that's probably only dry-cleaned once a season.

Lincoln sighs and slips his phone back in his pocket. "Well, let's just hope we win this game. Not that I care about football or anything. You ready?"

I look out the window and start to feel dizzy. "Can I just take a second?"

Lincoln and Jenni exchange a quick look. "How about we go get you some hot chocolate?" Jenni asks.

I smile weakly. "You know the way to my heart."

Lincoln holds out a pinky. "I need you to promise me that you're still going to be in this car when we get back."

"I am not going to pinky promise. We haven't done that since you were five years old."

Lincoln just stares at me, his pinky still in the air.

"Ugh, fine." I pinky swear, then Lincoln makes a big show of putting his car keys in his pocket.

"So you can't ditch us," he explains. He and Jenni get out and wave to me before heading off to the concession stand.

I'm alone. In the peace and quiet. I mean, sort of. I can hear the occasional bleat from a tuba and a few taps of a snare drum. The marching band must be warming up. A lone cowbell rings. The back of my neck starts to sweat.

Talk to someone who makes you feel comfortable, I think. I pull out my phone. But on We Are Not Alone, the red light glows beside BeamMeUp's name—even though he started a new thread about ten minutes ago—a reminder that he's still ignoring me.

"Crap!" I mutter. A huge group of cheerleaders breaks around the car like a river around a rock. I slide down in my seat and peer at them over the edge of the window. Pia and Caroline, both wearing their cheerleading uniforms, run by, laughing at unreal decibels because of who-knows-what.

Maybe they're laughing at how much you're going to humiliate yourself tonight, says a tiny voice in my head. I try to breathe in, only to find that I can barely get air. Why is it so hot in here? The scent of the pine tree–shaped air freshener hanging from the rearview mirror is suddenly choking me. I frantically press the button to roll down the windows, but the car's not on, so nothing happens. My heart beats fast, threatening to burst out of my chest like that scene from *Alien*. I wipe the sweat off my face, probably smearing all my makeup in the process.

Focus, I think, staring at the glove compartment. A loud screech comes from right outside the car and I jump out of my seat and plop back down. A group of little kids runs by, waving foam fingers, shouting something unintelligible. I put my hand on my heart, try to inhale. Seriously, *why* is it so *hot*?

"I'm sorry, Lincoln," I whisper to the empty car. I open the door and run.

CHAPTER TWENTY-TWO

I RUN LIKE I'M in a disaster movie and the pavement is crack-ing into pieces behind me, my eyes glued to the ground so no one will see that I'm on the verge of tears. Even the thought of my mom checking me into a "recovery" center somewhere doesn't slow my feet. I narrowly miss running into several people but manage to shoulder-swipe someone at the edge of the park-ing lot.

"Sorry," I whimper. A fiery pain races through my shoulder, but I keep going.

"Mal?"

Someone grabs a handful of Brad's jersey, whipping me around. Jake.

"Are you okay? Did something happen?"

I inhale shakily. "I . . . fine. I'm just going home to grab something." I try to focus on him—he's carrying an armful of brown-gray fabric and, I think, Artie the armadillo's head.

"Let's just take a time-out, okay?"

He grabs my hand and leads me behind a row of cars and under the bleachers. The costume almost slides out of his grip. The bleachers muffle the sound of the band members practicing scales and the stomp of the fans' footsteps on the metal stands enough for my heartbeat to slow. I don't want to tell Jake why I was running through the school parking lot crying and hyperventilating, so I preempt his questions with a question of my own.

"You know I'm going to have to report you to the proper authorities for kidnapping Artie, right?"

Jake laughs and tosses the costume on the ground. "Yeah, right. You don't think I have better things to do than steal a high school mascot?"

I look at him uncertainly.

He scoffs. "Point taken. But no, I didn't steal it. I saw a couple of little douche bags from Mayfield trying to shove the costume in the bushes behind the elementary school playground after I dropped Brad off. I just asked them what they were doing and they practically begged me to take it and not hurt them."

I let out a giggle and feel some of the tension evaporate. "Let me guess. They thought you just got out of prison?"

Jake shrugs. "Or rehab, gang, whatever. I guess having a reputation pays off."

"And tattoos," I add. A cheer erupts from the bleachers above us, sending a wave of *get home* through me. "Anyway, I'm feeling a lot better, so I'm just gonna go—"

I turn to walk away, but Jake grabs my arm. "Don't you have to be on the field in, like, two minutes?"

As if on cue, the band starts playing the fight song. The sound's snaking closer, and I know that they're marching onto the field.

"Do I?" I bite my lip.

Now Jake puts both of his hands on my shoulders and looks me right in the eyes. The silent-but-waiting treatment. "Were you trying to bail?" he asks quietly.

I used up all my energy running, and there's none left to keep the truth from pouring out.

"Yes, okay?" A brief, cool wind sweeps up my bangs. Tears spring into my eyes. "Adventure's Peak went okay, and I'm trying to do better and Lincoln said I could do it, but I just *can't*. I can't do this. There are all these people and the noises and the lights and . . ."

I swallow.

"Hey," Jake says, rubbing my shoulders. His hands are strong and his fingertips press into my shoulder blades. "I know what will make you feel better."

I look up at him, eager to hear whatever brilliant solution this genius guy has for me.

"The mascot costume," he says.

I wait a beat before asking, "I'm sorry?"

Jake smirks a little, and I wonder what the hell kind of "beautiful smile" gene the Kirkpatrick boys got and if it could ever be used for cloning purposes. "Hear me out."

The people in the stands above us stomp their feet and ring cowbells. Instinctively, I move closer to him. His arms wrap around my back far enough that his hands meet, making a warm knot between my shoulders.

"So before I went to Harvard," he says, "I started getting these . . . I guess you could call them panic attacks. You know what I'm talking about?"

I nod slowly, inches away from his chest.

"I'd get them whenever I felt like I was under too much

pressure, whenever my mom was hounding me about some new deadline or possible internship I might want to get. It was bad."

"Yeah," I say, eager to hear that someone understands what I've been dealing with.

"But what always helped me was being in a small space. I mean, sometimes when I would freak out, I'd climb into my closet. Don't, like, psychoanalyze that or try to figure it out, because I'm pretty sure there's some sort of weird, return-to-the-womb stuff going on. . . ."

I can't help it. I laugh.

"But just being in a small space made me feel . . . safe."

Safe. Secure. Capable. I get it. Jake lets go of me and bends down to pick up the mascot costume. I shout, "No!" and I'm not sure if it's because I don't want to wear the costume or I don't want him to let go.

Principal Lu's voice comes booming over the field. "Good evening and welcome, players and fans!"

A cheer erupts. More cowbells. Jake holds the armadillo head and costume out to me. "No one will see your face. You'll be totally hidden, Mallory." He unzips the costume.

The way he says my name gives me a little zing that rico-chets through my whole body. The crowd is screaming now; the noise is hitting me over and over again, like a huge wave. Do I run? Or do I walk onto the field? The thought of walking out in front of everyone makes me feel sick.

But I know, as I look at Jake's encouraging face, that I'm way past the point of hiding from everyone and everything. And if I have a chance at winning—and, maybe I'm crazy, but I think I do—then I need to go out there on the field. Winning means more than finding my dad now. It means showing everyone, like Mom and Lincoln, that I'm okay.

It means that everything can finally go back to normal.

I close my eyes and sigh. "Zip me up, Jake."

I step into Artie's (giant) feet and Jake reaches around me to zip up the back. With the screaming, the smell of the costume, and the nausea climbing up my body, I hardly have time to think about the nerves that fire at the touch of his hand.

"Please welcome to the field the members of your Reardon High School homecoming court! Caroline Fairchild and Luis Valdez!"

Holding Artie's head, Jake asks, "You ready?"

I have approximately ten seconds before Principal Lu calls my name, so I frantically say the words I never imagined would come out of my mouth.

"Just put the mascot head on me!"

Jake complies and the world around me disappears. With Jake, I stumble out from under the bleachers and toward the field. Thank God I have him to hold on to—I can barely see through the tiny eyeholes of the armadillo head and I have no idea where I'm going.

"Mallory!"

Someone else grabs my arm. I maneuver the head around until I can see who it is.

"We're up!" Brad says. "Where have you been?"

Brad and Jake say something to each other, but I can't hear them. This armadillo head makes it sound like I'm listening to everything through a seashell, but Jake's right—it's way better than being crushed under an avalanche of noise. Brad wraps his arm around me and leads me to the field. We step onto the sea of manicured, bright green turf.

"You found the mascot!" Brad yells so that I can hear him. "You're a hero! Again!"

The combination of Brad's compliment and the heat inside the armadillo shell is making me melt. Principal Lu's voice calls out, loud enough that there's a tiny echo in the costume.

"And, last but not least, Mallory Sullivan and Brad Kirkpatrick!"

I put one giant fuzzy foot in front of the other, following Brad's lead, as the crowd screams and rings those godforsaken cowbells. They're chanting something. . . .

"Mal-lor-y! Mal-lor-y! Mal-lor-y!"

My name. They're chanting my name . . . and not because they're making fun of me. Not because I'm the freak who's too scared to leave the house. Not because I'm Skyping into class.

Because I saved the day. Well, Jake did, but still. I was there.

And now I'm here.

The rest of the ceremony blurs by. After a lot of announcements and one squeaky performance of a Bruno Mars song by the marching band, Brad's already leading me off the field. Once we're safely to the parking lot, I yank the armadillo head off. My hair is plastered to my head with sweat, and my face feels tacky with makeup. Jenni would be horrified.

But I don't even care. I let the armadillo head fall on the ground and heave a huge sigh of relief.

"That was amazing, Mallory!" Brad shouts.

A smile swallows my face. I must look like an idiot. "You think?"

He shakes his head in disbelief. "You are the best. No one else had the balls to show up dressed as an armadillo."

Before I even understand what's happening, he gives me a

huge, lifted-off-the-ground hug. As he spins me around, I catch a glimpse of Pia Lubeck shooting us death glares, Jenni and Lincoln walking toward us from across the field, and . . . Jake, who stops dead in his tracks a few feet away, staring at us.

Brad puts me back on the ground. "Can you believe it?" he asks Jake, his face still lit up.

"Nope," Jake says. The flatness in his voice makes my stomach flop.

"What the hell?" Lincoln says. "I thought you"—he stops himself before saying "spazzed out and ran home"—"were kidnapped or something."

Jenni throws her arms around me. "You were fantastic. Oh, this fabric is so gross." She pulls back from me and wipes her hands on her skirt before she unzips me. The armadillo costume falls to the ground, and I'm once again wearing just jeans and Brad's practice jersey.

Brad puts a hand on my arm. "Hey, the cheerleaders are forming the tunnel and I need to get on the field. But I wanted to ask you something. Would you . . ."

I almost stop breathing. My heartbeat picks up. Jenni and Lincoln and Jake watch us.

"Want to go to Shauna Macgregor's party with me? She throws one after the homecoming game every year and it's usually pretty fun."

"Yes!" I say, and then immediately clap my hand over my mouth.

Jenni and Lincoln look at each other, clearly as shocked as I am about what I just said.

"I'm gonna split," Jake says to Brad, avoiding my gaze. I ignore the confusing feeling pooling in my stomach. I need to focus on Brad. "I'll catch you at home."

"Oh, wait, dude." Brad grabs his arm. "Do you think you could give us a ride to the party, and maybe pick us up, too? I hate to ask, but we're going to be celebrating, and I don't really want to drive home. . . ."

Jake looks at me, his mouth a straight line as he puts artificial pep into his voice. "Sure. Anything to help my baby brother the quarterback avoid getting a DUI."

"Awesome!" Brad says, looking just as genuinely happy as he does 95 percent of the time.

As Brad runs onto the field, the reality of what's going to happen tonight sinks in. *What did I just agree to?*

"Thank you," I call weakly after Jake, but he's already too far away.

CHAPTER TWENTY-THREE

"I STILL DON'T GET why we couldn't stay at the game," Jenni says, taking a spoonful of Ben & Jerry's Half Baked before passing it on to me. "You were doing so great!"

"And that's why we had to leave on a high note." I take a huge bite of ice cream.

Lincoln hoists himself onto the kitchen island and swings his legs. "Whatever. All I care about is going to Shauna's party with my sister, her best friend, and my boyfriend."

My phone lights up with a text from Brad.

Can def pick you up. See you in a few!

Jenni leans over my shoulder to read the text. "Look at that punctuation! He likes you, for sure," she says quietly.

"Brad's a human exclamation point. I wouldn't read into it too much."

The doorbell rings, and Lincoln hops off the counter to answer it. When he and Scott walk into the kitchen holding hands, all I feel are a million champagne bubbles of happiness for him. It helps that Scott's carrying a plate of chocolate chip cookies.

"My mom made these and she wanted me to bring them over." He shrugs. A faint blush flares over his face. He must have gotten a haircut for the party; it's shaved close to his head, which only serves to accent those eyes Lincoln won't stop talking about.

I'm still musing about how handsome Scott is when the doorbell rings again. Fluffing my hair up, I jog to answer it. Jenni's already fixed my makeup, post-armadillo sweat, and I changed out of Brad's jersey and into a black scoop-neck T-shirt.

I answer the door and I'm almost blinded by Brad's smile. "Hey, you ready to go?"

"You don't mind a . . . *few* extra people, right?"

Brad laughs when he sees Lincoln, Jenni, and Scott. "Of course not."

We stream out of my front door and walk to the Kirkpatricks' driveway. Brad opens the passenger door.

"Mallory?" he asks, gesturing toward the front seat.

"Oh!" I say. Of course Brad's holding the door open for me. Of *course* he is. I hop in, bumping right into Jake in the driver's seat. I jump. "I forgot you were going to be here."

Jake waves. "Nice to see you, too." He checks the rearview mirror. "Everybody in?"

I look over my shoulder. Brad, Jenni, Lincoln, and Scott all crammed into the backseat. It was nice of Brad to let me take the front seat, since it's so packed back there that Jenni's practically on his lap.

Jenni immediately peppers Brad with about a million questions about the game, which she'd been following online, so I take the opportunity to whisper, "You know, Lincoln could have taken us. You've already done a lot for us today."

Jake looks left and right at a stop sign before plunging ahead.

"Don't worry, I'll just be here at your beck and call, whenever you need a ride or to impress everyone or someone to actually give a shit about you."

His comment physically burns. I can feel pricks of frustration on the palms of my hand. I inhale, trying to feel safe, secure, and capable instead of angry and confused.

My friends *care*. Brad *cares*.

Jenni pipes up from the backseat, "Mal! Your poll numbers are through the roof! ReardonsFutureQueen.tumblr.com is blowing up!"

"Was IAmSoTiredOfHearingAboutHomecoming.com taken?" Jake mutters.

Jenni shakes her head in disbelief, still looking at her phone. "I don't know how you managed to steal the armadillo costume in the first place, but that was a great plan. A little dishonest, and possibly illegal, but still great."

"That's not what happened—" I start.

"So how many people do you think will be at Shauna's?" Jenni asks Brad.

"Yes, how many people *will* be at Shauna's?" Jake asks me with faux interest. "This party sounds *totally* great."

Jake's comment still stings. "Yeah, it's not really your thing," I mutter.

Lincoln laughs hard and loud in the backseat, and I glance back to see him holding hands with Scott. By the way his eyes flick to the mirror, Jake sees it, too.

"You sure you're gonna be okay?" Jake asks, softer.

I study the dashboard. "Why wouldn't I be?"

Jake reaches over, grabs my hand, and gives it a quick and gentle squeeze. Before my gasp has even made it out of my throat, he drops it suddenly and jerks his hand back, as if he's thought better of it. I watch him out of the corner of my eye, but he keeps his eyes on the road like nothing just happened. My hand feels like it's on fire. I wonder if there's some sort of weird magnetic force between us that draws us together and then instantly reverses and pushes us apart. He drives in silence and I half listen to the animated conversation going on in the backseat. Brad is laughingly insisting that *The Fast and the Furious* series is better than the *Godfather* films, and Lincoln is horrified. *Focus*, I remind myself.

"You know," Jake says, his hands gripping the steering wheel as he pulls up to the curb in front of Shauna Macgregor's house, "I could go back and get the armadillo costume. If that would make you more comfortable."

I think about walking into the party in the costume and I can't help but laugh.

"Thanks for driving, Jake," Lincoln says, clapping him on the shoulder as he and Scott slide out of the car.

"Yeah, thanks for driving," I say. Brad opens my door. "Sure you don't . . . ?"

Jake shakes his head as I hop out. "If you go to a high school party after you graduate, you automatically earn your Creepy Old Man certification."

"Mal!" Jenni calls. "Come on!"

Jake's already driving away.

"You guys ready?" Brad asks.

I take in Shauna's house. All of the lights are on and there are dudes leaning against the porch railings. The front door is wide open and a Rihanna song drifts out to the sidewalk.

"Totally ready," I whisper.

Jenni grabs my arm and smiles at me encouragingly as we walk through the front door.

The entryway is like the entryway of a house in a movie: a

high ceiling and a huge staircase that Shauna's probably going to walk down in her homecoming dress tomorrow as her mom takes pictures. To my left, I see two kids I don't recognize making out on a love seat. They don't seem distracted by the group of bros cheering on a guy chugging from a red Solo cup.

To my right, Pia, Caroline, and the rest of their friends are giggling about something. A bunch of other girls hang around the periphery of their group, probably hoping to be invited in. Pia waves at Brad, then sees me and makes a face like . . . well, like she just saw Brad walk into a party with me.

The music, the yeasty beer smell, and the dudes yelling swirl around my head. Even before I stopped leaving the house, my idea of a party was inviting Jenni and sometimes a couple other girls over for pizza and a Netflix marathon. This is the kind of thing I thought only happened in teen movies. There are people coming down the stairs, people pushing past us to get in the door, people crammed into the corners, people everywhere. My heartbeat quickens and I sort of *do* wish I had that armadillo costume.

Jenni pushes me into the living room toward Pia and Caroline and their other friends in neon-colored dresses. Someone's waving for Brad.

"Brad!" Lauren DeStefano coos. "Come here! We were just talking about the game!"

Brad puts his hand on my shoulder. "You don't mind, do you?"

I can barely speak, so I just shake my head.

"You're the best." He smiles before joining the girls on the edge of a huge blue sofa.

"This is . . . a lot of people," I say to Jenni as we make our way through the crowd. She waves to Lincoln, who's in the kitchen, Scott's arm casually slung over his shoulder. They're with some kids from film club. He raises his eyebrows at us and turns back to his conversation.

I fight an urge to rush to him, but he looks happy. It's not like Lincoln is often *un*happy, but this is different. He looks comfortable, accepted, content.

He looks *at home.*

"This is sort of overwhelming," I say to Jenni, but she doesn't respond. I turn around and see her crowding into a group picture with some of her friends from yearbook.

Okay. So all my friends have abandoned me, recluse-in-recovery, at this party full of people. That's fine. I can handle it.

I take a few steps and almost get knocked off my feet as Pat Sapperstein runs into me, sloshing a full cup of beer all over my shirt.

"Whoa, sorry," he slurs. "Wait, are you armadillo girl?"

"Just one of the many names I go by," I say with a polite smile, trying to edge past him.

He points at me like I've just said something particularly insightful. "That was . . . that was badass, Melinda."

"Mallory."

"Right, right." He touches a hand to his forehead, as if he's just forgetful and is not incredibly, disgustingly wasted. "Melissa."

"It's been great, Pat," I say, finally pushing my way past him. I find a corner in the hallway that isn't occupied by anybody puking or making out or both.

I crouch behind a giant decorative vase filled with fake palm fronds and pull out my phone. Maybe all of my IRL friends are having a great time without me, but that doesn't mean I don't have anyone to talk to.

The little light beside BeamMeUp still glows red. I lean harder against the wall.

"Mallory?"

I look up and see Shauna Macgregor staring at me, her hands on her hips.

"Oh, hi." I stand up and almost knock over the giant vase. I grab it as it wobbles and try to hold it steady. "Sorry!"

Shauna squints. "Are you doing okay?"

Can she tell that I'm panicking? That I'm totally out of my element and sort of freaking out? Is it that obvious to everyone?

"I thought you had some sort of skin disorder where you couldn't leave the house. Like, you're allergic to air or sun or something?" she asks, tilting her head. "It's just that my mom doesn't need another lawsuit hanging over her head, you know?"

I raise my eyebrows. "Allergic to air?"

She tilts her head like she's unsure what to say. "That's . . . just what I heard."

At least she doesn't think I'm a ghost. "Thanks for throwing the party, Shauna. I'm gonna go find Brad."

I wander down the hallway and wind up back in the living room. Shauna's house is like a weird maze that smells like Axe body spray.

Brad is still sitting on the edge of the sofa, listening to Caroline, Pia, Lauren, and a bunch of other girls with beautiful hair talk about who knows what. I pass a group of band kids playing strip poker around a coffee table before I can make out what Caroline is saying.

". . . it was just super weird, from what I heard. She totally threw up, like in the middle of the party, on someone's shoes. Because she was, like, allergic to dogs or something?" She laughs, as if the mere mention of an allergy is comedy gold.

I can already feel my face starting to get hot, but when I see Brad's shoulders shaking with laughter, my heart sinks somewhere down around my feet. Brad wouldn't do that, would he? He wouldn't be nice to my face and then laugh at me behind my back. He wouldn't bring me to a party just to turn me into a joke. I mean, life isn't some weird teen movie that plays on TBS in the afternoon.

But why else would he be laughing at Caroline, I wonder. I slowly back up, tears trying to push their way out of my eyes. All I want to do is get away from all of these people and get back to the comfort of my house, the place where I don't have to worry about seeing anyone.

I back into Pat Sapperstein.

"Hey . . . are you the armadillo girl?" he asks again.

I nod and gulp back my tears. "Yeah, Pat. That's me. Armadillo girl."

Pat grabs my arms tight. I freeze. "'Did you ever know,'" he sings quietly and off-key, "'that you're my heeeeerooooo?'"

I know Pat Sapperstein's drunk. I know he doesn't technically know my name. And I know he's doing a very bad job of singing an '80s karaoke standard at me.

But he's right. I'm not the same girl I used to be, the one who would hide under her blankets while watching *The X-Files* whenever she has a problem. I'm out of the house. I'm at a party. I wore an armadillo costume tonight, for God's sake. I'm Pat Sapperstein's hero, and I'm not going to let Caroline say whatever she wants about me.

"Thanks for the pep talk, Pat," I say, gently breaking his grasp and pushing past him. I walk up behind Caroline and tap her on the shoulder. She turns around and, seeing me, frowns.

"Are you lost?" she asks.

"I don't know, are you a massive bitch?"

She gasps. "What?"

"Seriously, Caroline, what did I ever do to deserve being treated like shit all the time?"

"Um . . ." Caroline looks around her, and that's when I

realize that everyone in the room is staring at me. The stoners. The half-naked band kids. Pat Sapperstein. Brad.

"Sorry I made fun of you puking?" Caroline offers, looking earnestly confused.

"Oh, it is not just about the puke," I say, crossing my arms. A whole new kind of warmth is spreading throughout my body. "You know what you did."

Caroline widens her eyes but says nothing. I can't stop.

"I'm talking about you nominating me for homecoming court as a joke. What's even wrong in your messed-up head that you thought that was funny?" I gesture to all of them on the couches. "What's wrong with all of you?"

"I didn't nominate you," Caroline says, looking even more confused than before.

"What are you talking about, Mal?" Brad asks, his green eyes full of concern.

"Don't act like you don't know," I say to Brad, barely able to fight back tears. "I saw you laughing when Caroline was making fun of me. You guys all think this is hilarious, don't you? Nominate the weird girl who Skypes into class for homecoming court. Sure, why not! Who cares about her feelings? She—"

"Mallory!" Brad stands up and looks me right in the eyes. "I wasn't laughing at whatever Caroline said. I didn't even hear her say anything about you. Lauren was showing me a video of a Great Dane trying to fit into a tiny dog bed."

I look at Lauren, who's still sitting on the couch. She holds up her phone. "It's, like, a really small dog bed," she offers in explanation.

I close my eyes and shake my head. "Okay, fine. But that doesn't change the fact that you guys nominated me for homecoming court as a joke."

"None of us nominated you," Pia says. "Jenni did."

CHAPTER TWENTY-FOUR

I LOOK BETWEEN CAROLINE, Brad, Pia, and Lauren, who's intently studying her phone again. "Jenni?" I ask. My mouth is dry.

A tiny "Mal" comes from behind me, so I turn around. Jenni and Linc are in the doorway. She opens her mouth as if she's about to say something, but I turn back around.

Brad shakes his head slowly. For the first time ever, he looks disappointed in me. "How could you ever think I would do that, Mal? You're my friend."

I swallow again. No one else is really paying attention to us anymore, and the chatter is picking up. But Brad's looking straight at me, and I feel a familiar tremble creep into my body.

I run toward the bathroom.

"Mallory!" Jenni shouts as I open the door and try to slam it in her face. "Would you just listen to us?"

"No," I say through my teeth. Head spinning, I sit down on the edge of the bathtub.

"Then we're coming in." Lincoln pulls Jenni into the bathroom before he shuts the door.

"I'm so glad we get to talk about this here," I say, gesturing to a sign above the toilet that reads PLEASE DON'T SPRINKLE WHEN YOU TINKLE.

"I wasn't trying to hurt you," Jenni starts.

Someone knocks on the door. "Just a minute!" Lincoln shouts.

"Did you know about this?" I glare at him.

Lincoln nods. "Jenni nominated you, but it was my idea."

I stare at him in disbelief. "Why would you do this? Why would my best friend and my brother humiliate me in front of everyone?"

Jenni holds out her hands. "We weren't trying to humiliate you! We wanted to help you!"

"By making me look like an even bigger loser?"

"No!" Lincoln looks frustrated. "By helping you act more like yourself . . . like your *old* self, before Dad left."

I gnash my teeth together as my whole body goes hot. "That's not how this works."

"Admit it, Mal," Lincoln says softly. "You've left the house more in the past couple weeks than you have in the last two months. We wanted to give you a reason to get out of bed. That's all we wanted . . . to help you get back to normal."

A bitter laugh escapes from my throat. "Normal. Right. I was totally normal without your help, thanks."

Lincoln gives me a hard look. "Listen, there is nothing normal about practically dropping out of society and becoming a hermit."

Someone knocks on the door again, even louder. "Anybody in there?"

"Just a minute!" I yell, then cover my face with my hands.

"I didn't mean to be a jerk, okay?" Lincoln leans into me. "You're making so much progress and I'm so proud of you. I mean, soon you'll be on the Europe trip, and—"

"What Europe trip?" Jenni asks, her eyes narrowing.

My body goes from hot to cold. I lift my face up from my hands to look at Jenni.

"The class trip? Mallory didn't want to tell anybody, but that's why she wants that five hundred dollars so much, so she can register."

"That deadline was months ago," Jenni says, her eyes darting back and forth between Lincoln and me.

Lincoln steps back, which is hard to do in this tiny bathroom, and he almost falls over the toilet. "Mal, did . . . did you lie to me?"

I form my hands into fists, concentrating on pushing all of my fingernails into my palms. "No! I mean, yes. I *do* want that five hundred dollars, but I didn't want to tell you why."

"Mallory," Jenni says in a low voice. "Do you have a drug problem?"

I roll my eyes. "God, no! I need the money because . . ."

Lincoln and Jenni stare back at me, their eyes wide. I can feel tears forming in mine.

"Because of Dad, okay? Because he's going on that stupid birding trip and registration costs five hundred dollars and if I could just *find* him, I know I could talk to him and convince him . . ."

"Of course," Lincoln says flatly, shaking his head. "Of course that's what it was."

"Why is this the first time I've even heard about this?" Jenni asks, looking hurt.

"Maybe because every time I try to talk about my dad you just change the subject?"

Jenni stands up straighter and, even though she's wearing a dress covered in tiny hot air balloons, I'm a little bit afraid for a second. "Excuse me? I don't know how you can say that I don't listen to your problems when all we ever talk about is *you!*" she says, shaking.

"What?" I ask.

"Guess what? *I* have stuff I want to talk about, too. You aren't the only one who has problems! But you never notice that, do you?" Jenni shouts.

"Seriously!" a male voice shouts from the other side of the door. "I have to go!"

"Just a minute!" the three of us yell in unison.

I shake my head. "I can't believe this is what we're talking about right now. Pia just embarrassed me in front of practically the whole school because of you guys, I feel like an idiot, and Brad barely even said a word—"

"Oh, don't bring Brad into this," Jenni says, even angrier than before. "When has he ever been anything but nice, and the sweetest guy in school, and basically perfect?"

I stare at her hands, clenched into fists, and start to ask her a slightly more sophisticated version of the question *Yeah, well, if you love Brad so much, why don't you marry him?* when Lincoln speaks, his voice dangerously quiet.

"You know what your problem is, Mallory?" While Jenni's screams let me know she's furious, Lincoln's relative calm lets me know that he's seriously upset.

"No," I say. "But I'm sure you'll tell me."

"It isn't that you're afraid of going out. It's that you're afraid of moving on."

He opens the bathroom door, letting Jenni storm out before he follows. It would be a lot more dramatic if the bathroom weren't so small and they didn't have to push the trash can out of their way to get past me. But in the pit of my stomach, it feels heavy.

Pat Sapperstein pokes his head in. "Are you done in here? Oh, hey, Mandy."

"Go pee outside, Pat!" I shout, slamming the door in his face.

I'm starting to feel dizzy, so I clutch the bathtub tighter and go through what's happened so far tonight. I've managed to yell at almost everyone I know and alienate my friends and family members. And now I'm locked in a bathroom at Shauna Macgregor's house.

I might be seventeen, but this is one of those times when I need my mom.

I pull my knees up toward my chest and call her phone, trying to steady my breath as I wait for her to pick up. It rings five times before I get her very professional-sounding voice mail greeting. "Damn it," I mutter, my heart beating faster and faster. I need to talk to someone, so I do something that shows I'm really desperate: I call Dr. Dinah.

After a few rings, I hear, "You've reached the phone of Dr. Dinah Martinez. Please leave a message after the beep."

There's no way I'm leaving a voice mail for my therapist on a Friday night. So I sit, waiting for my heart to just slow down. I lean my head against the wall and try to breathe in deeply, but the air gets stuck before it reaches my lungs.

The loud thump of a rap song is banging down the bathroom door. My heartbeat speeds up and I put my hand over my chest. My hands feel tingly, like they're falling asleep. The edges of my vision are filling in with black.

This is worse than the time I puked at Puppy Playtime, worse than the time I tried to walk to school. Am I having a heart attack? Will Pat Sapperstein be the one to find my body when he finally breaks down the bathroom door?

I need to talk to somebody, or I might actually die. I dial Dr. Dinah's number one more time, and this time, I listen to the entire voice mail greeting as I breathe in gasps.

". . . if this is a true emergency, please do not hesitate to call 911. Otherwise, I'll return your call as soon as I can."

That's it, 911. I might be dying, so this is definitely an emergency, and I'm sure the operator is trained in talking people down from panic ledges, right? I punch the numbers in and a woman's voice greets me almost immediately.

"Nine one one, what's your emergency?"

"I think . . . I think I'm having a heart attack," I squeak.

"What's your location?"

I give the woman Shauna's address. "I just need someone to talk to because I'm freaking out and all my friends hate me and . . ."

"We're dispatching someone right now. Can you take a deep breath for me?"

I try, and find that breathing is slightly easier. Even talking to this anonymous 911 operator is better than nothing.

I hear a siren and, suddenly, the music cuts off. Someone shouts, "Shit!" as another voice yells, "Cops! Get out!"

I stand up and open the door a crack. People are running in every direction, some of them shutting themselves in rooms and others running out the front door. People are screaming and slamming doors. A band kid runs by without pants.

"Ma'am?" the operator asks.

Shauna spots me peering out of the bathroom. "Some

asshole called the cops on us! Oh my God, I am in such deep shit." She scampers off and I cover my mouth with my hand.

Did I call the cops on this party?

"Ma'am?"

"Sorry, gotta go!" I shout into the phone.

I run into the kitchen and see a bunch of people streaming out the sliding glass door that leads into Shauna's backyard. I don't see Jenni, Lincoln, or Brad.

I leap off Shauna's deck and run through the trees in her backyard, like I'm in *The Hunger Games* or something. My heartbeat still pounds in my ears, but the air on my face makes me feel a little bit better. I run through several yards, dart across a street, dash through a park, and keep running until I can't.

I end up leaning against a swing set in a darkened, unfamiliar backyard. No one's here, and I can't even hear the sirens anymore. I catch my breath, then creep past the house until I'm standing on the sidewalk. *Where am I?* I wonder as a sharp pain stings my foot. I look down and see that one of my sandals is missing.

I'm alone, I called the cops on a party, and I only have one shoe. It's hard to think of a way this night could get worse.

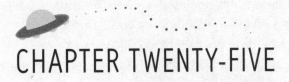

CHAPTER TWENTY-FIVE

THE WEAK, FLICKERING STREETLIGHT keeps an unsteady pace with my breathing. I listen to the phone ring. It's hot against my ear.

"Just pick up," I mutter, but all I hear is Jenni's professionally perky voice mail greeting.

I groan. The window of the house in front of me has an aquatic glow; the television is turning the whole room blue. If Jenni's not answering my calls, she must be really mad.

I dial Lincoln's number. Blood is thicker than rabid anger. He has to pick up.

Nope. All I get is the robotic voice that gently informs me, "The number you have dialed is currently unavailable. To leave a message . . ."

I hit END and let out a pathetic whimper. I'm feeling the opposite of safe, secure, and capable as I run my fingers through my hair, catching something in the process. A leaf. Oh God, I'm lost and covered in foliage.

I send a group text to Lincoln and Jenni.

Currently lost/dirty/panicking. Where r u?

Even if I think I'm having another heart attack, there's one person I'm absolutely not texting: Brad. The look on his face in Shauna's living room plays on repeat in my head. He wasn't angry; he was disappointed. I made the happiest person I know sad, and I don't think anything could feel worse.

Until I remember that I'm still lost and alone.

I look at the map on my phone and stare at the little blinking dot that symbolizes me. I'm on Canard Street. I zoom out and realize that I'm miles from my house. I sink to the curb and let my head fall in between my knees. *Think, Mallory.* Jake said small, closed spaces can help when you're panicking, but this, right now? This is the opposite. The expanse of sky and stars wink at me like they're making fun of my misfortune.

I finally cry—really cry. Tears don't threaten to spill over or leak out, they're suddenly just flowing down my cheeks. Sure, I've freaked out, almost *passed* out, been unable to breathe, and even puked, but it takes a lot to make me sob. I didn't cry when I broke my arm on the monkey bars in fourth grade. I didn't cry when my dad left. I'm not a crier, but I let it all out right here on the curb.

If I were just safe at home, wrapped up in blankets and watching Agent Scully be really skeptical of Mulder's far-out theory, I'd be safe. And now I'm alone, covered in dirt and wearing ripped clothing. I can't believe I ever thought I could do this . . . any of this. Get a guy to like me. Be homecoming queen. Find my dad. I really thought I had it all worked out, but sitting here at almost midnight all by myself, I know the truth. I don't have anything at all.

My phone buzzes, and I wipe my nose as I look at the screen greedily.

It's Jake. Of course.

When do I need to pick you up? Brad's ignoring my texts. Too busy doing keg stands?

I hit CALL, close my eyes, and focus on my breath. In through my nose. Hold. Out through my mouth.

Jake picks up after two rings. Before he can say anything, I croak, "Jake, I need you to come get me."

"Mallory?" he asks, confused. "What's wrong?"

"I'm lost," I say, picking another leaf out of my hair. "No one's answering my texts and I didn't know who else to call."

I can hear keys jingling in the background. "I'm on my way. Wait. Shit. Where are you?"

"Canard Street. Or at least that's what my phone tells me."

Jake exhales noisily. "How the hell did you get all the way over there? Shauna's house is on Alameda. Never mind. Just sit tight. I'll see you in fifteen minutes."

Fourteen minutes and twenty-three seconds later (I timed it), Jake's car turns onto Canard and inches down the road. I stand up and wave both my hands like I'm stranded on a desert island and he's the first boat I've seen in weeks.

Jake pulls over and rolls down the window. "Get in."

I open the door and curl up into a ball on the seat. "Thanks," I say, and sniff. I wipe my nose and realize that the entire lower half of my face is covered in snot.

We drive in almost silence. The radio is on some nightly call-in station and the DJ is talking to a man who wants to dedicate a song to his high school sweetheart.

After about five minutes, Jake breaks the silence.

"Did someone hurt you?"

I almost laugh at how ridiculous that is, but the seriousness in Jake's voice stops me.

"Just tell me who it was and, I swear to God, I will murder them. I don't even care what happens to me."

This time I do laugh, but it comes out bitter and angry. "No one hurt me, Jake. I did this. Me. Because I'm such a royal screwup."

The radio plays some slow Adele song. Jake reaches over and switches it off.

"Listen, I don't know what happened to you, but I can guarantee that you're not a screwup. And I should know. You're speaking to the king of screwups."

I snort. "If you know me so well, King Screwup, then why don't you tell me what you think my problem is?"

Jake doesn't speak as he eases the car over a speed bump. I wish Adele was still playing. Another voice in the car would make this a little less awkward.

"I don't think you have a problem," Jake says carefully. "But you seem like you have some anxiety, which isn't a big deal. I have anxiety, too. That's why I take medication."

"'Anxiety,'" I say, making air quotes, "makes it sound like I just worry about things once in a while. Like I get stressed out about a test or what I'm going to wear. It's not like that."

"Okay," Jake says, his voice betraying no impatience at all. He makes a complete stop at a stop sign and turns right. "Why don't you tell me what it is like?"

I look at him out of the corner of my eye. "You really want to know?"

Jake nods, keeping his eyes on the road.

I inhale like I'm about to dive underwater. "This is the farthest

I've been from my house in over two months. After my dad left, I had a freak-out in the middle of the Cheesecake Factory. And then I stopped leaving my house. Like, at all. That time you saw me in the yard, when I fell out of the tree house? That was my first time outside in months, and I only went out there because my therapist told me to, and she's kind of scary."

I pause to take a breath and Jake starts to say something, but I hold up a hand. "I'm not done. So whenever I leave the house I get panicky and sick and I feel terrible and I think I'm going to die, but I've been doing it. Because I want to be on homecoming court, because I need the five hundred dollars to go on this birding trip with my dad, who, FYI, apparently doesn't miss any of us because he hasn't even called."

Jake pulls to a stop in front of my house and unbuckles his seat belt. "Get out," he says, opening his door.

My heart is still beating super fast as I watch him walk around the front of the car, but that doesn't stop some anger from creeping in around the edges of my anxiety. It's not like I expected Jake to go all Dr. Dinah on me, but seriously? Just ordering me out of his car?

He opens my door. "Out."

I wipe my eyes, probably further smearing my makeup in the process, and hop out of the car, ready to tell him to go to hell before I stomp into my house and collapse into my bed.

But that's not what happens, because before I can say a single word, Jake wraps his long arms around me and pulls me into his chest.

"Close spaces, remember?" he says.

With the softness of his T-shirt against my cheek (and the hardness of the chest that's under that T-shirt), it's not easy to remember much of anything. I suck in a breath, taking in Jake's particular brand of boy smell—the deodorant, the faint sweat. He rubs his hands over my back and I know, I *know* I shouldn't be thinking this, but this doesn't feel like a friendly hug.

Maybe he's right about the close spaces, because I don't feel panicked anymore. Or, if I do feel panicked, it's about something else entirely.

I lift my head off his chest and slowly let my eyes meet his. His blue eyes look back at me and one of his hands moves up to the back of my neck. I stare at his crooked nose, at a tiny mole on his left cheek that I never noticed before, at his lips. God, his *lips*. It would be so easy to push myself up on my toes and close the gap between us, to totally relax into him, to kiss him. . . .

Then I push away, backing up so quickly that I almost trip over my own feet.

"I can't," I whisper. "Brad."

Jake drags his hands over his face and into his hair. "I don't want to think about my brother right now, if that's okay."

"No," I say, and I can feel the tears coming back to my eyes. "You don't get it."

Jake drops his hands and looks at me. "Then explain it to me, please. Do you . . . do you have a thing for him? Because I never would have . . ."

I shake my head, and I don't even know if I'm saying *no I don't like Brad* or *no you don't understand*. "Brad was supposed to ask me to homecoming. He's supposed to like me."

A beat of silence passes. "You're right," Jake says. "I don't get it."

Frustrated, I let my voice rise. I need to explain. "I need to be homecoming queen, and I can't get there without Brad. If people see me with Brad, I'll get more spirit points, and if I get more spirit points . . ."

Now it's Jake's turn to back away from me. "So this whole thing . . . was for a dance?"

I want to scream, I'm so angry. "Have you even been listening to me? It's not about the dance. It's about my dad, it's about—"

Jake holds up a hand. "No, hold on. You just almost kissed me, but you didn't because of my brother. But you're using my brother so you'll get to wear some shiny crown?"

"I don't think you really have any room to judge," I spit. The safety of his chest, his shirt, his smell feels miles away. "You're just scared and hiding from your problems, too."

He raises his eyebrows and takes another step backward, holding up his arms like he's surrendering. "You know what? I'm sorry. I'm sorry any of this happened. I thought I knew who you were, but clearly . . . I don't."

"Jake." I take a step toward him, already feeling bad about what I just said.

"I'll leave you alone so you can go check out ReardonsNext PrettyPrincess.com or whatever," he calls over his shoulder.

He turns around and walks toward his house, leaving me standing on the sidewalk. I watch him unlock the front door and go inside without looking back. He doesn't even give me the satisfaction of slamming the door. He just shuts it quietly.

I stare at his closed door for a moment. Jake says he doesn't know who I am, but right now, I don't really know who I am, either.

My phone buzzes in my pocket, but it's not Jenni or Lincoln assuring me that they're not mad, or Brad asking if I want to talk.

It's my mom, and in the perfect, abbreviation-free texting language she always uses, her text reads:

    Mallory, please come home right away. Lincoln
    was arrested.

CHAPTER TWENTY-SIX

Many of us have found our way to WANA because we simply have too many questions that can't be answered. When society won't be honest about what's happening right in front of our eyes, we have to find our own answers.

—*We Are Not Alone welcome post by user StrangerInAStrangeLand*

I DON'T WAKE UP until almost noon on Saturday, my head pounding—but not from the effects of a hangover. Unlike Lincoln, I didn't have anything to drink last night. But that's the nasty little thing about anxiety that no one tells you: It's exhausting long after it's over. A panic attack leaves me feeling like I just ran a marathon, even though all I did was feel like dying.

I peel myself out of bed and trip over the sandal I have left from last night. Instantly, it all comes back. The football game. The party. Calling the cops. Jake. Lincoln.

When I came in last night, my mom was hunched over the island with a cup of coffee after bringing Lincoln home from the police station. He only had one beer, he swore, but since he didn't run out of the house quite as fast as I did, he got busted.

I can only assume that Jenni was safe because she's never even let a sip of alcohol cross her perfectly lined lips. It ages you, she always says. Plus, her parents would kill her. Luckily, as Mom told me, Lincoln got off with a mark on his record that gets wiped when he turns eighteen, twenty hours of community service, and an alcohol education course.

I shove my sandal out of the way and freeze when I hear my mom's voice carry up the stairs. I crack open the door.

". . . I think it was pretty nice of me to let you get a good night's sleep after I *bailed you out of jail*, but it's a new day. Why don't you tell me what went through your head last night? Because the police seem to think you don't deserve much punishment, but I'm inclined to disagree with them."

I run downstairs, still in my giant THE TRUTH IS OUT THERE T-shirt and the baggy boxers I sleep in. "Wait!" I shout, running into the room.

My mom turns around, and Lincoln stares at me from his perch on one of the island stools. His hair is rumpled and he's even wearing his glasses. For only having one beer, he looks terrible—kind of like the time he got food poisoning from eating calamari at a buffet.

"Honey, go back to bed." Mom waves me off. For once, she's not worried about *me* doing something wrong, and I'm tempted to savor the feeling. But I know what I have to do.

"This whole thing. It's my fault," I say, taking a seat next to Lincoln and facing my mom. I can feel Lincoln staring at me, but I can't bear to look at him.

My mom tilts her head. "Unless you force-fed Lincoln a beer, I don't see how that's possible."

"Maybe I didn't literally give him that beer, but I figuratively made him drink it," I say.

"Mal," Lincoln whispers. "You're not really helping."

Mom points at him. "You. Shut up. I'll let you know when I want to hear from you."

She looks back at me encouragingly, so I continue. "It's my fault because I'm the one who wanted to be on homecoming court. We were only at that stupid party because of me. And I lied to you. I didn't want to win so I could get better or so I could prove anything to anyone. I mean, okay, that was sort of why. But it wasn't really."

I stop, unsure if I can even force the words out of my mouth. Lincoln and Mom are both watching me, waiting for me to go on.

"It was because of Dad. The excursion."

"The excursion?" Mom says, looking at me like I just told her I was abducted by aliens again. "You mean the one where a bunch of middle-aged men go camping with their binoculars in Nevada for a weekend?"

I almost fall off the stool, but Lincoln grabs my elbow and steadies me. "Wait . . . what do you mean, Nevada? You have to pay five hundred dollars to even find out where the excursion is."

Mom rolls her eyes. "That birding society likes to act like everything is some big secret, but they've been going to the same spot in Nevada for the last fifteen years."

She stops and I can almost see everything clicking into place in her head, like Tetris blocks. "Five hundred dollars? Oh, honey. You didn't . . ."

I stare at the swirls of pink on the counter. Mom walks around the island and wraps her arms around me.

"When did we become a hugging family?" I say, but it comes out muffled because her arm is covering my mouth.

"You too, kid," Mom says, pulling Lincoln in. "Get in here."

"This is ridiculous," Lincoln says, but I can hear the smile in his voice.

Mom gives us both big, over-the-top, lip-smacking kisses

on our foreheads. "Don't think this means you're off the hook," she says to Lincoln as she releases us. "I'm still mad. In fact, I'm going to go get part of your punishment right now."

As soon as she walks out of the room, Lincoln sighs. "I'm mad, too. I really thought that if I ever got arrested, it would be for something much more sophisticated than having a Bud Light Lime."

I snort. "Listen, I'm—"

Lincoln stops me. "Can we skip the apologies and just go straight to the forgiveness? That hug maxed out my emotion for the day."

I smile and bump my shoulder into his. "Deal. I need all the forgiveness I can get, since everyone probably hates me for calling the cops on the party."

"Well, if you ever checked the ReardonsFutureQueen tumblr, you'd know that you're number one in the polls this morning . . ."

"What?!"

". . . and everybody thinks Pia called the cops to get back at Shauna for making out with Pat Sapperstein."

"Ew!" I say. "I thought Pia liked Brad! How could anyone like Pat Sapperstein?"

Lincoln shrugs. "Love is weird. Speaking of which, I sort of owe you a thank-you, because Scott thinks my criminal record is super badass."

"It's not," Mom says, walking back in with a bottle of Windex.

"Yeah, dude," I say. "You were drinking a Bud Light Lime."

Mom hands Lincoln the Windex. "I'm really looking forward to having a spotless house. Go forth and clean, young one. Every window downstairs, okay? And after that, the bathrooms."

"I want to be able to eat out of those toilets!" I shout.

Lincoln trudges out of the room, dragging his feet.

My mom leans on the counter. "So . . . five hundred dollars, huh?" She sighs heavily. "I should've talked to you more about your dad. Lincoln, too, but especially you. I saw how hard it was for you."

I hold my breath, afraid that if I say anything she'll stop talking.

Mom toys with the bracelet she's wearing. "Your dad's always been like this, since before you were born, and I've always known it. Do you remember, when Lincoln was a baby, that time he left for three months?"

Do I remember that? Tiny bits of memories float into my head. Mom feeding Lincoln baby food, just the three of us sitting at the table. Grandma Barb being over here all the time.

"Yeah," I say slowly. "I guess I do."

"That's just . . . your dad." Mom shrugs. "Some people have alcohol, or drugs. Your dad has leaving. And there's nothing that you or Lincoln could've done about that."

There are approximately one million thoughts going through my mind, but only one rises to the surface. "Do you know where he is?"

Mom meets my eyes and nods. "I didn't want you to obsess over it, so I didn't tell you. But . . . well, it's pretty clear that was the wrong decision. You deserve to know."

I hold up my hands. "Wait."

Knowing is not going to bring him back, make me feel better, or turn him into the kind of dad who's going to stick around. I've spent the last month following a ridiculous plan to figure out where he was, but I'm starting to realize that's never what the plan was really about.

"I don't want to know," I say. "Not now, anyway."

Mom's face breaks into a smile—a kind of sad, but definitely proud, smile. "Okay. But if you ever do, we can talk. Promise.

No more secret plans to get five hundred dollars and register for a trip."

I can't help but laugh.

"Hey!" Lincoln says, walking into the kitchen. "Are you guys having fun in here without me? Because—"

"Windows!" Mom and I shout at the same time. Lincoln rolls his eyes and walks back out of the room.

We look at each other and laugh together for the first time in months. "You're going to make him really pay for this, right? Because I don't think you've ever punished him in his life."

Mom shrugs. "That's because he's usually in front of a screen. But yes, he's going to be grounded for a long time. Except for tonight."

I give her a mocking, scolding nod. "The youngest gets away with everything."

"Somebody has to look out for you," Mom says.

The reality of what she's saying sinks in. "You think I should go? Even after . . . everything that happened?"

Mom nods. "You spent weeks trying to win. Don't you want to go and see what happens? And see Brad? I know this is probably the last thing you want to talk about with your mom, but you like him, right?"

"Yeah. I like him," I say slowly, thinking about standing in the moonlight and that almost-kiss last night.

I shake my head. Wrong Kirkpatrick.

"Okay," I say brightly. "You're right." She pulls me into *another* hug.

But first, there's one other thing I need to do. I climb the stairs to my room, passing Lincoln muttering to himself as he cleans the glass in our front door.

I pull the birding map out from under my bed, fold it up,

and toss it in the trash can. On my computer, I find the folder of Dad's pictures. Deleting them feels wrong. Won't he want them when he comes back? *If* he comes back?

A Mountain Bluebird stares at me with its beady eyes. These are pictures of birds, and my dad took them. But this isn't my family. These pictures aren't of us, aren't of memories we shared. These pictures of birds are just . . . *pictures of birds*. I click DELETE and shut my laptop.

I pull on an actual, non-pajama outfit, and as I glance at myself in the mirror, my eyes catch on the picture of Jenni and me tucked into the corner. Me, Lincoln, and Mom . . . we're a weird, crazy, messed-up family, and I know that the same thing is true of me and Jenni.

Before I can talk myself out of it, I dial her number. She picks up on the first ring.

"I'm sorry," I say before she can even say hello.

"Me too," she responds immediately. "Last night got kind of out of control."

"I'll say. Lincoln got arrested, I got lost in the woods, I almost kissed Jake, I accidentally called the cops on a party . . ."

"Back up. You almost kissed who?"

I quickly run through everything that happened last night and Jenni murmurs sympathetically and gasps appreciatively at all the right times.

"Brad's so nice, and sweet, and cute," I say.

"And he's got that little dimple on his left cheek when he smiles," Jenni adds.

"But there's something there with Jake. And I don't understand it, but it pulls us together and pushes us apart over and over."

"Well, you know what they say," Jenni says wisely.

"Everything exerts force on everything else. Maybe there's just a really strong force between you and Jake."

I get a feeling in my chest like my heart hits a speed bump.

"Jenni, what did you just say?"

Jenni pauses. "Everything exerts force on everything else?"

"Where did you hear that?" I ask frantically.

"I heard Jake say it last time I was over at Brad's," Jenni says, sounding guilty. "We were just hanging out as friends, and I swear I'm not trying to mess up your homecoming plan—"

"Jenni," I stop her, realizing that I've been wrong about a whole lot of things. "Do you think you can come over right now?"

"I'm already halfway there," Jenni says, and hangs up.

"Lincoln!" I yell.

I've been the biggest idiot in Reardon, in the world, in the galaxy. Brad and I aren't meant to be—we never were. There's someone else who's been encouraging me, helping me, making me feel better this whole time. There's another person who gets me more than anybody. The person who shares my belief that there's something else out there. The person who knows what it's like to deal with anxiety that feels like it's crushing you.

The person who knows me, even when I didn't.

I still have to apologize to Brad for assuming the worst, and I still have to go see if my classmates think I really deserve to wear that crown.

Lincoln walks in, still holding the Windex. "Please don't tell me you want me to clean your windows. I have my limits."

I turn to face him. "I'm going to the dance."

Lincoln drops the Windex. "Screw cleaning. Let's do this."

CHAPTER TWENTY-SEVEN

JENNI'S TINY FORD FIESTA screeches to a halt outside.

"What is it?!" she shouts as soon as I answer the door. Her high ponytail is just the slightest bit askew, the only sign that she rushed over here. Otherwise, she looks flawless. I herd her into the living room, where Lincoln is dumping out the giant garbage bag full of dresses we looked through before.

"You're going!" She claps her hands together.

"I want to finish what I started," I say. "And—"

My mom walks into the room. "I'm sorry, did I hear the sound of someone not cleaning?"

She stops in her tracks when she sees the three of us huddled around the pile of tulle. Ever practical, Mom doesn't waste any time. Instead, she asks, "What are you wearing?"

Lincoln holds up a very sequined, very neon-green dress. "One of our Nickel and Dime treasures."

Jenni puts a hand on my arm. "I'm only saying this because I'm your friend. That dress looks like a Post-it note."

My mom wrinkles her nose, clearly skeezed out by the

236

prospect of a pre-worn dress. "You're not seriously going to wear one of these, are you?"

"Don't worry," I say, waving a hand in the air. "I won't wear the one with bloodstains."

Mom crosses her arms, then starts walking away. "Wait here."

Lincoln angrily paws through the dresses. "Frankly, I don't appreciate her disparaging thrift stores. It's one of the few ethically conscious fashion choices you can make."

"It's true," Jenni nods. "Fast fashion is *way* bad."

"Uh, guys?" I look back and forth between them. "No time for a discussion about ethics right now, okay? Jenni, when you said that thing about everything exerting a force on everything else, it made me realize—"

"Ta-da!" Mom steps into the room, holding a pale pink dress in front of her.

Jenni and Lincoln gasp in unison, but for different reasons.

"It's beautiful," Jenni exhales.

"That would get so much money at Nickel and Dime," Lincoln mutters.

"Well, it's not for you," Mom says. "It's for Mallory. If she wants it. This is something I've had since high school. It was old-fashioned at the time, and I know it's not necessarily in style. . . ."

I hold it up against my body. It couldn't be more different from the yards and yards of shiny, crunchy fabric that Lincoln brought home. There are no sequins or rhinestones, for starters. It's shimmery but not sparkly, with short scalloped sleeves, and it looks like it will hit somewhere above my knees—and I have to admit, I love it.

"It's a classic shift dress," Jenni explains. "With the right hair and makeup, you're going to look like you stepped straight out of the sixties."

"I'm going to try it on," I say, running to the bathroom.

A bit of tricky zippering later, I pop out of the bathroom and do a spin for everyone.

Jenni covers her mouth with her hands. "You look like Audrey Hepburn! Or Kate Middleton on a casual day!"

"Are you sure you don't want to let me sell it?" Lincoln asks, and Mom smacks his arm.

I look down at myself. I have to admit, I do look pretty good. At least I know no one else at the dance will have this dress. "Wanna do my hair?" I ask Jenni.

"Let me grab my emergency supply bag," Jenni says before she runs out to her car.

Several hours later, Jenni has coaxed my hair into a sleek high bun and arranged her own hair in a complicated braided updo.

I check my makeup in the mirror one last time. The winged eyeliner Jenni gave me really does make me look like I'm from another era. Lincoln, in his slightly-too-small gray suit, swears that my cheekbones "could cut somebody!" He says this like it's a good thing, so I'll just believe him.

Jenni, as usual, looks gorgeous in a lacy teal dress that fans out below her waist.

"You look like a very sophisticated figure skater," I say, trying to repay the Audrey Hepburn compliment she gave me earlier.

"Thank you?" she says tentatively, staring at me in the mirror as she swipes on coral lipstick.

My mom pops her head into my room. "Picture time!" she shouts, waving her iPhone.

Lincoln sighs. "Like I want this tiny suit immortalized on film."

"Shut up and smile!" I say, throwing my arms around him and Jenni and pulling them close. Lincoln sighs and leans his head on my shoulder; Jenni pops out her arm and tilts her head in her classic photo stance. My mom snaps picture after picture, and I flash a genuine smile.

No matter what happens tonight, even if Brad doesn't want to talk to me ever again after what I said, even if things with Jake are too far gone to repair, this is the moment I want to remember. Getting ready with my best friend and my brother, feeling more beautiful than I ever have in my life, and being with my family . . . the people who really matter.

Someone honks in the driveway. Lincoln wiggles his eyebrows goofily. "I've got a surprise for you guys. Scott borrowed his dad's old Cadillac so we can show up to the dance in style."

Jenni does a little hop in the air. "Oh my God, this is just like an old movie. But, like, I'm showing up with you guys instead of a cute date. I mean, no offense. But at least we're dateless together, right?"

I want to ask Jenni a million questions—what are her feelings for Brad? What does she think about Jake? Why has she clearly been putting her own feelings on the back burner while helping me win? But I don't have time to ask anything, because Lincoln says, "Scott's a-waiting!" and ushers us both downstairs.

We say our good-byes to my mom, who's already parked herself on the couch with a glass of wine and a marathon of *Property Brothers* (she swears she watches it to get ideas for houses and not because she just thinks they're cute, but I've seen the way she stares at those twins). Outside, Scott's leaning against the front of his Cadillac, looking for all the world like Jake Ryan at the end of *Sixteen Candles*, another movie Jenni made me watch when I would way rather have been watching *Alien* for the five hundredth time.

Except that instead of leaning against a fancy, bright red sports car, Scott is leaning against a more than slightly rusted blue Cadillac.

"So what I failed to mention," Scott says before any of us can get a word out, "is that my dad's Cadillac is so old that it may have been driven by dinosaurs."

Lincoln puts an arm around Scott. "I love you despite the fact that you expect us to ride in this jalopy."

Jenni and I look at each other and raise our eyebrows. *Love?*

"Please just say it runs," I say, getting anxious to get to the dance and talk to Brad.

Scott nods. "I promise that it will get us to the dance and back. I *cannot* promise that the ride will be smooth."

I look at the rusted car and think about how much could go wrong in the two blocks between here and the high school. A blowout. Hitting a wayward pedestrian. A sudden, inexplicable bout of road rage from Scott that kills several civilians and lands us all on the news, saying things like, "He just seemed so nice. This is a total shock."

But nothing in my life lately has been a smooth ride. Being on homecoming court, hanging out with the Kirkpatricks, leaving the house . . . it's all been rough. As I look around at my friends, I think, *Hasn't it been worth it?*

I turn around and give my house one more glance. To my surprise, I see my mom looking out the window. She waves at me, and I raise my hand.

The house isn't going anywhere, and neither is my mom. They'll both be waiting for me when I come home tonight.

"Let's do this," I say, reaching to open the back door.

The door handle comes off in my hands.

"Oh God," Lincoln sighs. "The perfect start to a perfect night."

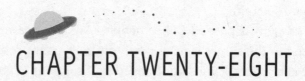

CHAPTER TWENTY-EIGHT

Some people think they can't wear a bold lip. But people think they can't do a lot of things, like wear yellow or pull off an asymmetrical haircut. The truth is, you can pretty much rock anything if you're willing to step outside your comfort zone. My friend Mal taught me that.

—Just Jenni, 2015

WE WALK INTO THE dance as the beat of a Nicki Minaj song pounds into my head with the force of a hammer. The home-coming committee did their best to make the gym look less like a room where sweaty basketball players practice every day, and I have to admit they sort of succeeded. The blue and gold streamers draped across the ceiling make the room feel like a circus tent. There are GO REARDON! banners everywhere and even a chocolate fountain in the corner. Already, my classmates are dancing in ways that must violate Reardon's code of conduct.

Lincoln spies the chocolate fountain immediately and lets out a gasp. "We need to go check that out. Oh, wait." He turns to me and Jenni. "Are you guys going to be okay?"

I wave him off. "Go enjoy the fountain. Just don't get anything on your tiny suit."

Lincoln frowns. "Young lady, that attitude is not becoming of a queen."

Scott pulls on Lincoln's arm. "Hurry up before somebody eats all the strawberries."

"Duty calls," Lincoln says, saluting me before joining Scott.

I clutch Jenni's hand as I crane my neck, looking for Brad. "Do you see him?"

The gym is packed full of people. And since every guy is dressed in the same basic uniform of dress pants, a button-up shirt, and a tie, they all blend together. I step out of the way of an aggressive dude whose dance moves seem to consist entirely of moving his elbows.

Jenni says something to me, but I can't hear her over the sound of Nicki's high-speed rap.

"What?" I ask, cupping my hand behind my ear.

"I said," she yells, "do you really like Brad? I mean, really?"

I'd hoped to have this conversation when there wasn't a girl in a scratchy sequined dress bumping and grinding with her date so close to me that she's grinding her sequins into my arm. I shake my head. "I thought I did, but . . . as a friend. That's it."

Jenni opens her mouth to say something, but the music fades out and Principal Lu shows up on stage. "Reardon High, I want to welcome you to this year's Homecoming Dance!"

The crowd cheers. Out of the corner of my eye, I see Pat Sapperstein and another dude lean over to light a joint. Classic Pat.

"Tonight, we'll find out who earned the most spirit points and votes to become your homecoming king and queen."

Another round of cheers. Even over the rest of the crowd, I can hear Lincoln's distinctive "Woo!" I look to my right and see him by the fountain, hands raised in the air.

"But first, there is one more way for the candidates to earn spirit points. Our homecoming committee is here and ready to judge the final speeches from each candidate . . ."

I turn to Jenni. "Speeches?"

". . . and then, after the final spirit points are added to our current tally, I'll announce your Reardon High School homecoming queen and king! But now, I'd like to welcome to the stage our first candidate, Brad Kirkpatrick!"

"Jenni!" I hiss over the applause. "What the hell? I need to give a speech?"

Jenni looks at me helplessly. "I thought you knew!"

I can't focus on anything Brad's saying because (A) I can feel my heart sinking as I remember the mean things I said to him yesterday, and (B) I'm trying, desperately, to think of what I'm going to say in my speech.

The crowd claps as Brad ends his speech, and Pia walks up to the microphone. I look at Jenni and stick out my tongue.

"Be nice." She wags her finger playfully.

Pia gushes about how it's "such an honor" to be on court. Then, as she looks out into the crowd and seemingly right into my soul, she says, "And to me, unlike some members of this court, nothing is more important than showing my Reardon pride. I'm at every football game, cheering on the team; at every pep rally, getting people pumped up; and even at every swim meet, and those are at, like, seven a.m. on Saturday. And I want you guys to ask yourself: Who loves Reardon more than that?"

I can feel myself shrinking down as the crowd claps for Pia's speech. There are a few random "Woo!"s as she takes her place beside Brad, and I feel sick as I see her give him a quick hug. I'm about to melt into a puddle of shame on the floor when I hear a loud "Boo!" come from my right.

I turn and see Pat Sapperstein, his hands cupped around his mouth. "Pia sucks!" he says, pointing toward the stage. "You know who should win?" Pat grabs the arm of the guy next to him. "Hey, Marc, you know who should win?"

Marc raises his eyebrows and tentatively points at me. "That girl?"

Pat gives me double thumbs-up. "Yeah! We voted for you, Mallory. You're gonna win."

Pat actually got my name right this time. I'm sort of touched. "Hey, Pat," I say, leaning over. "Thanks. And I think you might want to take it easy tonight, okay? There are a lot of teacher chaperones here."

Pat looks at me in awe. "That's why you're so great, Marlena. You care about us."

I turn away from Pat and see Jenni watching the stage as Caroline speaks. "Hey," I say. "I'm gonna go wing it, okay?"

Jenni nods encouragingly, as if me "winging it" has ever gone well before. She pulls me into a hug. "Good luck. You're gonna kill it."

I squeeze her back. "Thanks."

"And up next," Principal Lu says, "we have Mallory Sullivan. Mallory? Are you here tonight?"

Fearlessly, I push my way through couples and groups, making my way up to the stage. From the edge of the stage, Brad holds out his hand to help me up. I give him a grateful smile, and he tentatively smiles back.

Principal Lu interrupts our smile-fest by handing me the microphone. "Mallory? Would you like to say a few words?"

"Yes!" I say, grabbing the mic. A squeal of feedback hits the gym and everyone groans.

"Sorry," I say. The lights of everyone's camera phones look like a bunch of fireflies. I realize they're taking videos of me.

Swallowing so hard I think it echoes in the mic, I keep talking. "I don't have a lot of practice speaking into microphones. Or being in front of crowds. Or, well, doing much of anything lately."

Everyone just looks like shadowy blobs and, even though I can't see their faces, I know they're all staring straight at me. It's enough to make me feel a little wobbly kneed and I feel a sharp pang of longing for home, where Mom is currently sitting on our couch and lusting after the clean-cut Realtor Property Brother or the rugged contractor Property Brother.

Safe. Secure. Capable.

I take a few seconds and breathe in, hold it, breathe out. Principal Lu looks at me expectantly. Out of the corner of my eye, I see some motion at the left side of the stage, and I look over to see Lincoln giving me a big, goofy wave. My friends are here. I can do this, because I *am* safe and secure, and I'm feeling more capable than I ever have in my whole life.

"So you've all probably noticed that I haven't been at school for a while. All year, actually. And I guess this is a good time to explain that. It's not that I think I'm too good for anyone or that I don't like Reardon, it's just that . . . I was scared. I don't even have enough time right now to explain it, but I was scared to leave my house. Scared of what would happen, scared of what people would say, scared of . . . everything, really. So I stayed home. But through everything, my real friends"—I pause, giving Lincoln and Jenni a smile—"were there for me. Pushing me to take small step after small step, until finally I took one big step onto this stage."

I pause and take a huge breath in and look out over the crowd. No one's laughing at me. A few people look confused, sure, and at least one girl is way more concerned with the chocolate fountain than she is with my speech, but almost everyone is just . . . listening.

"I guess what I figured out is that we all have things we're afraid of. And that's okay. But it's what you do with your fear that really sets you apart. Do you let it force you into hiding? Or do you face it, even when it's hard, even when it hurts? I'm not going to act like I have all the answers, but I do know that the past month has been one of the best ones of my life, even though this past year has been the worst. And I just want to say thank you to a really good friend of mine who helped me realize that I am not alone."

I look behind me and smile at Brad. He smiles back at me encouragingly, and I turn back to face the crowd.

"I'm honored to be on your homecoming court, Reardon, and I just want to say thanks for making me feel like I'm home."

I hand the mic back to Principal Lu, who pats me on the arm and calls on Luis Valdez to give his speech. I'm filled with adrenaline and my ears are buzzing so much that the applause just sounds like static, but even in my slightly freaked-out state, I can tell that there's a *lot* of clapping. Before I can even make it a few steps to the homecoming lineup, Brad envelops me in the biggest, warmest hug. "You did so great, Mallory," he says sincerely.

I beam as I get in place between him and Pia. She ignores me, but Caroline leans over her to tell me how great I did. "You too!" I say, even though I didn't hear a single word of her speech. I try to listen to Luis's speech, but I can't concentrate.

Applause brings me back to the moment, and Principal Lu takes the mic. "Let's give a big round of applause for this year's Reardon High School Homecoming Court!"

Brad puts his arm around me and I whisper, "I have to talk to you."

"Our homecoming committee will score the speeches and determine our final scores," Principal Lu continues. "In a few minutes, I'll announce your next junior king and queen!"

Bruno Mars's voice fills the gym as we make our way off the stage, and despite Pia's apparent hatred of me, not even she can resist the allure of "Uptown Funk."

"Brad! Dance with me!" she whines, grabbing his hand and pulling him toward the center of the dance floor.

"I promise we'll talk right after this," he says helplessly as Pia drags him deep into the heart of the dance floor.

"That really was a great speech."

I turn around and come face-to-face with Caroline.

"I just wanted to say sorry." Caroline looks me right in the eyes. "It was really mean of me to make fun of you at Shauna's party. And it's okay if you're mad at me," she continues. "I mean, I'd be mad, too. But, like . . . I hope I'll see you around or something?"

"O-Okay," I stammer as Jenni, Lincoln, and Scott finally find me.

"You were amazing!" Jenni squeals, wrapping her arms around me.

"Seriously great," Lincoln says as Scott nods.

Bruno Mars fades out and we all look toward the stage. Principal Lu is standing there with a piece of paper in her hand, and I feel like my heart is trying to claw its way out through my mouth. You know, if hearts had claws. I didn't even realize quite how much I wanted to win until this moment, but now, I know: I want this more than I've ever wanted anything.

"Ready?" Jenni asks, grabbing my hand. To my surprise, Caroline grabs my other hand as she gives me a small smile.

Breathe in. Hold it. Breathe out.

"After tallying up all the votes and spirit points, it's time to crown the king and queen!"

Everyone claps. Lincoln wolf whistles. Jenni gives a tiny "Woo!" I just breathe.

"Please, give a huge round of applause to your king and queen, Brad Kirkpatrick and Mallory Sullivan!"

I don't even have time to react before I'm nearly crushed in a group hug among Caroline, Jenni, Lincoln, and Scott. *Oh my God.* I did it. I'm actually homecoming queen.

A tiny freshman appears out of nowhere and puts a shiny plastic tiara on my head and a million hands push me toward the center of the gym, where everyone has formed a circle. In the middle, Brad's waiting for me, wearing his own plastic crown and smiling.

"Hey," he says as I walk toward him.

"Um," I say. "Hi."

"Can I have this dance?" he asks with a smile.

I look around us at all the people who are watching, taking pictures on their phones, or just texting and ignoring us. I'm suddenly conscious of everything, of every streamer hanging above us and of the shiny, scratched gym floor under our feet. Brad's perfectly fitted black suit and the way my dress makes me look exactly as pretty as I feel. The low murmur of everyone in the gym talking as I take my place directly in front of Brad. All the tiny little details that add up to this, the moment I wanted but never really thought would happen.

Brad places his hands around my waist, still looking at me with those eyes full of genuine kindness. Some Ed Sheeran song starts playing, but I can't even focus on how much I want to make fun of it, because this is it. This is my moment.

"I'm sorry about what I said at the party," I say quickly as everyone around us starts slow dancing, too. "That was stupid, and I know you better than that."

Brad shakes his head. "Mallory, don't worry about it. You were upset. And nothing will stop us from being friends, especially not some stupid fight."

I swallow hard. "Can I ask you something?"

"As long as it isn't about physics or football." Brad smiles. "I'm taking the night off."

"No, not that. Jake spends a lot of time online, right?"

"Yeah. He's a total nerd," Brad says nonjudgmentally.

"Does the phrase 'beam me up' mean anything to you?"

Brad bites his lip and I can see the gears turning in his head. "Oh!" he suddenly says. "Yeah, that's Jake's handle for basically everything."

I stop dancing. "You're sure?"

Brad nods. "Mal," he says, leaning in again, "I'm pretty sure he likes you. Don't tell him I said that or anything."

Before I can stop it, a giggle escapes my lips.

"Mallory?" Brad's eyes widen.

"I'm sorry," I say through laughter. "This has been a really weird month. I'm just . . . really glad we're friends."

"Me too," Brad says, and as the song ends, he pulls me into a totally platonic, nothing-more-than-friendly hug.

"Okay," I say, determined. "I'm gonna go talk to Jake. But can you do me one favor?"

Brad nods.

"Can you and Jenni just get together already?"

Brad runs his hand through his hair. "Is it that obvious? Does she like me?"

I give him a look full of friendly pity. "Yeah."

A group of football bros run up behind Brad. "All hail

King Kirkpatrick!" one of them shouts as they hoist him in the air.

"Good luck!" I give Brad a thumbs-up.

"You too!" he shouts, looking a little panicked as they carry him away.

I push past couples making out and try to find Jenni. I can't stand to think about her hanging out forlornly by the chocolate fountain, alone, when she should be dancing to this sickeningly sweet song with the love of her life.

She *is* by the chocolate fountain, but she's the opposite of forlorn. Standing in between Lincoln and Scott, Jenni holds a finger under each eye as she laughs.

"Stop it!" she shrieks as I walk up. "My mascara's going to run!"

"Scott's reenacting Pia's angry speech," Lincoln explains when he sees me. "You know, the one where she verbally subtweeted you."

Scott shrugs. "It was pretty mockable."

I ignore them. "Jenni! Why are you not with Brad right now?"

Jenni looks back and forth between Lincoln and Scott. "Um . . ."

"We're not stupid," Lincoln says.

"We were both in that backseat with you," Scott reminds her.

Jenni gives a little sigh and looks at me. "I had a teeny-tiny crush on him. But it was no big deal, and I know you like him, and best friends come first. . . ."

"Sisters before misters." Lincoln nods.

"I don't like him!" I interrupt. "I mean, I *thought* I did, but . . . well, it's too hard to explain right now. The point is, you need to go find him right now. He likes you."

Jenni stands up straight. "He does?"

I nod. "I'm sorry I ever stood in your way. But you should've told me you liked him!"

She reaches into her purse, grabs a compact, and looks at her reflection as she brushes something over her lips, totally ignoring me.

"Don't you want to, like, go see Brad?" I ask.

Jenni smacks her lips together and tosses the compact in her purse. "That was to hold my lipstick in place. I don't want it to get smudged."

And with that, she pushes her shoulders back and marches off through the crowd.

"Whoa," Lincoln says as she disappears into the horde of gyrating bodies. "She's really something."

I laugh. "Yeah. She really is."

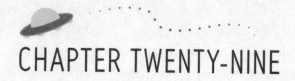

CHAPTER TWENTY-NINE

95% of reported UFO sightings can be attributed to air-
planes, weather balloons, or satellites, a figure skeptics
cite as conclusive proof that aliens are not, in fact, among
us. But for true believers, that 5% chance is just enough
hope to believe that we're not alone.

—AllenHuntress, 2015

"WHY DO YOU NEED to go right *now*?" Lincoln asks. "They haven't even played the Cupid Shuffle yet, and you *know* you want to watch me kill at that."

"Because!" I shout, then lower my voice and lean in closer. "Jake."

Lincoln looks smug as he puts his arm around Scott. "So you're finally realizing what everyone else has known the whole time."

"Oh, shut up. Don't act like you knew."

Lincoln looks offended. "Have you even seen the way he looks at you?"

"Like he wants to eat your face," Scott offers, concerned.

"But in a good way," Lincoln adds.

I wince. My palms are tingling, remembering the look in Jake's eyes the night before. "I have to go now, before I lose my nerve."

They cheer for me as I dodge the slow-dancing couples and run through the gym. I see Jenni and Brad with their arms wrapped around each other and their foreheads touching, but I keep going right through the double doors and into the parking lot.

And I run. I run through the parking lot, where a girl hanging out the sunroof of a late-arriving limo yells, "Go, Mallory!" as I offer her a wave. Thank God this dress isn't floor length or tight. But, as I hobble and almost trip over a crack in the sidewalk, I realize that these shoes just aren't working. I pull them off my feet and tuck them behind a bush, silently apologizing to Jenni for temporarily hiding her silver heels in the dirt. "I'll come back for you," I whisper.

I keep running toward the Kirkpatricks', pushing a million thoughts out of my mind. What if I step on a rusty nail and get a tetanus infection? What if a pack of rabid dogs attacks me? What if a freak storm occurs and I get struck by lightning and become the topic of a Buzzfeed article? *This Girl Was Homecoming Queen . . . Until Tragedy Struck.*

Until I realize that this time, I do have something to be afraid of. What if Jake hates me and never wants to talk to me again?

But I keep running. I push the thoughts out of my brain and focus on putting one foot in front of the other, dodging rocks on the sidewalk. When I finally reach Jake's house, I stop and place my hands on my knees, trying to catch my breath.

"Mallory?"

Jake's standing inside his garage, bent over his motorcycle.

My heart skipping, I stand up and walk into the light that spills onto the driveway.

"Sorry," I say between inhales. "For showing up. Unannounced."

"Are you okay?" Jake stands up straight and looks at me.

I take another step toward him. "Yes. I mean, no. Well, sort of. I will be, I hope?"

Jake just stares at me. I can't read his face or tell if he's still angry or just confused. So I go for it.

"I'm sorry," I say. To my embarrassment, tears start to form in my eyes. "I'm sorry I was a jerk to you, and that it seemed like I was using your brother. I guess I sort of was, but he's really my friend. But I mean, he's *just* my friend. I don't have a crush on him."

Jake fidgets a bit, switching his wrench from his left hand to his right hand, but he doesn't say anything.

"I know you're not just some guy hiding out at his dad's. I know you're a physics genius, and I know that you're a lot more than one stupid mistake. And I hope I am, too. Because I know you're BeamMeUp. And I just hope that I haven't messed everything up forever, because listen, I know I'm not perfect. I'm just figuring out how to leave my house, for God's sake. And sometimes I talk too much when I'm nervous or else I don't talk enough, and I love my family but we're a mess, and that one time I puked in front of everyone—"

"You won," Jake interrupts.

"What?"

He tosses his wrench down on the concrete floor. I don't flinch at the sound or try to run when he takes a step toward me. "Your crown." He reaches up to touch my tiara and I feel like my head might seriously burst into flames.

"Yeah," I say. I'd like to say something more intelligent or at least something that involves a few more syllables, but he moves his hand a little bit lower to stroke my cheek.

"Wait here," he says, cruelly pulling his hand back and jogging inside. Standing in his driveway, wearing a dress and a tiara, it hits me how weird this situation is. Weird and completely wonderful.

Jake pops back out the door and jogs over to me, holding a bunch of Twizzlers wrapped with a green ribbon. "For you."

I take the bag delicately and run my fingers over the ribbon.

"You know on We Are Not Alone, when I told you a hug wasn't all that romantic?"

I squeeze the Twizzlers to my chest. "And I said I'd hold out for a bouquet of Twizzlers? You remembered that?"

"Yeah, well," Jake says, rubbing the back of his neck. "I've had them since that day. I was going to put them in a vase, but I thought you'd be at the dance longer."

I never thought I'd get choked up over a bag of candy, but here we are. "This is perfect."

Jake nods toward the backyard. "Come see something."

He grabs my hand and curls his fingers around mine. We walk around the house. All I can focus on is the sensation of his rough hand . . . that is, until I see what's in the middle of the yard, illuminated by the light on the Kirkpatricks' back porch.

Our physics project. Finished.

"Did you do this?" I ask, kneeling beside it.

"Yep." Jake puts his hands in his pockets.

"Oh my God," I say, afraid to even touch it. "I can't believe you did all this work for us."

"I have a slight confession to make," Jake says, and I stand up to face him. "I helped Brad a lot when you weren't around. . . ."

"I knew it!"

"But honestly . . . I made it a little bit harder than it had to be. I just wanted an excuse to hang out with you."

I let it all sink in. "You did?"

He nods.

"Even though I called you a pompous asshole?"

Jake looks confused. "You did?"

Whoops. "Um . . . that might've been in my head."

Jake laughs, but the smile fades from his face quickly. "Listen, I'm sorry BeamMeUp ditched you. That guy's kind of a jerk."

I shrug, wrapping my arms around myself. "He's okay. I'm sorry AlienHuntress tried to make her life sound a lot cooler than it really was."

Jake raises his eyebrows. "I think she's always been pretty cool. Maybe that's why BeamMeUp had to stop talking to her—he wanted to see her in real life instead of on a screen." He points to the project. "Speaking of being a pompous asshole, I took the liberty of naming the rocket for you. Not sorry."

"It's more of a parachute," I start, but then I see what is painted on the side—*AlienHuntress*, in big, bold, red letters.

"You named it after me." My voice shakes.

"I like you a lot, Mallory," Jake says, stepping even closer to me so that our bodies are touching and our faces are just inches apart. His voice saying my name sends a shiver down my spine. "It's like a guy on the Internet once said, 'Everyone exerts a force.'"

"You more so than others," I finish.

He closes the gap between us and presses his lips against mine. I wrap my arms around his neck, and this is absolutely, positively better than being homecoming queen. This is better than any dumb plastic crown. It's at least as good as an *X-Files* marathon. Kissing Jake is even better than I thought it would be last night in the driveway. It's like a parachute expanding in my chest and a million rockets going off all at once.

Jake Kirkpatrick is a lot of things: physics nerd, forum member, pretend juvenile delinquent, and now I can say with full certainty that he's also a very, very good kisser.

He pulls back and I wobble a bit. All of the words I had in my head are suddenly gone. He smiles and it's so cute that I just want to grab his face and kiss him again, but then he says, "So you want to launch this rocket?"

It takes me a second to realize that this isn't some weird sexual euphemism. "But . . . won't Brad be mad if I finish our physics project without him?"

Jake gives me a look. "Has Brad ever actually cared about physics?"

I think back to Brad's sad, confused class notes. "Good point. We'll make another project tomorrow."

Jake kneels and tinkers. I stare at the back of his neck, the skin I touched just a minute ago, and I feel my whole body blush.

"I put a message in it," Jake says without looking at me.

"A message?"

"Yeah." He turns and looks up at me. "To the aliens. I mean, I know that wasn't the point of the project. I know this is for physics class, but I thought"—he shrugs—"why not?"

I kneel beside him. "What's it say?"

"'We're here,'" Jake says. "I was going to try to do something clever, or use a Ray Bradbury quote or something, but . . ."

"I like it," I say, taking it all in. The dirt of the Kirkpatricks' backyard on my bare feet, the electric warmth of Jake's arm lightly touching mine, the way his face looks half-illuminated by the back-porch light.

As those two little words repeat in my head—*we're here*—I let everything go. Maybe Brad and I won't get the highest grade in the class on this project, and maybe it doesn't matter, since I'm going to try going back to school. Maybe our project will crap out and fall into some trees two blocks away without recording anything. Maybe I can't protect Lincoln from everything—and maybe he doesn't even need protecting. Maybe I'll puke in front of everybody again (God, I hope not).

I know my life isn't suddenly perfect, that *totally making out with Jake* doesn't fix everything. It's not like I'm Anxious Beauty and the touch of his lips is going to cure me. I still have my problems, and he still has his. And things with my dad aren't ever going to be perfect, even if I do ask my mom to tell me where he is.

But I know where *I* am. Here. Here with Mom, here with Lincoln, here with Jenni. Here with the classmates who don't dislike me as much as I always thought they did, the ones who chose me to be their homecoming queen. Here with Jake, the guy I really thought I hated until I found out that I really, really didn't.

"You ready?" he asks.

I lean over and give him one quick kiss. This is it. This is where I belong. This is home.

"I'm ready," I say.

AlienHuntress Is Out of This World

ACKNOWLEDGMENTS

A huge thank-you to everyone at Paper Lantern Lit for being so amazing. I can't imagine a better first book experience. Alexa Wejko, you've been the editor of my dreams and I'm so grateful for all your work. And to Angela Velez, thanks for all your help and that delicious meal at The Pearl.

Giant thanks to Anna Roberto for taking a chance on me and making my dreams of seeing my book in print come true.

Thank you to all the readers, writers, and bloggers I've met on Twitter: You are the best. As a shy weirdo, I never would've imagined I'd meet so many great people online.

To everyone at HelloGiggles: Thank you for giving an unpublished girl a space to write about YA.

Thank you to the Young Writers at Kenyon workshop for being the first place I ever felt like a real writer. Thank you for existing, for making me feel special, and for helping me meet one of my best friends, Dan Rosplock.

Thank you to all the fantastic teachers I've had in my life, including Mrs. Kurdzel, Mrs. Orr, Mrs. Stevens, Mr. Jacox, and Steven Bauer. Thanks for showing me how to read better, how to write better, and how to be a better person.

Thanks to all my girlfriends and Billtown: You make my life so great. Thanks to my BFFAE and cowriter on some really impressive friend fiction, Dr. Catherine Stoner. You've always been so supportive, even when it involved reading all my terrible poetry in high school. Thanks to my #1 writing pal and the best writer/reader I know, Lauren Dlugosz Rochford. I really don't know what I would do without our daily e-mails.

Thank you to my family, including the Davises. Thanks to my favorite little brothers, Alex and Chase. You're the most creative and hilarious people I know and I feel so lucky to be your big sister. Special thanks to Alex for taking my author photo and making a perfect book trailer! Thanks to my parents for taking me to the library when I was little, never stopping me from reading "inappropriate" books, and only sort of trying to get me to major in something more practical than creative writing. I wish everyone had parents like you.

And, most importantly, to Hollis: Thank you for taking care of Merlin while I was locked in my office, for bringing me Chinese food and Skittles when I needed to eat, and for making me go on walks when I was getting stir-crazy. You're my Ben Wyatt, my Luke Danes, and my Ron Swanson and I love you forever.

KERRY WINFREY Q+A

1. When did you realize you wanted to be a writer?

It sounds very clichéd, but I knew I wanted to be a writer basically the first time I ever read a book. I used to dictate stories to my mom and have her write them down for me. (They were mostly Disney retellings, so I got an F for originality but an A for effort.) I always wanted to write books, but I didn't get "serious" about writing until a couple of years after I graduated from college. That's when I realized that (a) being a writer means you actually have to, you know, *write*, and (b) narrating the plot of *Sleeping Beauty* to my mom and having her write it down wasn't gonna cut it.

2. What were your hobbies as a kid? What are your hobbies now?

Okay, prepare to understand what a total dork I was. When I was too little to actually have homework, I used to give *myself* homework because it sounded so glamorous when the girls in the Baby-Sitters Club did *their* homework. I would check out a bunch of books from the library and then write a research paper on cats that no one wanted or asked for. When I got to high school and realized that homework was neither fun nor glamorous, my favorite thing to do was listen to depressing music while obsessively journaling. Also, my best friend and I wrote a story that was what Tina from *Bob's Burgers* would refer to as "friend fiction." It was hundreds of pages long and I still have it somewhere. I was extremely straitlaced in high school (and I still am!), so I was not at all interested in parties but totally interested in creating elaborate fictional worlds that involved people in my real life. My hobbies now involve a lot of reading, baking, sewing, and hanging out with my dog. Not much has changed.

3. Did you play sports as a kid?

Definitely not. I've always been comically uncoordinated. I was (literally) picked last in gym class most of the time, and I still hold a grudge against anyone who made fun of my inability to catch a softball. (To be fair, I *really* couldn't catch a softball.) The closest I got to a sport was the marching band in high school, which was a much more fun way to get in some physical activity (even if it did involve a very unflattering uniform). The sound of sneakers on a gym floor still gives me flashbacks to terrible gym class experiences, and I live in fear of winding up in a situation where I'm forced to play volleyball.

4. What book is on your nightstand now?

I have approximately one million books on my nightstand, including a Laura Lippman murder mystery, *100 Years of the Best American Short Stories*, and a Morgan Matson book. My reading life contains multitudes.

5. Where do you write your books?

I'm lucky enough to have a home office, and writing there makes me feel very official, like, "Wow, I'm such a real writer, look at me in my OFFICE." But I just as often write on the couch, because then my dog can sleep on my feet.

6. What sparked your imagination for *Love and Other Alien Experiences*?

The initial spark for *Love and Other Alien Experiences* came from something that really happened in my high school. Then, several years ago, there was a news story going around about a girl who was nominated for homecoming court as a joke. It seems unbelievable that anyone could be that cruel, but obviously it does happen! I started thinking about what it would be like to be that girl, and what it would be like if you decided to show everyone up by winning. Since then, *LAOAE* has evolved so much that it's not really about bullying and it involves so many different story lines, but originally it was based on something very real!

7. What challenges do you face in the writing process, and how do you overcome them?

My main challenge is my own brain. I have the hardest time just sitting down to do the work, because my internal voice always tells me, "Ugh, this is going to be rough." I just have to force myself to sit down (usually with a food or drink bribe) and commit to pushing out a small amount of words, even if they're terrible. And then once I get going, I usually end up writing much more than my original goal. "You can't revise a blank page" is my mantra.

8. If you could live in any fictional world, what would it be?

Okay, so this is from a television show and not a book, but I would love to live in Stars Hollow from *Gilmore Girls*. It always looks so cozy and comfortable, and everyone's a character (but in a fun way, not a rude way).

9. What was your favorite book when you were a kid? Do you have a favorite book now?

I loved *Little Women* as a kid, and I still do! Jo March is my hero—she's courageous and confident, she sacrifices for her family, and she never gives up on writing. I also like that she's full of so many messy emotions, like jealousy and anger. As a kid, I totally thought Jo should have ended up with Laurie (specifically Laurie as played by Christian Bale in the 1994 movie), but now I sort of wish she didn't end up with anyone and just kept writing whatever she wanted to. I still love *Little Women* so much because it's a book that means different things to you at different ages.

10. What's the best advice you have ever received about writing?

"Butt in chair." As much as I hate to recommend advice that uses the word *butt*, it's true. One of my writing professors in college used to say this, and I found out while writing *Love and Other Alien Experiences* that he was right. You're not always going to get some special flash of inspiration that will make the words flow out of your fingertips. All you can really do is sit down, write for a while, and work with what you've got on the page.

11. What advice do you wish someone had given you when you were younger?

I wish someone had told me that I could write a book. It's not that I didn't have a lot of people in my life who were encouraging—I had parents and teachers who really believed in me—but I didn't understand that "normal" people could write books. Even when I was a creative writing major, I still thought that people who wrote books had to have some sort of special credentials or connections. Nope! I firmly believe that anyone who wants to write a book can do it, and that's what I would tell all young writers. Writing a book is hard, but it's doable! Even if it takes you a long time or involves a lot of terrible first drafts (and it most likely will!), just keep at it.

12. What do you want readers to remember about your books?

The main thing I want my readers to know is that there are good moments even when you're dealing with bad stuff. My books are pretty light—I love comedy and kissing—but deal with real, tough problems that many people have. I hope someone reading *Love and Other Alien Experiences* sees that severe anxiety doesn't mean you can't experience true friendships or the kiss of your dreams.

13. Do you believe in aliens?

I've watched far too many episodes of *The X-Files* to completely reject the idea of aliens. I'm pretty skeptical, like Scully, but in my heart I'm Mulder. I want to believe.

14. Have you ever received or given a Twizzler bouquet?

No, but sometimes when I'm deep in a writing binge, my husband brings me a bag of Skittles, and that seems just as romantic (and cavity-inducing).

15. It's no secret that you're a romantic-comedy movie fan. Do you have any favorites? If so, why?

I have a lot of romantic-comedy loves (*The Wedding Singer, What If, Just Wright*), but my all-time favorite is *You've Got Mail*. For starters, it's written by Nora Ephron, the queen of the rom-coms. And Tom Hanks and Meg Ryan have fantastic chemistry. But my favorite thing about it is how sad it is. I like romantic comedies that are happy and hopeful but still understand that love doesn't solve every problem or make your sadness disappear.

16. Are rom-coms what inspired *Love and Other Alien Experiences*?

In a way, yes! I watch a *lot* of romantic comedies and I'm constantly thinking about the tropes they use, so I really wanted to try out some of those tropes myself. My all-time favorite scene that's in almost every romantic comedy, for example, is when the two main characters almost kiss but then get interrupted by a small child, meddling old person, or momentary misunderstanding. I hope I can put an almost-kiss into every book I write.

17. Did you research agoraphobia? Did you learn anything interesting and unexpected about it?

I did a lot of research on agoraphobia—although anxiety is something I have a pretty decent understanding of, agoraphobia isn't something I knew a ton about before I started writing. I read a lot of articles and Reddit forums to find out what real-life people with agoraphobia experience. The most interesting thing I learned is that agoraphobia isn't as simple as just a fear of leaving the house—it's a lot more complex than that, and just like all mental illnesses, it's different for everyone.

18. Mallory spends so much time online that her mom installs an app that limits her Internet usage. How addicted to the Internet are you? Be honest, this is a safe space.

I'm pretty embarrassingly addicted. While the app that Mallory uses (Focustime) is made up, I'm a BIG fan of Freedom and Anti-Social. I tend to get distracted and start going down true-crime Wikipedia wormholes or catching up on celebrity gossip if I don't have something to force me to stay off the Internet.

Thank you for reading this
Feiwel and Friends book.

The Friends who made
Love and Other Alien Experiences
possible are:

Jean Feiwel
Publisher

Liz Szabla
Editor in Chief

Rich Deas
Senior Creative Director

Alexei Esikoff
Senior Managing Editor

Kim Waymer
Production Manager

Holly West
Editor

Anna Roberto
Editor

Christine Barcellona
Associate Editor

Emily Settle
Administrative Assistant

Anna Poon
Editorial Assistant

Follow us on Facebook or visit us online at mackids.com.

Our books are friends for life.